The
Falling Sky

D0109559

The Falling Sky

Pippa Goldschmidt

FREIGHT BOOKS

First published April 2013

Freight Books
49-53 Virginia Street
Glasgow, G1 1TS
www.freightbooks.co.uk

Copyright © Pippa Goldschmidt 2013

The moral right of Pippa Goldschmidt to be identified as the author of this work has been asserted by her in accordance with the Copyright, Designs and Patents Act, 1988

All rights reserved. No part of this publication may be reproduced or transmitted in any form by any means, electronic or mechanical, including photocopying, recording or any information storage or retrieval system, without either prior permission in writing from the publisher or by licence, permitting restricted copying. In the United Kingdom such licences are issued by the Copyright Licensing Agency, 90 Tottenham Court Road, London W1P 0LP.

All the characters in this book are fictitious and any resemblance to actual persons, living or dead, is purely coincidental

A CIP catalogue reference for this book is available from the British Library

ISBN 978-1-908754-14-1
eISBN 978-1-908754-15-8

Typeset by Freight in Garamond
Printed and bound by Bell and Bain, Glasgow

the publisher acknowledges investment from
Creative Scotland toward the publication of this book

Pippa Goldschmidt grew up in London, and now lives in Edinburgh. She is a graduate of the renowned Masters course in creative writing at the University of Glasgow. She has a PhD in astronomy and worked as an astronomer for several years at Imperial College, followed by posts in the civil service including working in outer space policy.

In 2012 Pippa was awarded a Scottish Book Trust/Creative Scotland New Writers Award. From 2008 to 2012 she was writer in residence at the ESRC Genomics Policy and Research Forum, based at the University of Edinburgh. The Falling Sky is her first novel.

For my family

Nothing is as certain as death.

At first, the image is just a blur in the darkness, so Jeanette refocuses her telescope and the blob becomes clear and sharp. A young girl, twelve years old, in a blue and white gingham dress. She's immobile, fixed against the blank, dark background.

Now, and for ever more, she hovers just above the event horizon of the black hole. And when Jeanette tries to reach out to her, she's not really there. All that's left is this last photo of her, static on a summer's day in the garden.

NOW

Jeanette may as well be invisible. She's standing on the stage in the auditorium in front of about two hundred other astronomers, presenting the results of her PhD work at the annual British conference. But she can tell no one's listening.

She doesn't blame them. She wouldn't listen either, if she didn't have to. If she could only find a way of drowning out that slightly tremulous voice in her head, which is going on and on about dust in early galaxies. Still, not long now. She's reached the final slide, showing the actual data. That may interest them more.

She shines the red dot of the laser pointer onto the screen, wishing it didn't betray her nervousness. She's trying to show them the centre of a galaxy, the point where the contours on the map converge into the peak of intensity, and the dot is dancing around it, refusing to settle down. Perhaps it doesn't matter. She's only just finished her thesis, she's expected to be young and overawed by the prospect of speaking at a conference.

But they're not interested in this slide either. Some of them are working on their laptops, others are talking to each other. Several people are fiddling with their phones, reading the conference programme, even reading newspapers. Her boss, the Death Star, is asleep. That's to be expected, he always sits in the front row and sleeps, only waking up at the end to ask some horribly pertinent question. She wonders what he'll ask today. Because it's not enough to give the talk in a whisper and be ignored; the experience isn't complete without the ritual of questions afterwards, to allow the (mostly male) audience to do the verbal equivalent of showing their tail feathers off to each other.

She gets to the end, clicks off the laser, stands and waits. She doesn't have to wait long.

'Why haven't you used visible wavelengths as well as infrared?' from someone who appears to have been playing a game on his mobile phone and clearly hasn't listened to the main point of her talk, which was the comparison of visible and infrared images.

'Have you considered an alternative explanation of the results?' This is from someone she fears, a Bright Young Thing not long arrived here from Harvard and keen to demolish all before him.

'What sort of alternative explanation are you thinking of?' She certainly can't think of any and he obviously wants to enlighten everyone. He sets off on an elaborate discussion, gargoyled with words she has never heard of. When he finally stops talking she can't even summon the energy to reply to him, she just points silently to someone else who is waving his hand at her, as if summoning a waitress to remove his dirty plates.

'Why haven't you referenced my paper on this galaxy?'

'I have.' She hopes she sounds rude.

The Death Star wakes up and stares at her as if he's never seen her before. 'What does it mean?' he asks before his eyes snap shut again, not bothering to wait for her reply.

What does it mean? It means what she has already explained to him and everyone else, that the peak of infrared emission from this galaxy is spatially offset from the peak at visible wavelengths, implying a large amount of dust must be present which is obscuring some of the stars, soaking up the light and re-emitting it at longer wavelengths. The dust is made by exploding stars come to the end of their lives, so this is an old galaxy, it's already produced at least one generation of stars. Interesting enough, if you want to know the detail of how galaxies work.

It means she has fulfilled the obligations of her PhD and carried out a suitably non-controversial (i.e. boring) project, proved herself capable of slogging away at a telescope night after night to gather data of dubious quality, writing software not obviously riddled with errors to reduce and analyse the data, and then copying the style of thousands of other equally boring academic papers to report what she has discovered, so that she can get a job and carry on doing this for the rest of her life. If she is lucky.

This is what it means right now. But she knows that it means other things too.

It means she gets to spend time using real telescopes, ones large enough to see galaxies near the beginning of the Universe, or the edge of time, or whatever fancy phrase you want to use. Telescopes a long way away, in deserts and on the tops of mountains, in places so remote that they seem scarcely less odd than the galaxies themselves.

It means she has knowledge. She knows how to unpick apparently simple statements such as 'the sky is dark at night' to get at the information contained inside. She knows about the past, present and future of stars, of galaxies, of the Universe itself. She knows how to decipher the light of the night sky.

It means she has escaped. Escaped from home, the depression in the sofa, the radioactive glow of the TV, the outer space vacuum in the house, and the cigarette ash sprinkled over everything like earth on a coffin.

The Death Star starts snoring again before she has finished answering him. Afterwards she realises he might have done her a favour, by getting her to repeat the main point of her talk. Perhaps he thought she hadn't made it clear enough during her presentation and was giving her the opportunity to reiterate it. Or he may simply have missed it when she said it the first time. Or, and this is probably the most likely explanation, he's just bloody-minded and enjoys trying to wrong-foot the speakers.

She's been working for him for a year now but she still hasn't fathomed him. Nobody knows who first came up with his nickname or what its original meaning was, but it's endured because it suits him in its neat combination of his main research interest; supernovae, those massive stars that die in a spectacular explosion of light, together with the fear he instils in other astronomers as he rumbles up and down the corridors at the Observatory.

Later, as they're going into the hall where the conference dinner is taking place, she sees Richard, the other post-doc at the Observatory, surrounded by a crowd of people she doesn't know. Richard is laughing, an awful braying sound that's much louder than the underlying burble of words in the hall. She knows what the laughter means, it is supposed to signify that Richard is comfortable talking with these people. She's tempted to go over and join him, anyone can sit where they like at these things, and all it takes is a battle of nerves to go and sit next to the Astronomer Royal. Why shouldn't she belong too?

So she starts to work her way through the groups of people. A couple of people recognise her, maybe from the talk she gave that afternoon, and nod. Most people don't pay any attention to her. As she reaches the table where Richard and the Astronomer Royal are sitting, she pauses for a moment, but nobody notices her. So she pulls out a chair and sits down in silence. She's sitting beside two men she doesn't recognise. She appears to have interrupted their conversation, because after a brief pause they start to talk to each other as if she isn't there. She fights back the impulse to look down at her body to check she's still visible. Opposite her, the Astronomer Royal is staring into his empty wine glass as Richard explains to him with equal amounts of enthusiasm and inaccuracy a new technique for imaging very faint objects.

She glares at Richard but she knows she shouldn't feel so cross; she's partly responsible for him being here in the first place.

It was just after they both started work as post-docs, about a year ago, after being students for so long. At lunch that day she found Richard sitting at the furthest table in the canteen, listening to a man in a dark suit who was unknown to her. The man was talking about galaxy surveys; large projects to gather information on thousands of galaxies to determine how they change and evolve with time. There were many such surveys going on at telescopes all over the world. The man was explaining that his survey was one of the largest, involving hundreds of nights of telescope time, and hundreds of astronomers working together. It sounded like a job advert, and Jeanette realised what was going on. He was part of the consortium, a shadowy group of top astronomers collaborating on a vast project running for years, slurping up time on telescopes and promising to answer all the remaining questions in cosmology. It sounded like he was trying to get Richard involved in this work. Superficially it sounded appealing; Richard would get his name on lots of papers. But Jeanette guessed that they wouldn't actually let him do anything interesting on the project, all the big names would have divided the interesting analysis, the really sexy stuff, between them. They needed grunts like Richard to help out on the grindingly boring data reduction, to turn the computing handle and crank out zillions of images and spectra of galaxies.

She glanced at Richard, at his glossy hair and pink cheeks. He reminded her of a well-bred dog, sitting there eagerly gazing at the man in the suit, as if he expected a pat on the head. She couldn't be doing with this sort of work, the endless data collection where all the questions are pinned down in advance and all that's left to do is the drudgery. And it's not as if the consortium had actually published that much. They kept appearing at conferences, trailing their latest data like an advert for a future film that never got released. Rumour had it that they were sitting on thousands of images of galaxies. She would have liked to get her hands on that, but not at the cost of actually having to work with them. She'd leave that to the Richards of the world.

Perhaps it was because she was a woman, she thought, as she watched the two men. Up until the early twentieth century, women

7

were trained to be human computers in astronomical observatories, to do mechanical tasks that ostensibly required no intellectual ability. She'd seen photos of them, rows and rows of girls in white pinafores seated at desks examining glass plates, their expressions a mixture of boredom and earnestness. They were trained to look for variable stars by spotting minute differences between the plates. Perhaps it was better than anything else they could hope to do, but still she resented any notion that she might have something in common with them, and so she would avoid being the invisible cog in the wheel.

After lunch when she was back in her new office thinking about her future research, Richard came in. She carried on staring at her computer screen, trying to look busy. She wasn't desperately keen on having to talk to him about his plans. But he stood there, obviously waiting for her to finish what she was doing, so eventually she had to look at him.

'So?' she said, trying to sound cheerful, 'did you succeed?'

'Not yet,' his smile was a bit lop-sided. 'I really want it, though.'

She looked back at her work, she wasn't used to people being so obvious about what they wanted. It made him seem naked, somehow. It was unseemly. She was aware that she was blushing.

He carried on. 'They've asked me to do something. As a sort of test, I think.' He was fiddling with his hands, and she realised that he was there because he needed her help.

'Well?'

'I have to work out a strategy for observing galaxy images down to a certain surface brightness. To get the details.' He paused, as if waiting for her to make the connection between this and her own work. This was the sort of calculation she did all the time. How long would it take a telescope to be able to detect a feature on a galaxy, such as a spiral arm?

'I've done that,' she said, surprised at the briskness in her voice. If he was hoping that she would be able to cover up the inadequacies in his ability to do his job, she needed to pretend, for both their sakes, that it was simply to save time. 'No point in you doing it again.' And she scrabbled around in the pile of papers that had accumulated on her desk to find what she needed, a table of numbers from her last observing trip. 'This is for a four metre telescope, for a five sigma detection. This row shows surface brightness, and this shows length of time in seconds needed to achieve that level of statistical significance. Just scale it up or down for different sizes of telescopes.'

'Thanks, Jeanette,' he said, and she saw for the first time just how unnaturally white his teeth were. 'You're a star. Just give me a shout if you ever need my help. For anything.'

Now, she realises that the two men she's sitting next to are from the consortium. One of them might have been the man in the canteen that day, she can't be sure. Sometimes she's not so good with faces, galaxies are easier to remember. Perhaps it's because they're further away.

The other face that keeps looming up from the past is the ice woman. She takes a slug of wine and tries not to think of the ice woman, hardly noticing someone sitting down next to her in the last empty chair left at their table. It's an older man, old enough to be retired. Probably an emeritus professor. The conference is full of them, men who defined the subject forty or fifty years ago. Who set off like pioneers, with new telescopes to map the Universe, to chart its strange galaxies and different types of matter. She smiles shyly at the old chap next to her. These old geezers tend to be more courteous than the awful Bright Young Things, and as expected, this one smiles shyly back.

'Are you an open-minded young woman?' he says, so quietly it's almost a whisper.

Not again. God knows it's not the first time this has happened, but they're usually drunk and this one looks quite sober. She doesn't know if that makes it better or worse.

'I heard your talk and I thought you might want to see this,' and he looks around him, before he starts fumbling around theatrically in his trouser pockets. The whole table falls silent as he finally manages to produce a stained and crumpled roll of papers and slaps it down next to her soup bowl, so that the roll unfurls and she can read the title; 'An enquiry into the effects of the planets on the human psyche.'

'So what did you do then?' Later, in the bar with her collaborator, Maggie. Maggie's snorting with laughter.

'I had to politely listen to him talk about astrology for the rest of the entire bloody meal, didn't I?'

'Astrology! How embarrassing...Maggie purses her lips in disgust.

She just shrugs, not really wanting to talk about it any more, not wanting to consider why she seems to attract the freaks and nutters at conferences. Perhaps she looks too sympathetic. She sneaks a look at Maggie standing there, one arm balanced on the bar, nursing her first and only glass of wine that evening. There's no clutter about Maggie. Nothing to distract her from her purpose in life.

She's been collaborating with Maggie for a few years now, has watched Maggie's fingers patter precisely over computer keyboards, has interrupted her quiet voice explaining the intricacies of galaxy formation, and has spilled coffee over her neatly annotated charts on countless observing trips at countless telescopes. Maggie's a comrade in arms.

'Let's talk about our next trip,' she says now to Maggie, who's pushed her wine to one side and is ordering an orange juice. 'We need to have a battle plan.'

Jeanette sets off on her journey to fetch her sister back from the dead. She dives down into the blue night, beyond the surface layer of planets and their moons, far below the Sun and the bubbles of comets at the edge of the solar system. There is still a long way to go, before she reaches the midnight depths.

Now she's travelling with the Universe itself, riding the back of it, surfing on its energy.

She circles early galaxies, swoops into the sea of primordial hydrogen, photons streaming brilliant light from her fingertips.
She finds her sister asleep, curled up at the bottom of the ocean. Kate dreams the world; its beginning and its end. She won't stop dreaming as long as Jeanette obeys the Universe's equations.

The next week, Jeanette is back in Edinburgh, sitting in her small office at the top of the Observatory's west tower, with the papers balanced on her lap because her desk is too cluttered with towers of books and data tapes. She's supposed to be completing yet another job application form. She reads the question on the form, trying to concentrate on the meaning of the words as if this is the first time she has ever seen them; "Why should your research be funded?" and her mind stops.

She stares at the posters on the walls. '3rd ESO-CERN conference on the early Universe,' claims one. '4th Hawaii workshop on shrouded stars,' states another and, oddly crammed in between these symbols of earnest work, is a small photo of a naked man with horns scribbled on his head in felt-tip pen. The graffitied photo has been in this office longer than she has. She refuses to take it down although she can observe her students gazing at it during tutorials, when they should be paying more attention to her. She likes having a piece of irrationality in this place which is a monument to science and logic. No one will ever know who the man is, or why there are horns drawn on his image.

She wonders how long she can sit here without having a coherent thought. It is the privilege of the dusty academic, she muses, to be answerable to no one and so I can sit here not doing anything and not feel guilty. But she knows that's not really true. She's answerable to the grant funders, to the students and to the senior staff. She's answerable to herself when she wakes up at three o'clock in the morning and lies in bed working out how many more months, weeks, and days she has left on her grant.

Sometimes she feels like Alice in Wonderland, chasing rabbits down holes and falling for ever towards some unknown destination. Like Alice, she can read and talk as she falls, and speculate on what's happening to her. She catches glimpses of galaxies as she whizzes past, their spiral arms reaching out to her like octopus tentacles. The faces of other astronomers slide by, elongated by gravity, their voices echoing down the hole.

'It's trivial to show that the Universe is closed so that every path in space-time loops back upon itself,' says Tweedledum.

'Nonsense, the Universe is expanding at an exponential rate. It's hyperbolic so all paths lead to infinity,' says Tweedledee.

She tries to talk to them but her words can't be heard. I wonder if I'm in a vacuum, she thinks. In space, no one can hear me argue. She sees herself reading books speculating on what caused the Big Bang and whether there will be a big crunch. She observes herself having apparently sensible arguments with apparently normal human beings about the precise number of galaxies in the Universe. She watches herself give a seminar, as if to the Queen of Hearts, at which her intellectual rivals stand up and shout at her that she must be wrong and that she should have her head cut off, or at least lose her allocation of observing time on telescopes.

She decides to give up work for the day and leaves her office, going down the spiral staircase. At the bottom, as usual, she runs her fingers along the scar in the brickwork.

The story of what caused the scar is hardly ever referred to, and when it is, the details are usually wrong. But Jeanette's read the original newspaper cuttings, and knows what really happened.

The standard story, usually told in a half-joking way, is that in 1913 a suffragette tried to bomb the Observatory, and failed, only causing a minor bit of damage to the library.

But in fact the bomb went off at the base of this tower, and did considerable damage to its structure, as well as to the telescope housed in it, causing some of the optics to be smashed and the metal casing to shear apart.

Jeanette wonders why the history is never told right, even though there's plenty of evidence for what happened. The then Astronomer Royal's apoplectic letters about the incident. The pale seam of newer bricks in the wall. Why do people here feel the need to dismiss their own history?

She's made an arrangement to go and meet her friend Paula. She walks down the steep hill away from the Observatory, through the streets of Marchmont, and into town. They always meet in the same pub, a basement dive off Rose Street.

When she gets there, it takes a moment for her eyes to adjust to the gloom inside, and then she notices that Becca is there too. They're both sitting at the usual little round table which is already covered with several empty glasses. They've clearly been there for some time.

Paula looks up at her and says, 'Oh, hi,' sounding surprised, as if they're not expecting her, as if she's interrupting them. Not for the first time, she wonders what they talk about when she's not there.

'Do you want a drink?' Paula says, and without waiting for an answer, she goes to the bar.

'She wants to ask you something,' Becca says.

'What?'

'Best wait until she gets back.'

Again, that feeling of being shut out. Becca just fiddles with her cigarette lighter until Jeanette feels compelled to say something. 'How was your day?'

'Oh, alright. Nothing exciting.'

They both watch Paula at the bar. Her head is thrown back and she's laughing with the barman. Becca twists to look out of the window so that Jeanette can see the hair cut short against the skin. The back of her neck looks as though it's not often exposed to the light, it looks pale and vulnerable.

Years ago, Jeanette was friends with Becca at university. Almost as many years ago, Paula was one of Jeanette's flatmates. Jeanette provides the official link between Paula and Becca, but sometimes when they both look at her, she feels like the odd one out.

Becca turns back, still half silhouetted against the window and smiles slightly. 'What mysteries of the universe have you uncovered today?'

Jeanette feels the need to entertain. 'I found a dead spider in my notebook. It probably smuggled itself into the country with me, when I came back from my last observing run in Chile.'

Becca seems to find this amusing. 'Perhaps it's the smallest illegal immigrant ever.'

'I can see the headlines now — "Eight-legged asylum seekers hidden in science notebooks".'

Becca snorts with laughter. 'Perhaps it could sell its story to the press — "My fear of being flushed down the plughole".'

'It wasn't a very successful bid for freedom though. It's rather two-dimensional now.'

But after this they fall silent again. Jeanette isn't inclined to say anything more. She's done her bit with Becca and now it's Becca's turn. Except it never is Becca's turn. Always beautiful, always remote, she sits there politely and waits for other people to entertain her. So they watch Paula flirt with the barman, until finally she wanders back with Jeanette's wine and rearranges herself on her chair.

'This chair's too short,' she says, and straightens her legs out as if to demonstrate their inconvenient length. 'How much rent do you pay each month, Jeanette?'

Jeanette is taken aback by this non sequitur. 'Um, a lot. Why?'

Paula touches her arm and smiles, showing very white teeth. 'Wouldn't it be good if you only had to pay half?'

Jeanette's still confused. Paula's wearing bright lipstick this evening, even redder and shinier than usual. Why is she so dolled up? 'Yes but no one's offering to pay half my rent for me. Are they?'

There's a pause while Paula takes a swig of wine. 'Well, I might,' she says.

'Why?'

'Because I need a place to live.'

'But you've already got somewhere.'

'It's too damn expensive. It's not easy changing careers and going back to art college.'

Becca says, 'It's not only the expense. You can't actually carry on living in that flat now.' She adds to Jeanette, 'Sex-kitten shagged her landlord last month.'

'He let me off the rent for a week.'

'You mean he *paid* you?' Jeanette almost spits a mouthful of wine across the table.

Paula just twirls her wineglass. 'It was fun when we lived together, wasn't it?'

Jeanette grins. 'We had a lot of parties,' she tells Becca. 'We had a toga party and everyone else was draped in dirty white sheets, but Paula was Louise Brooks in this vampy black dress and a wig.'

'Well, there you are. We'll have fun again.'

She can remember the way that Paula looked at them all on her first day in the house, when they were equally lined up on the sofa in front of the television eating their tea, and there was a motorbike disembowelled on the rug. She'd never minded the motorbike, but it soon disappeared after Paula moved in.

The first one to get sucked in was Wayne. He lasted a month, before she found him crying in the kitchen one day, his fat little-boy face buckled with grief.

She tells Becca, 'She slept with all the other flatmates, that's why she had to move out.'

'Oh for Gods sake! Not all of them.' Paula laughs, clearly delighted that Jeanette is making her out to be such a femme fatale. 'I didn't sleep with you!'

'You're not a lezzer.'

'Do you have to use that word?' Becca glares at Jeanette.

'I like it,' says Jeanette. 'I'm reclaiming it from nasty school kids and men's mags.'

After Wayne the details are a bit hazy, but she can remember gradually becoming aware of the night-time noises coming from Paula's room next door. The noises were muffled, as though underwater, and Jeanette used to imagine Paula enticing men under the sea, wrapping her arms around them in the turquoise water and making love to them until they drowned.

'Isn't your flat awfully small for two people? Where is she going to sleep?' asks Becca.

'It's big enough.' She wonders why Becca seems so against the idea. It will be a squeeze if Paula's camping in the living room. But if she can't get a new job, some more money coming into the flat will be essential.

Becca doesn't say anything else, just taps her fingers on the table in a sharp staccato rhythm like Morse code.

'Hang on, is your sofa bed a double?' Paula looks thoughtful.

'No, not really.'

'That should be alright. Mr. Landlord was so awful in bed it's put me right off. It was about as sexy as inserting a tampon.'

Jeanette laughs and even Becca smiles, but Jeanette is surprised to see that her smile is as thin and sour as a slice of lemon.

The next day she goes to visit Jon, one of the lecturers. Unlike most of the other scientists at the Observatory, Jon wears a proper white coat and works in a proper lab, tucked away in the basement of the newest building on the site. She enjoys watching Jon at work because everything seems so physical in the lab. He has dirt under his fingernails, and pieces of duct tape stuck to his sleeves. His biros are neatly lined up in his chest pocket. The wires on the lab bench are soldered together at junctions made by old tobacco tins. She thinks of Jon as an alchemist, transforming these physical components into pure knowledge.

Sometimes when she visits him in the lab, he tells her about the instrument he is building. This instrument is going to be part of a satellite, and once it's in space it will carry out detailed measurements of galaxies and transmit the data back to Earth. He's nicknamed the instrument Orion, the hunter. Its real name is the slightly more prosaic OIRS, short for 'optical and infrared spectrometer'.

This won't happen for at least another year. The instrument has to be shipped out to the satellite control centre, then bolted onto the satellite which will go the launch pad to be loaded onto the rocket that will be launched into outer space. It will fly until it reaches the right spot far above them, and then release the satellite.

She likes the sense of order in the lab; more than that, there is a sense that everything has a purpose. She's all too aware of her own slapdash approach to work, the ideas not followed through, the half written papers never finished. But Jon's instrument requires meticulous planning and teamwork if it is going to change from a sketch on a page to a piece of glass and metal, and then back again into more knowledge about galaxies.

Recently he's been running calibration tests on one of the components of the instrument. This component will capture light from galaxies, and then smear out the light into spectra; long ribbons of rainbow colours. With these spectra you can measure how much light is emitted by different chemical elements at different wavelengths. It's an old concept, a reliable method of studying stars and galaxies. But the instrument that Jon is building will be the most sensitive ever; it will look at the most distant galaxies in the Universe.

Jon used to be a chemist and has a chemist's love of matter that goes beyond words and symbols into something material. He likes to talk about the differences between the two forms of carbon. One is soft and malleable, and the other is hard diamond. They're the same carbon atoms, but the differences are due to the way that the electrons are arranged around their cores. It always amazes Jeanette that electrons; particles whose masses are thousands of times smaller than those of the atoms, can have such a profound effect on the physical nature of substances.

But today, Jon doesn't talk about his work, he tells her about his family. 'My great-grandfather was an astronomer too. He was the other man on Eddington's 1919 expedition.' As he talks, the pair of spectacles perched high on his head catch the light and glint at Jeanette. It's as if he has an extra pair of eyes.

Jeanette's puzzled. Eddington carried out an expedition just after the First World War to measure the curvature of light rays around the sun during a solar eclipse, and prove that Einstein's theory of general relativity was correct. She isn't aware that any other astronomers were involved.

Jon carries on, 'There were actually two expeditions to carry out the experiment, on separate islands. Eddington was in charge of one of the trips, and my great-grandfather led the other one. His name was Crommelyn.'

Still no recognition from Jeanette. Jon rolls his eyes. 'Don't you know anything? It was famous.'

'So, is it in your blood then? Did you learn how to use a telescope at your great-grandfather's knee?'

'Don't be daft, he died years before I was born. But I was intrigued by him. He took part in this world-famous experiment,

19

in fact it was his data and not Eddington's that were actually used. And he's forgotten now. He just went straight back to his country house and spent the rest of his life there. I'm not sure he was even particularly interested in general relativity. He was more interested in the practicalities of doing the experiment. You know, they had to lug a huge telescope halfway up a mountain on a tropical island off the north coast of Brazil. It was an amazing thing to do. It took them months and months. Eddington's expedition had bad luck, it was cloudy where they were, and they only got a few usable photographs. But Crommelyn struck gold. And then when it all became public it was Eddington who got the glory, even though it was Crommelyn's photographs that were used.'

'Didn't he want any of the glory?'

'Oh, I don't think so. From what we can tell, he seems to have been quite happy to slip away. He spent the rest of his life hunting for comets.'

Jeanette remembers something else. 'Wasn't there something odd about that experiment? Didn't Eddington just find what he wanted to find? The data were pretty poor.'

'He had great — intuition. He discarded the data that he didn't like, without explaining why.'

'That's terrible. You'd never get away with that nowadays.'

Jon laughs at her. 'Of course not, Miss Morality.'

The speed of light is a constant. This is so amazing Jeanette can't stop grinning whenever she thinks about it. Speeds of ordinary things like people, cars, or trains, are not constant. They vary depending on how they're measured. A train whizzing past a station at eighty miles an hour appears to be stationary to the people travelling in it. But light isn't like that. It's always moving, always the same.

Sometimes when she's whirring around the universe, trying to decide where to live, what to eat, and who to sleep with, she forgets about the constancy of light. She can only see the fireworks around her, and hear the boom boom boom of her heart. But when things are still and quiet, there is a flash of torchlight, and she detects it, and is grateful.

On the first evening of her week-long observing run in Chile, Jeanette stands on the mountaintop, examining her reflection in the metal dome. There's nothing else here. No people, apart from the astronomers and the support staff. No buildings, apart from telescopes where they work at night and the residential lodge where they sleep during the day in a curious inversion of normal life, like a photographic negative.

As the light drains from the sky, she hurries back inside to the control room to continue working with Maggie. Sunset is a precariously narrow time trapped between the fat certainties of day and night. Each evening they compete against the darkening sky to ensure that the telescope is set up correctly, so that none of the precious night is wasted.

At this telescope, the control room is off to one side, curved around the edge of the dome which houses the telescope. The astronomers and the telescope operator sit in this room all night, sending instructions to the telescope and scrutinising the resulting images.

There are no windows in the control room, so it feels small and claustrophobic. There is no way of actually looking at the night sky unless you go outside. She couldn't believe this on her first observing run. It seemed nonsensical, to cross the world to use a telescope and not even be able to look through it. Now she is resigned to the fact that the only way of understanding the world is to see it displayed in rectangles on the computer screen. She still wishes they could actually work inside the dome, but this hasn't happened in Chile for several years now. The heat from their bodies would make the air shiver and distort the images formed by the telescope mirrors, so they're hidden away. There's still one telescope in Australia where the astronomer has to sit in a small metal cage behind the primary mirror. She did that once, when she was a student, and remembers the view of the sky with the stars flashing past as she swooped around the dome, and the exhilarating feeling of being on a fairground ride in the dark, with the cage rattling around her.

They don't talk much to each other at this early stage. Maggie tells the telescope operator how they want to use the telescope, and gives him the list of coordinates of their galaxies.

Then the first image of the night appears; two galaxies entwined, with their dense white centres twisted by tidal forces. It's easy to see the dynamics of this interaction; the gravitational attraction between the galaxies making them move towards each other, and most likely merge together in the future after some unimaginably long period of time. But the image isn't quite right, the light from the galaxy centres spills over to contaminate the fainter, outer regions which aren't showing up well. Jeanette and Maggie adjust exposure times and try again.

Jeanette's worried that the set-up of the telescope is wrong, that their observations won't work. And then she wonders why she's worried about this. If things don't work out, if she can't get another job, this may be her last trip to Chile. Understanding galaxy evolution is such a small thing to worry about, compared to the rest of her life.

But the next image is stunning. The galaxies look like underwater creatures, trailing ghostly arms through the black sea of the sky. Jeanette starts to relax. It will work. She has a future.

She and Maggie go on several observing trips each year, and they always have the same conversations. They talk about the galaxy clusters they're studying, and the way that the larger galaxies in those clusters seem to interact and feed off each other, cannibalising smaller ones and spewing out stars and gas. They talk about the food at the residential lodge, and complain about the endless avocado sandwiches. They remind each other of the possibly apocryphal student who lost control or lost patience, no one is ever sure which, and froze a tomato in the vat of liquid nitrogen before smashing it against the curved wall of the telescope dome. Jeanette can imagine the tomato shattering on the metal, its brilliant red shards melting and congealing. There's no trace of red now. Everything in the dome is drab grey; the walls and floor, even the long tube of the telescope itself. The slot cut into the dome for the sky provides the only respite. If you go into the dome at night, the stars above your head seem more real than the dull telescope.

The night's routine is established and Jeanette is able to escape outside for a moment. As ever, after spending any time in the control room, her senses feel almost smothered in the new-found space, and the sheer weight of the starlight takes her by surprise. There are so many stars in this sky they seem like a substance, eating away at the blackness. Inside, it's easy to forget that the sky is not actually a paper chart or a database, but a reality rich with knowledge, an ocean teeming with discoveries waiting to be caught. Standing out here, with the cool air brushing across her face, and the dust beneath her boots, it's obvious that the control room is just a shadow-world, a bad copy of this one.

Out here, the sky can be overwhelming. It presses down on her and there's nowhere else to go, nothing else to look at. But it's not the same sky as at home, where only a few stars are able to hammer through the heavy, dirty air. There, they are so distant and spread apart that it makes her feel lonely just to look at their feeble light. Here, she is in a crowd.

She quickly gets her sea legs as she navigates her way around, from the jewels of the Southern Cross to the fragile puff of the Large Magellanic Cloud, and on to the crowded centre of the Milky Way. There is a rhythm involved in moving from star to star that she can match to her breathing, so at the peak of each breath she arrives at a star and then swings herself onto the next one, spanning the darkness.

Then she goes back inside and back to the relentlessness of the data gathering. The telescope acquires each galaxy, spends ten minutes locked onto it and then reads out the resulting image to their screen. The rest of the night is parcelled up into these ten minute slots, and

Jeanette and Maggie must spend their time staring at the screen, scrutinising pixels.

'I hate this job,' Jeanette mutters to herself at one point, aware that she is gritting her teeth.

'Pardon?' Maggie is so close to the screen, her nose is practically touching it.

'I mean, it's ridiculous. We're not looking at the sky, we're not even looking through the telescope.' She waves a hand around the dusty room. 'We're shut in here, cut off from reality, and we're trying to interpret it via a computer screen.'

Maggie turns away from the screen, and gestures at all the computers, the racks of tapes, the remains of their sandwiches and the crowds of dirty mugs. 'Looks pretty real to me.'

'I suppose so.' Jeanette's mood subsides. Right now, she just wants to go to sleep. She doesn't want to check images for cosmic ray glitches or dust in the telescope. She doesn't want to look at the spectrum of a galaxy and have to convert the numerical wavelengths into corresponding colours in her mind. Four thousand angstroms is blue, six thousand is green and eight thousand is red. Add them all up and you get a rainbow you'll never see, at least not here in the control room. This place is about controlling your emotions and analysing data, so she shuts up and carries on, trying not to yawn.

The next day she wakes up in the late afternoon and hurries outside to check for clouds in the sky. The observatory is surrounded by mountains and she finds herself disliking them for their perfection and unreality. The rocks are too jagged, the sky too uniformly blue, everything is too precise here. There are no distractions, no bushes or grass to blur the lines of the earth. No animals or birds to break the relentless silence. She wants to scuttle away and burrow under imaginary damp leaves and into forgiving earth. She longs for Edinburgh, with its uneven pavements and grubby shop fronts. She misses the unpainted windows of her flat, even the stains on the carpets. Shortcomings go unnoticed there. Here, everything stands out in sharp relief against the mountains.

She's vaguely aware that bad things happened in this country some time ago. The first time she came here, soldiers manned roadblocks all along the Pan-American highway. She remembers having her passport inspected by a bored teenager in an army uniform, when she was on an interminable bus journey up to the observatory from Santiago. But none of the people at the observatory, neither the European astronomers nor the Chilean telescope operators, talk about politics. They swerve around it, as if avoiding a dead animal on the road.

That night the sky clouds over and Jeanette and Maggie can't do anything. The telescope is set up and calibrated and the list of objects to be observed is marked in different colours according to priority, but they just have to wait for the cloud to clear. It happens occasionally even at such high altitudes, but there's still a sense of uselessness and fatigue in the control room.

Maggie's supposed to be writing a paper, but Jeanette notices that she spends most of her time staring at the wall, as if it's a proxy for the sky.

The telescope operator is talking on the phone in Spanish, and eating biscuits at the same time. His desk is covered with layers of newspapers and biscuit wrappers, archaeological evidence of years of observing.

'What happened with your last job application?' Maggie swings round to face her.

'Nothing.' Jeanette doesn't want to think about it.

'Was it a permanent lectureship that you were applying for?'

Jeanette just nods.

'Well, did you get any feedback, at least?' Maggie persists.

'Nope. Nada.' She may as well have flushed her application down the loo.

Maggie goes back to studying the wall. 'Perhaps you're being too ambitious. Nearly everyone at our age is still a post-doc. Just wait a bit. Be patient.'

Jeanette sighs. It's ok for Maggie, she seems content to be a post-doc, changing jobs every two years, moving house, shifting about the world with all her belongings in her suitcase. She's based in Heidelberg now, but before that it was Japan, and before that it was — Jeanette can't even remember. She wonders what it's like, being foreign all the time.

The telescope operator has finished his lengthy phone call and is now talking to Maggie, who can speak Spanish. Jeanette can't tell what they're talking about, and the meaningless words buzz irritatingly about her head. She looks at Maggie for enlightenment, but gets no response. She feels ignored.

She decides to check her emails for the nth time, but there's nothing interesting; just another one from the invisible woman, asking if she wants to meet up again. She contacted this woman through an advert a few months ago, after a particularly lean patch. But when they finally met, she walked past the woman three times before noticing her. Later, as they wandered along the beach at Cramond, and the wind hustled sand and rubbish around their feet, Jeanette found herself being hemmed in by the woman's small words. When she tried to respond, her descriptions of her own life sounded equally circumscribed. She hoped the physical act might rescue them. But in bed, she tried not to shudder as the woman said, 'That was nice,' with a wistfulness in her voice which infuriated Jeanette. She left shortly afterwards, slamming the front door behind her, and the noise it made gave her more satisfaction than the tiny orgasm she had had buried under the sheets, the woman's diligent hands working on her.

Now, she deletes the email without replying. Surely, it's better to be alone, with no limitations?

At three in the morning she's eaten her sandwiches and drunk a lot of coffee. They have to wait here all night, just in case the sky does clear. Now the wind is picking up, which may be a good sign; it may sweep the cloud off the mountains.

She gets up and walks around for a bit, but then Maggie sighs and puts down her pen. They look at each other but don't speak. Jeanette decides to leave the room.

It's not that dark outside; the cloud diffuses the moonlight and smears it out across the sky. Jeanette stands just outside the door and listens to the wind. It has a curiously tinny sound as it bounces off the metal domes; someone might be rattling a baking sheet in the sky.

She sets off down the path that leads away from the telescope. She knows she shouldn't be wandering around by herself at night without telling anyone where she is going. Those are the rules here. It's supposed to be dangerous. But Jeanette has had enough of being stuck inside; out here is better.

But out here is too windy. She battles against the wind like a cartoon character but she can barely stand up. She stumbles back up the narrow tarmac path, and by the time she is back at the telescope she's out of breath. She pushes at the door to the control room, but as it opens she can hear voices; Maggie and the telescope operator. She listens for a moment; the voices are hushed, as if they're telling each other secrets. She doesn't want to listen any more. She shuts the door and creeps around the side until she comes to another door. When she opens this one, it takes her straight into the dome.

Inside, she stands on the circumference of the room looking up at the rectangle of sky. When her eyes get used to the dark she sets out for the centre, where the telescope is. She has to resist an impulse to reach out and stroke it, as if it were an animal shackled to the concrete floor. The dome judders as the wind picks up and she wonders if it could be unpeeled from its base and made to sail into the sky.

The thin amount of light in here can only glint off small pieces of things. It hints at something else, something larger buried in the darkness. A nest of wires coils out of the back of the telescope and snakes away across the floor to the door on the far side. Beyond that is the control room. Here in this mysterious space, it seems impossible to go through that door and enter a world of other people, fluorescent light, and stained coffee cups. Perhaps she can shelter here, at least for the rest of tonight.

But suddenly there is a tearing, crashing sound above her, not safely in the sky, but right here in the dome. And as she stands, terrified, the light that she has grown used to diminishes and disappears. She is in darkness. And it's not the velvet-soft darkness that she imagined, the darkness that would wrap itself around her and make friends with her and stroke her face. This darkness continues to be filled with a sharp noise, no longer from above her but right in front of her. She senses something fly past her face, cold air brushes her cheeks and she screams. She falls to the floor.

Light hits her eyes.

'Jeanette?' Maggie's voice sounds thin. More footsteps; the telescope operator is there too. 'Are you ok?'

She manages to get to her knees, but realises she is shaking.

'For God's sake! What are you doing in here? Why didn't you tell us?'

She remains kneeling on the cold floor in front of them. Perhaps she is thanking them for something.

'It's a good thing we heard you scream. Juan managed to stop the telescope.'

So it was the telescope that almost hit her. She wants to shut her eyes again, to block it all out. People have been killed by telescopes. She's standing now, her feet reasonably firm on the floor. She can't see anything beyond the torchlight burning into her face. Someone grabs her elbow and she realises it is Maggie trying to steer her away. As she moves, something inside her mouth loosens and she's finally able to speak. 'What happened?'

'Juan was parking the telescope for the night. He didn't know you were in here.' They're back in the control room now. Maggie pushes her into a chair and sits down opposite her. 'Why did you leave?'

'Why not? Nothing was happening.' She can detect a tiny shred of guilt in Maggie's words. If this were serious, they would all be in trouble, not just her. But going into the telescope dome without telling anyone is a cardinal sin, she would be in the most trouble. Now, she's not sure why she did it. She just wanted to be in a different place. She stares over Maggie's head at a star chart pinned to the wall.

'What were you doing in there?'

Aldeberan, Betelgeuse... The names of the stars are comforting. And it must almost be the end of the night by now, almost time to go to the residence and sleep. She's aware that Maggie wants her to speak. Riga, Altair, Andromeda... Maggie's hair is twisted around one hand and her eyes look too small, as if they've retreated from something. Perhaps she is upset by what happened. How does Jeanette know what Maggie feels? Behind them, out of sight, she is aware of the telescope operator. He hasn't spoken since she entered this room. His version of events is unknowable to her, and she thinks she prefers it that way.

'Why did you take the risk?'

She wishes she knew the answer to that. 'It's alright, Mags, I'm fine.'

But Maggie persists. 'You can't do things like that. It's not fair to me or to Juan. You're not the only one here.'

'Look, I just needed a bit of space.' She tries to laugh. 'You know what it's like being cooped up in this room with the same people night after night.'

'That's our job, Jeanette. It's what we do.' And Jeanette realises, surprised, that Maggie's voice is hard. Perhaps Maggie really might be fed up with her.

Perhaps she should just throw herself into her work and not do anything else. She knows plenty of other astronomers who live like that. There's someone at Cambridge who never goes anywhere apart from his office and the canteen. He became a professor at the age of twenty-nine. She wonders what he thinks about on cloudy nights.

The next afternoon she sits in the canteen at a table by herself and watches the other astronomers staring out over the mountains and sky, waiting for the evening.

There are no differences to the days here; time goes round in circles and the sky rotates overhead. That's what makes Jeanette want to scream, to be boxed in by time as well as space.

That night the control room is silent. Jeanette and Maggie sit at opposite ends of the room, the telescope operator in between them. Jeanette knows she should speak, should explain why she behaved the way she did. But she's not sure if she can trace the thread of her actions from cause to effect. Why did she decide to go into the dome? She can't think of a reason. Boredom? Curiosity? No real reason at all. But that won't do for Maggie. So much of their work here is driven by routine; setting up the telescope each evening, taking the calibration images, working methodically through the list of targets. This is not a place to be impulsive, to take risks.

There are two ways of measuring time at a telescope; two separate displays on the console tell Jeanette the ordinary earth-based time, and also sidereal time. The time of stars. The two loop round each other, one lagging behind the other and then leap-frogging it, depending on the time of year. Tonight the sidereal time is two hours behind the ordinary time and Jeanette can't stop staring at the large red numbers ticking away, even though it reminds her of her mother compulsively watching the TV. Watching and waiting for the future to be brought to her, because the present is so unbearable.

'Jeanette, look at this!'

It's four in the morning, the dead hour when all you can do is try and stay awake, but Maggie sounds alert, excited even. This is almost the first thing that Maggie has said to her all night so, intrigued, she stands behind her to get a better look at the screen, yawning discreetly into her hand.

She sees oval blobs of different sizes, the largest as big as a thumbnail, and there are about thirty of them making up a cluster of galaxies. A thin arc, no wider than a couple of pixels, appears to join two galaxies near the centre of the image.

'Nice,' says Jeanette, but something is puzzling her. 'That's the wrong galaxy.' She points at one of them, at its faint whirlpool arms.

'What do you mean?'

'We already know its redshift — so it's not in the cluster.' Maggie doesn't reply, but Jeanette has to carry on. 'It must be an interloper.'

They're both silent now. Neither of them needs to say the obvious; that the interloper can only appear to be connected to the other galaxy through being superimposed on it in this two dimensional image. But according to its redshift that's impossible; the standard Big Bang model says that a galaxy's redshift is a measure of its distance. Two objects with different redshifts are at different distances and they can't be physically connected in the way that these galaxies appear to be.

'The link looks real, though.'

'It does, doesn't it?'

They smile at each other. They don't know what it means, but it is unexpected, and therefore interesting. Not many unexpected events happen in their work; usually they do observations for which they have already predicted the results. This is the drawback to working in a well-established science where the main theory is sketched out and all they are doing is colouring in the details.

Maggie pats the empty chair next to her, and Jeanette sits down.

'We should repeat the observation, make sure it's not just a cosmic ray or a random fluctuation,' says Maggie.

'Make it longer this time, we can probably go to twenty minutes before the centre gets saturated.'

The next twenty minutes take a long time. They don't normally repeat their observations. She thinks what a privilege it is to be able to wind back the clock and reconstruct a splinter of reality. You can't do this in everyday life, can't just say to a soon to be ex-lover, 'Hold on, rewind, let's go back to that bit where we still had hope and try again, differently this time.'

The repeat observation is finished and they hold their breath as the image is read out onto the screen. The link between the galaxies is still there and Maggie lets out a whoosh of air. The telescope operator carries on reading his newspaper, it's not his job to get excited about these things.

They spend the rest of the night analysing the images in more detail, their heads bent together in front of the screen. Maggie adds the images together and cleans them of contamination, while Jeanette does a quick calculation of the size of the link. Here, on this image, it's just thirty pixels long, but out there it's larger than the entire Milky Way. She squints at it from the side of the screen; perhaps it holds a secret, like Holbein's anamorphic skull. It's really very faint.

'Take a look at this,' Maggie says, a few minutes later. She's done something to the data so the link looks brighter, and more obvious.

'You've smoothed it?' asks Jeanette.

'Yup.'

'That's kind of cheating.' Now the pixels have been smeared over each other so each one shows some of the light from its neighbours.

'Makes it look good, though?' Maggie is grinning.

'Why don't we write a separate paper about this?' Jeanette asks, 'We could probably do it really quickly.'

'Does it warrant an entire paper?'

'Maggie!' Jeanette laughs incredulously. 'This could be amazing! This could be evidence against the entire Big Bang theory!'

Maggie sits up, 'You're not serious! One tenuous link between two galaxies at different redshifts? What about all the evidence in favour? We're not dismissing that.'

'I'm not saying one thing or the other. But it's a major observation.

Let's publish it and see what happens.'

'You actually think people are going to look at this and question — everything?'

Jeanette hesitates. 'Yeah, maybe. That's what we do. Or what we should do. Ask questions.'

She's asked questions all her life, and now she's an adult the questions get answered. Or at least listened to.

When she leaves the observatory a few days later, travelling down the tightly curled mountain roads back to bird song and rain, the realisation of what they want to publish begins to dawn on her. Are they seriously suggesting that they have evidence that the Big Bang model is wrong? They'll have to be cautious. As long as they stick to the actual data and avoid drawing any conclusions it should be ok.

But it's not until she's on the plane going home, listening to the comforting hum of the engines, that she's able to see the sky clearly again.

THEN

One summer, when Jeanette is ten years old, her home explodes. An intense flash of light slams through all the rooms, sucking up the air and noise and colour, making everything brilliantly white, impeccably silent.

When the light dies down, the house is empty. Oh sure, all the furniture's in the same place; the sofa where her mother sits in the afternoons, staring at air. The dining table and chairs where Jeanette and her parents eat without speaking, trying not to look at the empty fourth chair.

She wants to make it sound like it used to. When she gets home from school, she bangs the garden gate, flings open the front door, shouts, 'Hello,' and stamps down the hallway into the living room.

'Keep the noise down,' her mother whispers from a huddle on the sofa.

Kate used to get up early each morning and go to the pool for swimming practice. When she was very young she learnt how to tuck all her hair into her tight blue swimming cap, so that not a single wisp blurred her outline as she swam in perfect straight lines up and down the length of the pool. Occasionally Jeanette came and watched her. She liked the way Kate could push the water aside so efficiently. She always swam as though she was going somewhere, and needed to get there fast.

The other kids made a mess of the water, they splashed too much and churned it up, and the coach shouted at them. He didn't often shout at Kate, but walked along the side of the pool as she swam, keeping pace with her.

Sitting there watching Kate felt like sitting in a clean, hard box. All the kids had neat, tidy bodies. The coach was small and compact, with a bullet head and legs tightly corded with veins. Jeanette felt out of place as she lolled against the seat, surreptitiously sucking sweets and picking scabs on her knees, trying to remember when Kate had started swimming. There had always been swimming. Kate had swum for ever.

One night Jeanette hides in her bedroom to get away from her parents. She opens the window to get a better view of the dark-covered land outside. The sky's clear and she sees the stars; they feel like some sort of blessing. She tilts her face up to them for so long that she notices they're moving. They're not keeping pace with the moon, which is arcing high overhead; they have their own smaller motion. As they swing around she wants to grab onto a chain of them and be carried away from here. Fascinated, she watches a single faint star in the apple tree, its light just visible as it moves through the tips of the branches.

That night, she learns that it takes a star an hour to travel the width of the tree. An hour of not having to sit with her parents downstairs. An hour of feeling the air brush her face and cool the hot, sad, congested mess inside her.

At first, just after the explosion, everything seems shocking and clear, as if the world has been replaced by another one overnight. One that superficially looks the same, but which is a copy of the real one, like some sort of TV programme where actors try to be proper people, but you can tell they're faking it. When Kate returns, the world will be real again. But Kate doesn't return. Not after her funeral when Jeanette goes back to school and her parents to work, and they all have to pretend everything is normal. Kate could return now, Jeanette thinks, and it wouldn't be too difficult. She might be cross about the funeral, or maybe she would find it funny. Jeanette doesn't know.

Then more time goes by, and the actors get better at acting, or perhaps Jeanette forgets what's real and what's fake. But every now and then, she realises that the world isn't just pretend, it's wrong. And still she doesn't know why it happened. Kate's gone but she doesn't know why. Nobody will talk about it. There is just this heavy silence everywhere.

One evening as they're eating dinner she asks her parents, 'Why did it happen?'

They don't say anything, but her mother gives a sort of shiver as if she's cold, although it's quite warm in the house.

So she tries again. 'What happened to Kate?'

Finally her father speaks. 'She drowned.'

Drowned? But she was swimming. She was the best swimmer. The best one in the team, in the whole county. There was talk of Olympic trials. How can you drown if you know how to swim?

'But how could she drown? She didn't just suddenly stop swimming, did she?' She fiddles with her fork while she waits for them to answer, before she realises that they're not going to.

'How did it happen?' She taps the fork on her plate to break the silence. It doesn't make sense. Why won't they tell her what really happened?

'Jeanette.' They refuse to tell her any more so she gives up and lets the silence take over. That night she leaves them in the living room with the television blaring, and she goes upstairs to her room and leans against the window staring at the sky.

The swimming suits are still all around the house, like the discarded skins of dead animals. They lie curled over the radiators, and crumpled in the corners of the kitchen. Jeanette finds one of them in her own laundry basket, but she's afraid to touch it. When she does finally pick it up, it seems too light, as if it could float up into the sky. She's not sure what to do with it, so she scrunches it up and stuffs it under her mattress. She doesn't want to throw it away; Kate may need it. The swimming suits have a sour smell which Jeanette never really noticed before, but now it seems ominous, like a siren going off in her head.

Kate died.

She died because she drowned.

No, she didn't die. She swam down a river until she found a hill with a cave hidden in it. In the cave there's a bed draped in satin and she's asleep on this bed, with a knight standing guard over her.

Perhaps she likes being asleep. But Jeanette doubts that. Kate was good at getting up early for swimming practice. So perhaps she's lying on the bed just pretending to be asleep, but really she has one eye open and she's staring at the knight, wondering why he's wearing armour and why she's lying on satin sheets.

Perhaps she got ill and died in the swimming pool. But she hadn't been ill that morning. Jeanette can't remember the last morning, which means that it must have been a normal one; Kate crashing down the stairs at six o'clock, her father waiting by the front door, eyes half shut with tiredness.

Satin sheets would be very slippery. You'd slither off the bed. Velvet is better, Kate used to have a dark blue velvet hair ribbon. It's probably still in her room. Jeanette thinks about going to get the hair ribbon but stays where she is, gazing up at the sky and wondering what her parents know, and what they won't tell her, about Kate's death.

Jeanette's father spends a lot of time gardening. He used to give Jeanette and Kate things he found out there, handing them over as if they were priceless gifts. Rosehips or daisies, or, once, a tiny pale blue eggshell. One side of it was shattered, but if you turned it over you could pretend it was still whole. They argued over who could keep it and Kate won. It's still in her room.

There are lots of other things in her room, but Jeanette doesn't want them anymore. She wanted them when Kate was still here, but now that Kate has gone, something's happened to the things. It makes her feel heavy inside, just thinking about the bird's egg, or the oyster shells, or the swan feather. It makes her feel tired.

There's other stuff too, to do with Kate's swimming. All the medals and cups and certificates and curled up yellowy newspaper clippings used to be crowded together on the sideboard in the dining room. There wasn't enough space for all of it, not after Kate started winning really big cups with wide handles.

One morning Jeanette's the first to get up. This happens quite a lot, now that her father doesn't have to take Kate to her training session. There's no shape, no centre to their days without Kate's swimming to keep them in order.

But if nobody else is around, it's easier to pretend that things are normal, and that her mum is asleep and Kate and her dad are at the pool. This is what she's used to. On mornings like this, the lump inside her melts, just a bit, and she can breathe easier. But when she takes her breakfast into the dining room, all the stuff has gone, and the surface of the sideboard is flat and bare. There are faint rings in the dust, like ripples on a swimming pool. Jeanette blows on the dust, making it rise into the air. The rings are even fainter now.

Just one photo of Kate is left. A school photo; Kate in her uniform grinning at the camera. Jeanette can't work out how far away it is, even though she knows it's on the sideboard. Space seems to have buckled so that it's simultaneously in the middle of the room, hovering under the lightbulb, and also at the edge, near the garden. She can't look at it any more, the lack of perspective makes her feel dizzy.

Jeanette eats her breakfast in the kitchen to avoid the photo. In the evening, when they're in the dining room, she's aware of the photo lying in the dust. The three of them eating in silence and a photo of the fourth. Is this what happens when you die? Do you turn into an image?

One day, even the photo is gone and the sideboard is polished clean. The photo is never seen again, but that doesn't help the silent words.

They get ready to move house. This was planned when Kate was still here. In fact the reason for moving house was to live nearer to the big Olympic-sized swimming pool, so Kate didn't have to spend so much time travelling to her training sessions. Now, there is no point in moving house, but it happens anyway.

Before they move they have to pack up everything in the old house. It's like the end of an elaborate game, where all the pieces are scattered all over the board and they have to be put back into the box. Except that this game seems to consist of the pieces getting thrown away.

Jeanette's mother kneels on the kitchen floor and crams a crumpled cushion cover into an already overflowing cardboard box marked 'RUBBISH' in neat black pen on each side. Around her are heaped piles of stained tea towels, a crooked tower of saucepans missing their lids, a stack of postcards so faded that it's impossible to tell where they come from, a wind chime with its strings tangled together, and a dog collar.

'Whose is this?' Jeanette picks up the dog collar. It's old and worn, almost disintegrated in places.

'When I was a kid, we had a dog. A lassie dog.'

'And you've kept its collar all this time?'

'It's going now.' And the collar gets squashed into the box.

The door to Kate's room stays shut during all the packing activity and Jeanette is afraid to open it. She doesn't know what she's more afraid of, seeing a bare room, or seeing all her sister's belongings still endlessly waiting for her sister. The patience of things, the way they will just sit and wait like dumb animals, makes her want to cry.

Finally, the day before they move, she plucks up the courage to creak open the door. The room is empty. In fact, there's an astonishing absence of things. In every other part of the house, the packing cases are piled up in the middle of rooms and surrounded by abandoned tat and rubbish, like a beach at low tide covered in strands of seaweed and chunks of old plastic. Here, there is nothing. Not even any boxes. Just indentations on the carpet showing where the furniture was. Jeanette goes over to where the bed should have been and lies down on the floor, looking up at the ceiling. Perhaps there are clues up there. But the ceiling is bland white. She doesn't remember ever looking at it before. All she can do is take great bites of the air, gulping it down inside her. There's nothing else of Kate that she can take with her.

She's in her sister's bedroom, trying to tidy up. But something's wrong. The schoolbooks piled on the desk aren't covered in dust, the way they should be by now after all these years. The handwriting on the sheets of paper is still crisp and black, not faded.

She picks up the waste paper basket and tries to shake the contents into a bin bag, but the pieces of crumpled paper, old tissues and pencil shavings refuse to move. They disobey the force of gravity and stay poised in mid air, the way her sister used to hover above the diving board before plunging into the pool.

The swimming suit on the radiator is still wet, but the water isn't running down the grooves of the radiator and soaking into the carpet the way it used to.

Her sister's bedroom is the only place in the universe which defies entropy and time. Which stays locked in the past.

NOW

When Jeanette arrives home the observing trip, like every other observing trip she has been on, seems slightly unreal. Those journeys up mountains into air stretched out thin feel as if they take place in another life. Perhaps they're the scientific equivalent of going to a monastery. Perhaps the only way of understanding the universe is to retreat from normal life.

The first day back at work is always an ordeal. Her sleep patterns are disturbed from the combination of jet-lag and the topsy-turvidom of working at night. But she hasn't forgotten how much she longed for the grit of Edinburgh, the kindness of its dirt and noise, the whole multiplicity of life here, as opposed to the tedious singularity of purpose at the observatory in Chile.

Fortunately, there is one aspect of this trip that is different to the others. When she returns, the tapes of data collected during the trip are piled on her desk waiting to be analysed. Sometimes they wait for a long time, because it's never as much fun looking at data afterwards as it was at the telescope. The crucial sense of discovery has dissipated on the journey home. But this trip has been different. They actually have something interesting to look at.

She puts the tape in the computer and locates the image of the connected galaxies. The link between them is very small and much fainter than she remembers. Her heart sinks, but she carries on.

The first, crucial question she must answer is, is the link real? The best way to deal with this to turn it around — is it not real? That is the question everyone else will be trying to answer.

So. If it's not a real link between the galaxies then what is it? There are two types of possible answer. The first is related to the telescope.

There could be an artefact in the image that mimics a genuine link between the galaxies, caused by the way the telescope works, or dust on the lens. That's ok, she can quantify those possibilities because she has the necessary manuals and software to help her calibrate the image. To a large extent this work is routine.

Or the link could be caused by some real material being emitted by one galaxy, but not necessarily connected to the other one, and it's only a coincidence because they're looking at it from a certain angle. It's just a trick of perspective. This is less palatable because it's more difficult to quantify. It involves more conjecture. She doesn't like handwaving arguments.

She sets about calibrating the data so she can eliminate the first possibility.

Then she zooms in on the link, blows it up until each individual pixel is visible. There are no sudden jumps in intensity from one pixel to another. Good. That means it's unlikely the link is caused by a cosmic ray hitting the telescope.

She looks for evidence that the link is not actually joined to both galaxies, that it's superimposed on one or the other. She makes a contour map to identify the pixels at the same intensity across the image. The smooth transition in intensity implies a coherent link.

It seems real. It's unlikely not to be real. This is what she has concluded. She gets up and moves away from the screen and the sudden change in perspective takes her by surprise. Everything here seems far away, unlike the tiny chain of pixels she's been staring at for the past hour.

Time to go and look at different types of images. She's been invited to the end of year show at Paula's art college. She's keen to see what sort of art Paula has produced because she still can't imagine Paula creating things, but perhaps she only knows one version of her, and there are many others folded up inside, like extra dimensions. Paula's only been at art college for a year, and Jeanette isn't used to the idea of her being interested in painting. She never seemed interested in it when they were both students.

At the show she discovers she doesn't know anyone apart from Paula. Everyone else seems to know each other, or perhaps they're just better at pretending than she is. Fortunately she finds one of Paula's paintings and is able to stand in front of it, avoiding the need to talk to strangers. She's just remembered that this is another of the things she finds difficult after observing trips.

But the painting's good. She's surprised at how good it is. It shows a woman who superficially looks like Paula, but there's something different. It's larger than life, the face is about three times its normal size. There's a glowing intensity to the pale skin, it reminds her of the surface of the moon. Staring at the face makes Jeanette feel uncomfortable, so she works her way round the edges of the painting. Behind the face is a bed with a pile of white sheets on it. In another corner there's a man's suit on a hanger.

But when Jeanette looks closer at this dark suit she sees it's painted to look like fur. It's the skin of a large animal, maybe a bear. The title of the painting is 'My Life as a Man'.

'What do you think?'

Jeanette jolts round to find Paula grinning at her. 'It's amazing. I mean, I didn't know you could paint like this. It's so lifelike.' She looks back at the painting. Now the face seems more serious and somehow more real than Paula's own.

'You haven't asked about the title.' Paula steers her away from the painting and towards the wine.

'Well?'

'I tried to imagine myself as a man. I dressed in a man's suit when I was painting it. I wanted to be something different, the opposite of what I normally am. To see how it would affect the painting.'

Jeanette's intrigued. 'The opposite? Like anti-matter?' She can imagine Paula meeting male anti-Paula and both of them exploding into pure energy.

Around them, other people swirl and laugh. It's very hot in this room and Jeanette's thirsty enough to keep sipping the awful wine. She asks 'Where's Becca? Isn't she supposed to be here too?'

'She's not coming.'

'Oh? Why not?'

But Paula has seen someone else she knows, and she darts off.

Jeanette finds another of Paula's paintings. This one shows a woman lying on a bed, but only her legs can be seen, from the thighs down. Again, everything is meticulously depicted, the dark wooden floor, the white walls, the pale marble-like legs, even the crimson nail varnish on her toes. They're nice legs, thinks Jeanette. She wonders who they belong to. Somehow she knows that the woman is naked, even though the rest of her body can't be seen. There's an elegiac quality to the painting. It feels as if someone has just left the room. Something in the way that the legs flop to one side implies that the woman is alone, and has been abandoned. The room seems old, whatever happened here was a long time ago.

The third of Paula's paintings shows an ear, about two feet high, painted in shades of white and cream, with a few strands of dark hair. The title is 'Omphalos'; the Greek for navel. Is this a little joke of Paula, to get her anatomy deliberately wrong? But as Jeanette studies the ear she sees the point. The earhole does appear to lead away to the centre of something, something dark and profound.

The Ancient Greeks used to call the oracle at Delphi the 'Omphalos', the navel or centre of the world. The oracle made utterances. But ears don't speak, they listen.

She escapes outside, and bumps into Becca.

'We thought you weren't coming,' she tells her.

Becca shrugs. 'Is it crowded in there?'

'Yeah, packed.'

'Good.' She walks inside, Jeanette following behind her. At one point Jeanette loses her, but then she sees her at the far side of the big room, looking at one of Paula's paintings. It take Jeanette some time to work her way through the crowded room and get closer, but Becca hasn't moved. She's standing very close to the painting; the woman on the bed.

'Do you like it?' Jeanette asks her.

'Like it?' Becca turns to Jeanette, but her expression is odd. Jeanette gets the impression she's not really looking at her, she's still got the painting in her mind's eye. Her eyes glance around the room. 'Where's Paula?'

Just then they both hear a trill of laughter and Paula is next to them. She is flushed, her cheeks pink with the success of her paintings, and her performance here tonight.

'Darlings!' She flings an arm around each of them. 'Thank you so much for coming! For being here.' She squeezes them to her so that there is a sudden muddle of soft bodies and perfume, and Jeanette gets a strand of someone's hair across her mouth. Then Paula's off again, greeting someone else, and Jeanette and Becca are left together in front of the painting.

'Nice legs,' says Jeanette, gesturing at the painting.

'Thanks,' says Becca.

'That's you?'

'Yes. I had a short-lived career as an artist's model.'

When? When did Becca model for Paula, and why didn't they mention it? The label on the painting says it was painted last year. As usual, Jeanette feels like she doesn't know what's going on underneath the surface of things.

The next day at work and it's Jeanette's turn to lead a reading group for the students. This is an opportunity for the students to learn some new astronomy and demonstrate what they've learnt to their more senior colleagues. Most of the students tend not to see it as an opportunity, but as a threat.

Today's reading group is based on a review paper about the standard Big Bang model, summarising the basic building blocks of this model, the assumptions needed to construct it, and the most recent work which both reinforces and modifies it.

The post-docs take it in turns to lead reading groups, sometimes watched over by more senior colleagues, keen to see how their students are getting on. Today, Jeanette must make sure that she challenges each of the students and gets them all to contribute to the discussion.

The reading group is always held in the canteen, to give the illusion of informality. All the first and second year post-graduate students are required to attend; it's optional for the more senior ones, which means they never attend.

Today the students gather round one of the low tables near the white board, clutching their mugs of coffee and copies of the paper. The first year students look worried. The older ones just look resigned.

As they approach her, Jeanette remembers the incident in a reading group last year when a student started to quote poetry, something about the glory of heaven. Then he recited part of the Lord's Prayer, 'On earth as it is in heaven'. He left the Observatory shortly afterwards and was never seen again. There are always casualties.

She knows from experience how difficult it can be to get them all to participate. So she's prepared a list of questions for them to respond to, and to get the conversation moving. She reads the first one to them as they're still settling into their chairs. 'What do we need to assume to build a basic model of the Universe?'

She wants to get them to think about what is known, and what isn't known but can be reasonably assumed. They look down at their notes, shuffling through bits of paper. She tries not to sigh. This is such a basic question.

'Something about everything being the same everywhere?' says Clara. Clara doesn't look like she really belongs inside here, she's glowing with health, her hair is thick and butter-yellow, her cheeks rosy. She should be running through flowery meadows, surrounded by Alpine cows with long eyelashes. A black smudge of biro on her cheek only makes the rest of her look even cleaner and healthier.

'Yes, but what. What properties are "the same", and what do you mean by "the same"?'

Clara gives up and stares out the window. Her PhD is based in the lab with Jon, building part of the satellite instrument. The theory is not so relevant for her.

Silence. Part of the point of these seminars is to get the students to do the work, they shouldn't be spoon-fed. So she can't crack and reveal the answer, however much she'd like to. And perhaps a tiny part of her enjoys inflicting this pain on them, demonstrating how wide the gulf is between her and them, and how much she has achieved. Post-docs are the most junior level of the academic staff, but they are on the other side of the divide that separates her from this group. She has her PhD and they don't.

'Can you outline the two most basic, important assumptions?' she prods them. Sometimes the silence just gets too much and she's driven to speak. It can be horribly reminiscent of childhood dinners, sitting at the dining table wishing someone would talk to her. Answer her questions.

Clara tries again. 'The same wherever you look?'

Finally. 'Yes. We assume the Universe is isotropic, so it looks the same in all directions. This isn't true on small scales, but is true on larger ones. Now, what's the other assumption?'

She looks around. There are six of them present today; as well as Clara there is Giovanni, who hasn't managed to button up his check shirt correctly, so there is mismatched fabric bunching around his neck and crotch, and Mark who is wearing a tee-shirt with Maxwell's equations printed on it. She knows Mark knows this stuff and considers it faintly beneath him to be quizzed in this way. His silence has an air of disdain for the whole process. The others look more frankly baffled. She wishes they'd stop shuffling their papers around.

Mark finally decides to speak. 'You also need the Cosmological

Principle, which is just an extension of the Copernican Principle, namely that we're not in a privileged position in the Universe. The view from the Earth, which is isotropic, is the same as the view from anywhere else. On this Weyl hypersurface anyway...'

She stops him. 'Yes fine, Mark. But hang on. Let's not go too quickly. Go back to the Cosmological Principle. What do you get if you combine isotropy with the Cosmological Principle?'

He looks at her as if she were stupid. 'Homogeneity, of course.'

Of course. Bloody show off, she almost whispers under her breath. He's left the others way behind, and their paper-shuffling has reached epidemic proportions.

Giovanni says, 'Why do you have to assume anything?' He finally realises his shirt is not buttoned correctly so he starts to adjust it, revealing expanses of hairy stomach.

'Without any assumptions the problem's intractable. The Universe is just random squiggles on the sky. But you can test your assumptions. The cosmic microwave background looks the same in all directions, so that backs up isotropy.'

Giovanni still looks worried. 'So you must assume isotropy but you can derive homogeneity? What is the difference between them?'

Mark rolls his eyes.

An hour later the white board is covered in scribbles and they've managed to reach page two of the paper, so they pause to get more coffee. At this rate, it'll take them the rest of the day to get through the paper so Jeanette decides to hurry things along.

'Who can explain what redshift is, and its relationship to distance in the standard model?'

They get bogged down in discussions of Doppler shifts and speeding ambulances, and Bill does his impression of a siren, which seems to surprise some of the other people sitting in the canteen. Jeanette brings them back into line by reminding them that this is just an analogy. 'Remember it's space itself that is expanding, the objects are not actually travelling through space.'

'No?' Several puzzled faces turn to her.

'No. Now, can anyone explain the evidence for dark matter?'

'Umm, like, galaxies spin around too fast?'

'Too fast for what.'

'Too fast based on how many visible stars they have. So you need something else to stop them flying apart, something you can't see?' Bill looks relieved at being able to make the galaxies stable.

'Well done.'

'Hang on.' Giovanni's worried. 'Where does the Cosmological Principle stop?'

'Stop?' She's a bit annoyed that he's gone back to this. They need to get on.

'Yes. The Earth isn't in a unique place and neither is the Milky Way, and now ordinary matter is only 4% of the mass so the Universe is mostly dark matter, and perhaps even the Universe may be just one of many. At what point does it all stop and something become special again?'

' "Special"?' says Mark. 'That's not physics.'

But Jeanette feels almost sorry for Giovanni, still clutching his shirt as he's being spun around on a cosmic wheel that has no centre. What else does he have to hold onto?

She's sitting on a horse with rigid nostrils and a plaster mane moulded on one side of its bright painted neck. She's paid her pennies and she can ride as long as she wants. But every seminar she attends and every equation she solves sends her looping and spiralling further beyond the wooden circumference of the merry-go-round.

Each new size and shape of darkness projects her further into the night, holding on to whatever she can find as she gallops through the universe.

The door to her office opens, and she's caught resting her head on her desk.

'Sorry to disturb you,' says the Death Star and he waits while she removes the stacks of papers from the other chair to make space for him, before perching on the desk so that he's looking down at her. He's wearing a bow-tie. She realises she's staring at the bow-tie; there are cartoon pictures of planets on it.

'I've been interviewed for Radio 4, Melvyn's programme. They've asked me to speak about the end of the universe,' he says.

'Ah.' There's a silence and she realises she's required to say something, to offer some information in exchange for his. 'I've been rewriting my paper, the one that needed a bit of work after the referee's report.'

She tries to sound enthusiastic about this, although she first wrote the paper three years ago when she was a student, and the referee's indictment of it has been lurking in her desk drawer for the past eighteen months. Only occasionally she has the strength to take it out and read it before hiding it again. Phrases from it regularly appear in her mind at night when she can't sleep; phrases such as "the author clearly believes in the strength of her own argument without having to bother with the unnecessary, and clearly to her, irritating detail of testing it impartially and scientifically".

'Good. I imagine you've dealt with all of the comments? You'll need to get it back to the journal soon, the editors'll be wondering what's taken you so long. At that journal, they're daft enough to think that the referee might be right!'

Jeanette keeps an eye on him as he chuckles. She knows he likes criticising other people who attack his staff, but only because he thinks that activity is his sole privilege. Sure enough, he stops laughing and knots his hands together in front of him as a prelude to the inevitable lecture.

She fights back the impulse to mimic him and knot her own hands. She has observed plenty of post-docs who become their professors' doppelgängers. This is how the scientific method is disseminated, and it's a far more powerful way than simply studying textbooks. She has observed how a scientist speaks, how he (and it is nearly always a he) talks up his own work, rubbishes his critics, patronises his students and she knows that if she can replicate this behaviour she can become one of them, with a few minor modifications needed to allow for the fact that she's a woman.

It's necessary to jolt him off this topic of conversation. She doesn't want to agree meekly to yet another rewrite of her boring paper. 'I've got something interesting to show you,' She displays the image of the connected galaxies.

He stares intently at the screen for some time before speaking. 'What are the redshifts?'

She tells him.

'So this... link is just apparent, it can't be real.'

'I know, but look at it. It looks real.' She doesn't really have to say this. He hasn't come up for air yet.

'You're planning to publish this?' He finally twists round to face her and she's surprised to see he's smiling.

'Umm, yes. Probably. I still need to run a few more tests. Double check the calibration.' She's got what she wanted, he's interested, but for some reason this makes her nervous.

'Of course. Nothing hasty now,' he murmurs, and looks back at the galaxies. 'Would you be the first author on the paper?'

Her mind does frantic calculations. 'I don't know. Nothing's been discussed.'

'Could help you.' His voice is even quieter now, and she has to lean forward to hear him as he continues. 'Could be good for your career. Even if it's wrong.'

Later that night, she wonders if she heard him properly, if he did actually say that. In one way he's right. Most scientific papers are wrong at some level. They're superseded by more accurate papers with better quality data or more detailed models. This degree of wrongness is how the subject works, how things progress, how people learn. But what she and Maggie are considering is a spectacular amount of potential wrongness. They're not proposing an incremental change to an accepted model. They're proposing blowing it out of the water. And what's more, they haven't actually got anything else to put in its place. Could this really help her? She lies in her bed, staring at the ceiling and thinking, until morning.

Jeanette is eating lunch with Richard and the other post-docs in a corner of the canteen but she's not really paying attention to them arguing about football, she's still thinking about the connected galaxies. One of them sighs; the Death Star is approaching them.

Jeanette watches as he slowly makes his way up the centre of the room, tray clamped in his hands, his gaze sweeping over the staff and students. Finally he reaches their table. As he sits down, he accidentally knocks his bowl of soup which spills onto the table. But he doesn't make any move to clean up the steaming mess.

'Why does heat flow from a hot body to a cold one?'

This is why they dread eating lunch with him. Yesterday he asked them what the best course of action should be if someone were trapped in a free falling lift about to hit the ground. Should one jump up in the air just before the moment of impact? If so, why.

Today, Richard is the first to try and answer. 'It's the most likely thing to happen. It would be very unlikely for the hot body to get hotter and the cold body to get colder.' Jeanette just sits and waits. She knows Richard will get into knots. He always does this, always makes an attempt to answer the Death Star, and fails. She wishes he'd learn to keep quiet, but his justification is that it's better to have a go.

The Death Star turns his gaze onto Richard. 'Why.' He can say 'Why' as if he's prodding you along a tightrope, each question pushing you further and further into thin air.

Richard retreats into analogy. 'Well it's like a deck of cards. It's much more likely for the cards to be randomly shuffled, than in order. That's equivalent to a low state of entropy.' He bows his head at that point, as if trying to look at those imaginary cards.

Silence. The Death Star looks round the table. 'Jeanette? Can you help him out? Explain some basic physics to him?'

The tiny but audible emphasis on the word 'basic' is another reason why they hate him. He pits them against each other, humiliates them in public. She prods the remains of her mashed potato, heaps it up into a wall on her plate, and starts to tell Richard about the second law of thermodynamics, how to calculate the likelihood of disorder. After she's finished, Death Star clears his throat.

'An illuminating explanation, Jeanette.' As usual, it's impossible to tell if the old codger's being sarcastic or not. 'And shall I put you down for a seminar in a few weeks?'

She's puzzled. 'I haven't got anything new to talk about,' she says automatically.

'Oh, come, come. No need for false modesty here. You may have something immensely exciting.'

The others are staring at her now. Richard's mouth is slightly open. She feels a bit sick. 'It's really not ready.'

'What you showed me yesterday looked absolutely fascinating.' The Death Star is very slowly collecting up all their dirty dishes onto his tray, assembling a precarious tower of greasy plates.

'So you do have something.' Richard still looks vaguely cross about the second law of thermodynamics. But it's not her fault.

'Well...' Perhaps it would be quite helpful to talk it over with the people at the Observatory, and get a sense of their reaction before launching it wider. 'Ok.' She's aware she's avoided replying to Richard. The Death Star nods at her before abandoning the dirty dishes and shuffling away.

As she gets up to leave, she notices some of the lecturers gathered around the coffee machine looking at a piece of paper.

'Good news,' Jon shouts over at her.

It's an advert for a new lectureship. The university has been dithering about creating this post for some time, but now apparently it's going ahead. She breathes out and tries not to smile with relief. She must have a good chance, surely? Then Richard appears next to her.

'Ah, yes,' he says. 'I knew this was going to happen. The Death Star told me yesterday.'

She tries not to wince. Typical of him to imply that he gets access to restricted information. Why didn't the Death Star tell her about the lectureship too? Why didn't he tell all of them at lunch just now?

'Who do you think is going to apply for it?' Richard asks her.

She says she doesn't know, but that doesn't stop him. He talks for a long time about the other potential rivals for the job, and quantifies the possibility that each of them will get it. She shuts her eyes, trying to block out the dull sound. If she actually gets this job she will have to listen to this sort of conversation all the time. She will even have to speak like this herself.

'Richard,' she says. He stops and looks at her, so she continues, 'What would you do if you weren't doing this?'

'Oh, I don't bother thinking about that.' He laughs abruptly and leaves the room.

A week later she's avoiding the canteen and the other post-docs, eating her chips in peace outside, when Jon appears from his lab and ambles over.

'Apparently you're a contender,' he says to her, without any preamble.

'What?'

'For the lectureship. The Death Star was in the lab this morning and he said something about your fascinating data.' He leans against the stone wall and gets out his sandwiches. He's always organised enough to bring his own lunch, he never has to rely on the slop from the canteen. Perhaps Mrs. Jon makes his lunches, and Jeanette has a momentary vision of a woman peacefully cutting sandwiches into neat squares. But she's never met Jon's wife, the only evidence that she even exists is a thin gold wedding ring.

'Why is he so interested in it?'

Jon pauses between mouthfuls. 'Because it's controversial. High profile.'

'But it's probably wrong. It can't really be right.'

Jon laughs. 'Doesn't matter. It'll get loads of publicity, the research council will love it.'

Back in her office, she stares again at the apparent link between the galaxies, wanting to reach out and touch it to see if it's real or an artefact, and knowing that there are never any easy images in astronomy. It's always a struggle at the limit of what can be done. People initially disbelieved Galileo's discovery of Jupiter's moons, partly because they had no tradition of looking at the sky for external tests of ideas. And when they did look, his telescope was of such poor quality that it was difficult to distinguish the moons from the crowd of ghosts generated by the distorting glass.

She goes back to her analysis of the data and makes a map of the image which she displays on top of it, clear black lines delineate her calculated shapes of the galaxies and her estimate of the umbilical link between them. Clean contours overlaid on the grey blanket of reality. She deletes the grey and sits there contemplating the map. It almost pleases her more than the real image. She turns to look outside and instead of trees, cars, people, or buildings, imagines a neat world of thin black lines.

Paula and Becca are in the pub, sitting at the usual little round table. Everything in this image is crisp and clear; she can see the buttons on Becca's shirt, the lipstick mark on Paula's wine glass where her mouth has pressed against it.

They're talking to each other before they both slowly, simultaneously, turn to face her and they fall silent. They seem to be waiting for her to say, or do, something.

She knows they are looking at her but she can't see their eyes, because their faces are pixellated. No features. Just a handful of smooth blank squares. It reminds her of CCTV footage of crimes. But are they victims or perpetrators?

The lack of information is appalling.

THEN

The new house sits on a hill overlooking the rest of the town. One night, when Jeanette is in her room avoiding her parents, she looks out at the sky and sees the moon low down on the horizon. She has never seen it so low before, in the old house it must have been hidden by other buildings nearby.

Floating just above the land, like a balloon, the moon is huge and it glows fiery orange. But as it rises in the sky, it becomes paler and smaller. She watches it for over an hour, witnessing its transformation into the ordinary moon.

It's winter. At night, Orion is in the sky. He's always low down on the horizon, because he's hunting, hiding from the animals in case they see him and run away. Sometimes when she should be asleep, Jeanette watches him, as he creeps across the sky from East to West.

If she looks at the sky for long enough, she can find the pole star. At first it's anonymous; but if you watch and wait, you can find it. It's the one star that doesn't curl around the sky as the Earth rotates through the night. It looks quite ordinary, but it is the steadiest thing.

On some nights a fox sits in the garden, and stares back at her.

In the new house there is a room that was meant for Kate, but now it has no purpose. On the first day, she glances at this empty room from the doorway, but doesn't go inside. What's the point? When she gets up the next morning and negotiates her way past towers of cardboard boxes in the hallway, the door to the room is shut.

The hallway is decorated, the woodwork around the door to the room painted white. But the door itself is left alone.

A few months after they move, Jeanette realises that she's never been in this room. She stands outside and stares at the door. What's behind it? It seems impossible that there is just a room similar to her own. Something has happened to the room in her head, it has expanded and also shrunk. It can't contain her. She walks away.

Her mother spends weeks unpacking the boxes and arranging their belongings. But a lot of things seem to have disappeared. The new house has smooth, bare walls with no pictures or photos. None of the drawings brought home from school by Jeanette and Kate that used to cover the old kitchen walls are on display any more. Jeanette isn't even allowed to spread her school books all over the dining table, but has to take them upstairs to her bedroom.

'Your own desk! How nice!' exclaim her parents. She doesn't mind. She'd rather be up here than downstairs with them. But it is odd living in this sort of house. Even things like the towels that Kate used for swimming, that smelt like comforting old dogs, have gone. The rug with little smiling suns woven into it has gone. The shower curtain with goldfishes printed on it has gone. Her parents buy lots of new towels and rugs and sheets and curtains, but all these things seem to have the colour left out of them. Her mother calls them 'neutral'.

These new things match her parents. Her mother wears beige clothes and doesn't bother with lipstick anymore. She still has a few of her old lipsticks, these haven't been thrown away in the move, but they rattle around in the bathroom cabinet like forgotten dolls.

One day Jeanette takes out one of these lipsticks and, feeling sorry for it, opens it and dabs it on her mouth. The colour is startling, like creamy blood. She scrubs her lips with toilet paper and flushes the colour down the loo.

A few weeks later, she's hiding upstairs in her bedroom after school when someone knocks at the front door. This is odd, hardly anyone comes here. She shuts the book and listens to her mother pad to the door. Voices. She leaves her room and goes to the top of the stairs; from here she can see the hallway. Her mother is standing in the open doorway with a man. Kate's old swimming coach. She hasn't seen him since the funeral.

'...pure coincidence!' The coach's voice is as loud as ever. Perhaps he hasn't yet realised he doesn't need to shout in ordinary houses.

'How did you find us?' In contrast, her mother sounds very quiet.

'One of your neighbours has a son who I used to coach. I popped in to say hello to them just now and they just happened to mention that you've moved here!'

The two of them continue to stand in the hallway next to the open door, as if unable to decide what to do. Jeanette wonders why her parents haven't told the coach that they moved. Have they told anyone? Is that why nobody ever visits?

Suddenly his voice drops quiet. 'How are you all doing?'

Her mother is silent for a moment before she replies, 'Oh fine, fine. We're — I'm — starting a new business. Tidying up people's houses. Decluttering. It's good for the soul to get rid the stuff you don't need.' She still hasn't invited him inside.

'Hidden away here, aren't you?' he laughs. Jeanette's mother doesn't laugh.

'I expect you're busy,' she says and she makes a move towards the door. 'I know I am.'

Jeanette knows her mother will just go back to the sofa. Her decluttering business hasn't really taken off yet, she only spends about one day every fortnight at someone else's house persuading them to throw out all their belongings. The rest of the time she is at home.

'Well, no,' says the coach, 'I'm not that busy. Not at all. Not coaching so much nowadays.'

'I'm sorry to hear that,' says Jeanette's mother, but she doesn't sound very sorry. She sounds rather triumphant.

'Not since...' and he stops. He can't refer to Kate either, thinks

Jeanette. 'It's kind of done for my coaching activities. That's why I popped round to see your neighbour, to try and convince him to let his son carry on swimming with me.'

'Well.' And her mother breathes out a long sigh, like air escaping from a tyre. 'I'm not surprised, I'm afraid. If a child dies on your watch, then what do you expect? You were lucky at the inquest.'

The inquest? Jeanette knows there was one, but she doesn't know what happened at it. Now it occurs to her that there might be something written down as a result. Something that her parents might have, that would help her understand what happened to Kate.

From up here she can see her mother pointing at the coach, jabbing a finger at him. 'Lucky you didn't get more of the blame.'

'And how do you know what happened! You weren't even there —' There is an odd emphasis to this final 'you'. But Jeanette's mother hardly ever went to the pool. Who blamed her for what happened? Jeanette edges closer to the top of the stairs, hoping for more. But they must have heard her because they both look up and the coach falls silent. She stands on the top step, unsure whether to join them.

'Look.' Her mother beckons to her. 'There's no point talking about it. It doesn't help anyone, does it?'

When she reaches them, her mother puts an arm round her and pulls her close.

'Hello, Jeanette,' says the coach.

She's not often this close to her mother and it feels weird. She can feel her mother quivering slightly. 'Hello.'

He still smells of chlorine, even if he isn't doing much coaching any more. She wants to ask him what happened to Kate but the quivering is putting her off. The coach pats her on the head before he turns and walks away, and her mother releases her.

It's difficult to get the opportunity to look for any papers about Kate because her mother is nearly always at home. Finally, one day she gets a decluttering job on the other side of town and when Jeanette gets home from school there are instructions written on a piece of paper about boiling potatoes for dinner.

It's good being by herself in the house. Without the constant whine of the TV the house feels more peaceful.

Ignoring the potatoes, she goes upstairs to her parents' bedroom. She knows where important papers are kept, in a metal box inside the wardrobe. She's worried it might be locked. But it opens easily.

She rifles through the papers, not really sure what she's looking for. She finds a photo of her parents' wedding. Her parents standing on some grass, smiling and squinting at the camera. Her father in a dark suit and her mother in a veil which has flown up and over her head, like a white flag of surrender. Both their faces are rather bleached by sunlight.

She puts the photo to one side and carries on. She finds her birth certificate, creased into three parts. But although she reaches the bottom of the box, she can't find anything to do with Kate. It's as if Kate never existed, not officially. The metal box is cold against her fingers. The air in the bedroom feels cold, colder than the rest of the house. Perhaps they don't ever have the heating on in here. She gives up and goes to do the potatoes.

Her father spends even more time in the new garden than he did in their old one. But now, when he comes back into the house, he doesn't have anything for Jeanette.

So she has to go out and look for things herself; she finds delicate brown leaves that crumble in her hands, sturdy seed pods, the wisps of an abandoned birds nest.

And when she's out there she can see things change. First, crocuses spike through the lawn, then blossoms appear on the tree. The roses bloom, their ice-cream coloured petals scatter on her shoes when she goes outside to tell him tea's ready. Like a magic trick, the dead flowerbeds come back to life.

Later on that summer, her mother's doing the dishes after tea. Jeanette is still at the table, making her piece of cake last as long as possible. Her father is working in the garden.

The radio is burbling away in the background, so there's a reason not to speak. The radio voices make it feel almost normal. But as Jeanette picks at the final crumbs, her mother screams. The room is full of a funny flickering light and it takes a moment before she realises it is outside. Outside is on fire.

When they rush into the garden, her mother's rubber gloves still dripping water, they see her father. He's not attempting to get away from the flames around him. In his hands there is a plastic bottle, and as he jerks it around his feet, the last few drops of liquid scatter from it and catch fire.

Even as they run across the lawn to get to him, blades of grass are shrivelling and turning black. The rosebushes are turning into shivers of flame. There's fire everywhere, fire arcing across the flowerbeds, writhing through the vegetable patch, snaking up the new apple tree, and in the middle of it all is her father, just standing there.

Whenever she and her mother visit her father in hospital, he always seems to be asleep. Perhaps he's pretending to sleep because he's scared of her mother. They sit on either side of his bed, watching him as he lies there with his eyes shut. The room smells strongly of disinfectant, and underneath that there is the anger, just as strong, radiating from her mother, who sits with her lips pressed tight together, waiting. Waiting for him to wake up and explain.

Jeanette stares at the bandages wrapped around his arms, from his wrists all the way up past his elbows. If she concentrates hard enough, she can get lost in the furled landscape of the bandages. It's calm and pale in there. Not like their garden, which is still dark and sodden, stinking of smoke and petrol.

Her father is in hospital for some time, so now it's just her and her mother at home. They face each other across the table at meals, and this reminds Jeanette of all the cop shows that her mother watches. People smoking and drinking mugs of tea, and asking questions.

She sits opposite her mother and silently interrogates her. How could Kate drown? Why won't you tell me? Why did Dad set fire to the garden?

She almost wishes she'd seen him do it. Pour the petrol, its haze sneaking across the innocent lawn, light the match and fling it into the night. Listen to the grass begin to crackle as it deformed in the sudden heat. Perhaps she would be able to understand, then.

They eat their tea and listen to the radio. Then her mother lights a cigarette and pours a drink as Jeanette does the washing up. Her mother hasn't washed up since that night. Jeanette stares into the sink even though she knows that if she looks up, all she will see is the mirror world of the kitchen reflected in the window. But she keeps her head down anyway. When this is done she can leave the room and go upstairs.

But later that evening, when her mother is in the lounge, and the TV has replaced the radio, Jeanette surprises herself by tiptoeing downstairs, pushing back the latch on the back door and stepping over the threshold of the house into the garden.

It's the first time she's been out here since that night. The air is still heavy with fumes, and when she bends down to touch the scorched leaves, they feel greasy under her fingers. The petrol has poisoned the earth. But as Jeanette straightens up, she sees a flash of green. New stalks of grass, all mixed up with the wreck of the old. It is a miracle. But if grass can do it, why can't Kate?

And Jeanette thinks she knows why her father started the fire, or at least why he wanted to destroy the garden. It was dead the first winter after Kate died, after they moved in, and then it came back to life. At first it seemed as if Kate was surviving in some form. But as her dad tended the garden and watched it grow, he must have realised how blind all this activity is. There's no intent, no purpose to this new grass. It simply is. And Kate simply isn't. And then the grass became an actual affront. It must have taunted him with its ability to survive and renew.

When her father is allowed to come home, he finds it difficult to use a knife and fork, and so she or her mother has to cut up his food for him. Jeanette does this carefully, trying to make the lumps all the same size. But her mother just flattens everything into mush, smashing the sausages into the gravy, stirring the eggs and beans together into gloop. She doesn't like to look at her father as he manouvres the remnants of her mother's tiny violent actions into his mouth.

There seem to be many textures of silence. A few are simply the companions of eating, the easy, sloppy sounds of chewing and swallowing. But most are harder and more jagged; little mountains that have to be climbed at each meal.

She tries talking about school. She launches words into the thin air, but they fall down again, they can't get a grip on this ice. Her parents don't reply. Her mother wields a fork and spears a piece of meat. Her father shuffles some lettuce around the plate.

Nothing is done about the garden. When it rains, lines of sooty black water run across the patio. The petrol container is still lying on the ground at the back of the lawn, ghost-white.

NOW

One morning Paula appears at the front door of the flat, surrounded by boxes, even though they haven't actually agreed when she is supposed to be moving in.

'Couldn't wait any more,' she explains. 'The landlord turned up again and asked for extra payment.' She shudders at the thought of this, and Jeanette winces in sympathy.

Although she hasn't been expecting her, or at least not so soon, it is surprisingly easy to adjust to Paula living in the flat. Sure, some spaces have to be recalibrated. The living room is now a thin corridor of carpet around the permanently extended sofa bed. Distances have to be altered; it takes longer to negotiate the length of the kitchen, once Paula has stacked her boxes of cocktail glasses and vintage teacups on the floor. Things appear out of thin air. A painted wooden monkey takes up residence on the television, and kimonos are draped over chairs. An old Bakelite telephone stands on the floor by the sofa bed.

It's not until Paula's belongings are splashed around the flat that Jeanette realises she has been used to living in a pale world of cream walls, white bedlinen and beige rugs. Paula pins a poster onto the living room wall, and the giant face of Hedy Lamarr pouting at Jeanette whenever she goes into the room takes her by surprise.

Paula herself is not there that much. She has to spend a lot of time at the art college, she says, getting ready for the next show. She's usually still asleep when Jeanette eats her breakfast in the morning, stretched out in the sofa bed only a metre or so from where Jeanette is munching her cereal. There is hardly room to eat in the flat. There never was much room, but now they seem to eat most of their meals standing in the doorway between the kitchen and the living room.

Even when Paula is not there, there's evidence of her. A talcum powder footstep on the bath mat, which fits Jeanette's own foot. The air smells of Paula's perfume; something with geraniums in it. Not a sweet smell, but sharp, reminding Jeanette of crushed flowers.

Things move from one place to another as if a poltergeist has taken up residence. A bottle of sloe gin appears from the back of the drinks cupboard, where it has lived undisturbed for several years, and sits on the floor of the living room within reach of the sofa bed. Each morning Jeanette notes that the level of liquid in it has decreased; it is being drunk at the rate of about two centimetres a day. It lasts for a week before she finds the bottle, now empty, abandoned near the back door. She realises she's never actually tasted sloe gin, so she takes the lid off the bottle and licks the rim. It's like kissing lip-gloss; sweet and sticky. She glances through the doorway but Paula is still asleep, hair swept out across the pillow as if she is running somewhere.

Even after Jeanette brushes her teeth, she can still taste the gin.

One evening, Becca comes over for dinner. The sofa bed is folded away and the flat suddenly seems much larger. When Becca arrives, Paula and Jeanette are in the kitchen, making prawn paella.

'Very domestic,' Becca says.

'Well, we have been flatmates before.' For some reason Jeanette feels defensive. Becca stands on the edge of the room watching the two of them, making no move to take her coat off. Why doesn't she want to join in, Jeanette wonders? It's cosy in the kitchen, the paella's bubbling away, they're both sipping gin martinis, and there's some forties-style jazz playing on the radio. But Becca looks from one to the other and Jeanette realises she's being scrutinised, measured. She doesn't know why.

Later on, it gets better. They're all sitting on the floor, amongst the dirty plates and wine glasses, laughing at Paula's impersonations of Jeanette's colleagues.

More time passes. They're lying on the floor, singing and holding hands. They're swigging from a bottle of some anonymous liquor, passing it around like a communion cup. They're all smoking, sharing one cigarette between them, smudging out the ash spilt onto the rug.

'Paula's a great artist,' Jeanette informs Becca at one point.

'I know,' Becca smiles.

'Of course! You were her model. A great model. Great legs. Great...' She runs out of words. She smiles back at Becca.

'Shall I make some coffee?' Becca offers.

But Jeanette has to go to the loo. In the bathroom, she presses her fingers against her face; tries to be reassured by the feeling of her skin, flesh, and skull. She shouldn't drink so much; reality seems to race away from her when she does. Sound comes at her like bursts from a radio.

It's nice here in the dark. She rests her forehead against the mirror and breathes slowly, appreciating the cold glass against her skin. Eventually her feet become re-attached to her legs and they are capable of carrying her back into the living room.

But everything seems to have become very quiet in here.

'Becca's got to go now,' Paula announces. They're still sitting on the carpet, opposite each other. Becca's staring at Paula as she says this.

'I do,' she murmurs, but this sounds more like a question.

'Why? You could stay,' offers Jeanette. 'Crash with me or Paula. There's plenty of space.'

Becca looks at her, and she's astonished to see the sadness in her eyes. 'I can't do that.' And she picks up her coat and walks out of the flat. Paula's still sitting on the floor, her legs sticking straight out in front of her, like doll's legs.

'What's that all about?' Jeanette asks, but Paula doesn't answer.

A few weeks later Paula suggests they have a party. There were lots of parties when they were students but Jeanette's memories of them are blurred; puffs of cigarette smoke, and nebulous faces. She hasn't had a party since then and she wonders if the experience will be the same.

She invites the people from the Observatory and Paula invites the art students. Predictably, they don't mix. The astronomers stick to the kitchen and stand around in the glare of the fluorescent light, drinking various obscure types of beer and talking about bumps in the microwave background. The artists stay in the living room, dancing around in the shadowy dark lit up only by a string of fairy lights, and making fluttery movements with their hands. Jeanette stands at the edge of the room, watching them. The kitchen is too much like work.

'Boo.' Richard suddenly appears next to her. He squints into the living room. 'Is that your new flatmate?' Paula is rattling a cocktail shaker over people's heads, pouring gin martini into their upturned mouths, like a debauched mother bird feeding her babies. She's not wearing much, just one of her kimonos over a lace slip.

'Yup.'

'She's got them all in a tizz in there.' He jerks a thumb towards the kitchen. 'Long time since that lot have seen any female flesh.'

'Don't I count?' she says, laughing.

But he doesn't answer her question. 'Does she usually walk around in her scanties?' His voice is thick, his body threatening to topple over onto hers, before he smiles suddenly, as if he's discovered a secret. 'I bet she does all the time when *you're* around.'

The spectre of her sexuality is made visible in front of them both. Richard knows about her and the ice woman, he was nice about it. He took her out and got her drunk, tried to make her laugh with exaggerated stories about his own failed relationships. But now there is something new, and not so friendly, in his voice. There is something he wants here.

She looks at him more closely; his face seems blurred, and out of focus. But she's still quite comfortable standing there until he murmurs, 'Ever fancy a threesome? Think your flatmate would be up for it?'

She walks off. She gets fed up with being reminded about Paula's effect on people. On men. And she certainly doesn't want to be dragged into it herself, into Richard's sordid little fantasies. How ridiculous and unprofessional to suggest something like that to a colleague. And then she remembers the ice woman again, and blushes.

Some time later she's done a circuit of the flat, filled people's glasses, introduced people, and tried to chase her colleagues out of the kitchen. She feels too efficient. She should be lurching around the living room, swigging from a bottle. But this party hasn't really worked for her, she's been outside it all evening, stuck on the other side of the glass watching everyone else. At least Richard seems to have disappeared, presumably gone home. And she's back on the edge of the living room again.

A man, one of the art students, taps her on the shoulder and asks, 'Do you know where Paula is?' so she points across the room.

'Ah,' he says, sounding like he's found something he needs. He moves away from her, into the darkness and towards Paula.

She decides that the party is over. The best place to be is the garden. She stands in the middle of the lawn, a breeze soft on her cheeks, tilting her head up at the sky to get away from all this. When she looks back at the flat, and into the kitchen, it's empty. Her colleagues have all gone home. Then Paula comes in, and she watches her flinging open cupboards, before she pauses in the centre of the room, her lipstick blurred slightly by some flaw in the glass, so that it looks like blood smeared on her mouth.

To Jeanette's surprise, Richard appears in the kitchen and Paula turns to face him. They stand some distance away from each other, and she can see their mouths move as they talk. The only way back in is through the kitchen, and she doesn't want to interrupt them, doesn't want to know what they're saying to each other. So she has to stay out here and watch them. She's out there for some time.

Each week, on Wednesday afternoon, one of the staff gives a seminar on an aspect of their research. Today, as agreed with the Death Star, it's Jeanette's turn. As she stands at the front preparing to begin, she has a shivery nervous feeling in her stomach; she is going to tell them something different, something unexpected, and she is not sure how they will react. There is a silence in the room as they wait for her to start. She must remember that she is in control here. All she has to do is tell them what she knows. She's going to start with the easy stuff first.

Richard's sitting near the front, pretending to take notes. But she knows, from sitting next to him at previous seminars, that these 'notes' are in fact obscene doodles about the imagined sex lives of the older lecturers. She hasn't seen much of him since the party. She can't work out if he's been keeping out of her way, but now he grins at her as she glances at him. No obvious embarrassment. Perhaps he can't remember what he said. She wishes she could wipe it from her mind.

Most of the other post-docs are sitting clustered around the Death Star, like orbiting satellites. Jeanette knows that they're only listening to her in order to think up difficult questions. It's one way of proving yourself; spot an error in the speaker's logic, and trap them in the question and answer session afterwards.

She still finds it amazing that she can talk about galaxies, that she knows things about them; their distances, their brightnesses, their compositions. Nothing in this boring lecture room suggests that there's knowledge here. There's not much to look at; a bunch of star charts lying in a dusty pile on the shelf, a faded portrait of Hubble in which he has the appearance of a disappointed schoolteacher sucking on his pipe. The real knowledge is hidden away in the data stored on the computers, in symbols, in their heads.

Sometimes when she gives seminars, she knows she captures her audience and takes them with her. Today's one of those occasions; when she projects an image of the connected galaxies onto the giant screen behind her, and starts to explain about the link between them, the room falls completely silent.

The professor of theoretical cosmology sits up. 'How different are the redshifts?'

'They're 0.4 and 0.8' she replies, knowing exactly what he will say next. And he doesn't disappoint.

'So the distance between them is of the order of megaparsecs,' he barks. 'How can they be linked at that distance? A physical link would be orders of magnitude larger than any other known structure.'

She doesn't bother speaking, but just points again at the handful of pixels between the galaxies.

'Something wrong with your data calibration,' suggests one of the engineers. 'Has anyone else been able to verify this?'

'No, we haven't asked anyone else. You're the first to see this.' She means this to imply a sort of privilege, but a lot of them are still glaring at her. She glances at the Death Star. He has a sharp nose, she notices for the first time, and he is looking at her the way a dog points at its quarry.

And so her seminar continues. People don't like it but nobody can find anything wrong with it. People start shifting around in their seats, whispering to each other, and some of them actually get up to scrutinise the image of the galaxies on the screen.

One of the emeritus professors bellows, 'Are you trying to say that you've turned into one of those flat-earthers who worship Fred Hoyle?' and people laugh. She smiles tightly but doesn't reply.

'Are you going to publish it?' asks the Death Star.

'Why not? I'm neutral about it. I don't know what the correct interpretation is, so the best thing to do is to publish it and then see what people think. That seems to be the most honest thing to do.'

'Ludicrous! I don't believe a word of it,' exclaims the other emeritus professor and he gets up and walks out. The breeze from his departure causes the screen to flap and distort the galaxies. Jeanette reaches out to steady the screen, but realises that her hand is trembling.

'So you think it could be wrong, but you're going to publish it anyway?' This is from Jon. 'How is that honest? If you publish it, you should be prepared to defend it.'

'But if you truly don't know either way, how else can you let other people decide?' she replies.

'You can't be neutral. Either it's wrong or it isn't. You need to make a decision.' Typical Jon; he always sees everything in black and white. But these pixels, showing a link that shouldn't exist, span a whole spectrum of colour. Suddenly he sits up a bit straighter. 'How about Orion?'

'Orion?' What is he talking about? Orion is a useful constellation if you want to study star formation. That's got nothing to do with what she's been telling them. Then she realises; the instrument. Other people clearly realise at the same time, because a sort of rippling sigh goes round the room, some of the tension caused by her work has been lessened. There will be a test.

'Is it going to be sensitive enough to see this sort of structure?'

'Of course.' He looks proud. The Death Star sits back in his chair and smiles, almost to himself.

She thinks quickly. From what she knows of Orion, it should be able to get a much clearer image of this link than any ground-based instrument. If Orion can see it, maybe it's real. If not, not. One way or another, they'll know for sure. 'But when will it be launched? How long do we have to wait?'

She's not aware of how impatient she sounds until Jon starts to laugh. 'You'll have to wait at least a year. First light isn't scheduled until next Autumn, and that's assuming it gets launched in the next available launch window. That's a big "if". '

'Oh.' How can she wait that long? How can they all wait? The roomful of people looks back at her with varying expressions on their faces. She's aware of more warmth towards her than earlier. Perhaps, in spite of themselves, they like a bit of humanity.

Richard has the final word, 'Just wait until the media get hold of this,' and he raises an eyebrow. The Death Star smiles, and she wonders again what he's thinking.

Afterwards, when everyone's standing around drinking the obligatory glass of cheap wine, the Death Star comes over to her and murmurs, 'How's the paper coming along?'

'It's almost ready to go.' She swills the wine around her mouth before managing to swallow it.

Richard joins them, clutching his glass. 'Well done you,' he says. 'Talk about stirring things up.'

'Richard.' The Death Star glares at him. 'It's the science that counts at the end of the day. It's really very unlikely that these galaxies are actually connected, but Jeanette's right, she needs to let the scientific community see the images and decide.' He waves his finger at Richard, who continues to drink, not looking at him or Jeanette.

'Very honest of you,' Richard mutters.

'I've got nothing at stake here. It'd take more than this to bring down the Big Bang model.'

'Much, much more,' he agrees, and they all continue to drink their wine in silence.

Some time later that evening Jeanette is back in her office. Now that she's completed the seminar she wants to leave it all behind for the day, but she can't stop gazing at the image of the galaxies on her monitor. She knows that none of them really believes it, she doesn't fully believe it herself. But until there's a definite reason to discount it, she might as well carry on. It's a shame that publishing things makes them so definite; pins them like butterflies in glass boxes. It's very difficult to remain neutral, but she wants to try.

To get away from the galaxies, she swivels on her chair to look at the blackboard, which is one of those old-fashioned ones where a never-ending roll of black fabric loops round so that if her tutorials are long enough or enthusiastic enough, Jeanette can find herself confronted with her earlier work. When this happens it always feels a bit like travelling back in time, and meeting her earlier self.

Today it's a palimpsest of ancient chalk markings from various tutorials. But at the bottom of it there is some fresh chalk, so she looks closer. Someone's written 'GAG' in wobbly letters. And next to that is a tiny picture of a face in profile with an open mouth. It's nothing more than a curved line and a dot, and it's not recognisably her, but it is a face.

How long has this been here? Did someone creep into her office during the seminar? Did one of her students get particularly bad marks lately? It could have been easily done; she never locks the door of this room. She stares at it for so long that when she finally looks away, the face is stamped onto her retina and printed on every part of the room wherever she looks.

She's looking at a star chart, a map of the sky. Beside each star and galaxy on the chart is its name in faint blue letters; Altair, Riga, Aldeberan, Vega... Eventually she finds what she's looking for; the large off-centre triangle in the northern sky. But here in this version of the universe it's not named 'Andromeda'. Next to it is written her sister's name.

This gives her hope, and later that night when she takes her telescope outside, she does find her sister in the night sky. In the usual story, Andromeda is rescued from the sea monster by Perseus. But in this version, her sister is chained to the rocks as the sea rises, her mouth and nose filling with water, her hair streaked with foam. She never manages to break free.

She's scrolling through the abstracts of new papers published on one of the e-archives, when she notices a paper by the consortium. A long tedious-looking affair comparing the accuracy of different data reduction algorithms. The sort of paper she should read thoroughly and conscientiously, but never does. Skimming down the lengthy list of authors, she finds Richard. He's buried about halfway down the list, so whenever the paper gets referenced in the future, he'll be swallowed up in the *et al*. He'll probably never see the light of day again, now that the consortium has shackled him to his computer. Partly out of pity, she prints off the paper and flips through it. The same boring galaxy analysed in a hundred subtly different ways. Spot the difference on the hundred images. A pixel here, a pixel there.

'Saw your paper,' she says to Richard at lunchtime, as the Death Star lurches towards them. 'Looks absolutely fascinating.'

He frowns at her sarcasm. 'It's useful. We needed that algorithm.'

'Ah, the collective "we". And are you going to be so high up in the list of authors on the actual science papers?' She's not sure why she's being such a bitch to him, and then she remembers him and Paula, leaning towards each other in the kitchen while she waited outside in the cold.

Later, the phone rings.

'Jeanette?'

'Yes?'

'It's me. Mags.'

'Oh... Hi...'

But Maggie is too quick for her. 'I'm not sure we should publish the galaxies.'

'What? Why not?' Something thumps in her chest. It's difficult to speak.

'Because. It's too uncertain. I'm not sure it's right, and even if it is, what does it mean? What are we really saying about all this? And even if we don't say it outright in the paper are we really going to imply that redshifts aren't cosmological? And...' Maggie's voice sounds as if she is spinning off into outer space. Curiously, that makes Jeanette feel a bit better. She is the one on the ground here. Tethered to reality.

'Hang on. Let's start at the beginning. Remember what we actually saw; two galaxies at different redshifts that appear to be physically connected. That's what goes into the paper. We don't need any speculation about the implications, because that's all it would be, just speculation. We just stick to the data.'

'But we have to comment on it.' Maggie's voice is still thin, tremulous.

'What's the point? Everyone knows the implications. We say something like "this is an interesting finding, which we expect other people will want to examine more closely."' Jeanette looks at the blackboard again. 'GAG' is still there. 'I can't see anything wrong with that.' She pauses before continuing, 'There's a job here. It would really help.'

'Oh, Jeanette! You and your jobs!'

'The Death Star thinks it's interesting...'

'You showed it to *him*?' Maggie sounds incredulous.

And the rest of the Observatory, Jeanette wants to confess, but doesn't. Maggie carries on. 'You should have asked me before you showed anyone else.'

'Asked you? Why?' She's cross now.

'It's risky. We need to check it out more thoroughly before we do anything with it.'

Jeanette sighs and looks at her screen, where the image of the galaxies is shown. The link is just a handful of pixels. Who knows whether it actually exists? Is publishing it the right thing to do? If they sit on it, nobody else will be able to see it for themselves, or make their own judgment. If only the image was better.

'I think we should get more data. We could get time on the Hubble, maybe?' Maggie sounds a bit more amenable now.

'Could take at least another year to get Hubble time. We can't sit on it, we need to get a move on. If we don't publish it soon the image will be in the public domain and someone else will publish it. I think we've got about two months left before that happens.'

'You really think someone else will publish it?'

'Maggie! Don't be naïve. Of course they will. You would, wouldn't you? If you knew it was there and you could get your hands on it?'

Pause.

'Ok. But we damp down the discussion. Keep it sober. Avoid any discussion of how this may affect the standard model.'

'Whatever.' She feels impatient now. She flicks through Richard's tedious paper, at all the countless images of this galaxy that nobody will ever look at, and has an idea.

That night, Jeanette takes Paula up to the Observatory. It's already dark by the time they reach the top of the hill, the city glittering beneath them.

'Oof,' says Paula. 'I forgot it was so steep.'

'Have you been up here before?'

'When I was a kid.' Paula stops to gulp air before continuing, 'Sunday outing. With the dog.'

There are two telescopes at the Observatory, the little modern one at the back which is used for teaching and public demonstrations, and the old one in the west dome. This telescope was built in the 1920s and is so huge that you cannot reach its eyepiece from the floor; you have to sit in a specially constructed chair that ramps up several feet in the air. The surrounding dome is enormous, all creaking iron and copper. When she takes Paula into the dome, the feeble light makes the space look melodramatic enough for a mad scientist to come leering out of the shadows.

But no one comes in here anymore, the telescope hasn't been used for forty years and the whole space feels shut off from the ordinary world. Nothing in here is ordinary after all. There has never been anything ordinary in here. This is a space where only extraordinary things are allowed to happen.

'Wow', says Paula, 'This is incredible. You actually work in here?' She's wandering around, gazing at the chair, its seat even higher than Jeanette remembers.

'No, no. This equipment is ancient. It's all completely out of date.' She pulls at an old rope tied to the wall and manages to winch the dome open, so a thin slot of sky appears overhead. But the cloudy sky has a lumpy, doughy appearance. It's an everyday sky, nothing special, and it looks almost mundane compared to the rest of their surroundings.

Paula rummages around in her bag. 'This is just fantastic. It's enormous in here, truly monumental. I want to make a few sketches.' She fishes out a bundle of pencils and charcoal sticks, and then a notebook.

Jeanette's not sure what her role is, now. She has introduced Paula to this space, but is she supposed to disappear? Or is Paula sketching her too? Is she part of it, or separate?

She makes her way across the wooden floor to the far wall. From here the telescope is in line with the sky outside. Briefly, the clouds blow away and she gets a glimpse of an anonymous star before it disappears again.

'You know astronomers used to draw what they saw in the sky, before photography was invented?' she tells Paula.

'Really?' Paula looks up. 'No, don't move. Stay there.'

So she is in Paula's picture. She feels pleased, and then wonders why.

As they leave the Observatory and walk down the hill towards the bus stop, they pause to look back at the dark buildings behind them.

'Do you get used to working at night?' Paula asks. Jeanette can see why she's asked this. The building looks forbidding now. The towers are just black shapes blocking out the sky, from this angle they seem more like an absence of something. How to explain that you do get used to the dark, that you shed the natural human instinct to be in the light, that you welcome a moonless night? That a sunlit day can make everything look flat and artificial, like stage lighting?

When she sees Paula's sketches, she's a bit confused; they're difficult to understand. The paper is mostly blank with a few cryptic marks here and there. She can't see herself in them at all.

'I was trying to draw the space,' says Paula. 'Indicate an absence of things. But the actual painting won't be like this at all. I'm thinking it's going to be more like a portrait. I want to get across that sinister element with the fact that this is where people actually work...'

'But they don't, not anymore,' Jeanette interrupts.

'Stop being so pedantic. They used to work there. So I want something real, ordinary, almost superimposed on the space. Like it's been cut out and pasted on.'

'A portrait?' asks Jeanette.

'Yes,' says Paula, and now she's grinning. 'I'm going to paint a portrait of you.'

There's not enough room in Jeanette's flat for Paula to paint and so they go to her studio at the art college. It's a muddled, fusty space with piles of papers and rags scattered around on the floor. Two plastic chairs lean against each other.

'You'll need to stand for a bit, so make yourself comfortable. You have to maintain the pose for some time; make sure it feels ok.'

She watches Paula prepare, moving precisely and surely around the grot in her studio. She seems to know which pile of rags hides tubes of paint, and where the box of charcoal might be lurking. Various colours are squeezed onto an old china plate, and some brushes are laid out in a neat row. Jeanette is reminded of scalpels, and begins to feel as if this is an operating theatre. What's going to happen here? Will she be opened up and inspected?

Paula has asked her to wear her usual work clothes so she's wearing jeans and a t-shirt that says 'British Cosmology Summer School 98' in faded blue letters across her chest.

'Could you unfold your arms? That pose looks a bit defensive.'

But now her arms are hanging uselessly by her side and she's not sure what to do with them.

'Try not to fidget with your hands.'

Silence. She can hear Paula drawing. The pencil makes a scratching sound, as if a small animal were feeling its way across the paper. She could be using this time to think about work, but her mind feels oddly numb, almost cauterised in this new environment.

Paula's not talking and it takes Jeanette a while to realise this is unusual. She experimentally makes a comment about the large windows, but gets no response.

After a bit she realises there's a rhythm to what Paula is doing. Paula looks up at Jeanette for a few seconds and then down at the canvas. It's as if she's soaking up information about Jeanette in those few seconds before depositing it on the canvas. Or, Jeanette realises, there's a similarity to how a telescope observes a distant object before downloading the image.

Never before has she been the subject. She feels caught, trapped in a spider's web of Paula's gaze, rendered immobile. Usually she's good at judging how time passes, but now she realises she has no idea how long she's been sitting here. Ten minutes? Half an hour?

Again Paula's gaze is on her. This time she looks back and their eyes meet. Jeanette's head jolts back as if an electric shock has just gone through her. Paula's gaze is entirely, nakedly, neutral. It simply wants to know Jeanette. She feels Paula's eyes travel over each aspect of her face as surely as if she is touching her. The eyes take in her eyebrows, cheeks, lips, chin, and then dip down to observe her neck and strands of hair lying against her chest.

And Jeanette in turn sees Paula for the first time. Usually she only sees the brightly made-up, loudly laughing Paula. The one who does that exaggerated film star thing of asking men for a light and then half closes her eyes and sucks in air deeply, ecstatically, as it's being lit for her. Paula always acts like she's on display, even in private. When she's drunk, it's an exaggerated impersonation of being drunk.

She's a beautiful apple, Jeanette has often thought, but you never see the colour of the flesh inside.

But here in the studio, she isn't doing the act. Jeanette knows that Paula is no longer aware of her own appearance as she seeks to understand Jeanette's. I'm privileged, she realises. No one else has seen her like this. She watches as Paula tucks a strand of hair out of the way behind one ear. Except maybe her lovers. What do they see?

Only now is Jeanette aware of the colossal tension building up in her neck as a result of keeping still. The tightness is spreading down her back and into the base of her spine. She has to move.

Paula notices her discomfort. 'Can you keep still for a bit longer? I'll finish soon.'

Finally Paula releases her. 'All done.' And she flops forward like a puppet with its strings cut. But this doesn't really do it. The energy's still there waiting for its outlet.

Paula moves out from behind the easel but Jeanette stays bent over, looking at the floor. She doesn't want to look up, and see Paula there, too solid and three-dimensional and real. She wishes the usual Paula were here with her red lipstick.

'Hey.' Paula's feet are right in front of her. Still she doesn't look up. 'Are you ok?' She nods her head. Then Paula touches her hair and something shivers down her back. The touch is tentative, not how Jeanette imagines Paula normally approaches people. She wants Paula to go away and be normal again.

The next sitting is a week later. She's been thinking about it all week, wondering if it'll be the same experience.

'You can sit down this time,' Paula says, 'I think I'm going to concentrate on your face today.'

So she sits and watches Paula prepare, and thinks.

'Paula,' she says, 'Is it different painting people to painting things? Like chairs?'

Paula twitches, startled. A pause. 'Yes and no, I suppose. I'm trying to bring out the essence of you, but in the same way I'm trying to bring out the essence of that chair. It's more difficult with you, because I know you. It makes it more complicated because looking at you has all these associations. You have a history associated with you.'

'You make me sound like an old book. Or an old lover.'

But Paula doesn't reply, so the word 'lover' is left hanging in the air.

'Richard.' She waits in the doorway of his office until he looks up.

'What.'

She thumps his paper down on his desk. 'You're right, a nice piece of work. Very nice indeed.'

He narrows his eyes. 'You've actually read it?'

'Yeah. Well, some of it. Listen, how many galaxies do you have?'

'Dunno. Thousands. That's the whole point of the project...'

'I know. Umm — could I have a look at them?'

'Uh?' his mouth falls open.

'Just sort of — borrow them for a bit.'

'But they're still proprietary. I couldn't possibly let them out into the public domain.' He looks worried now.

'I know that! I'm not asking you to release the data. But I was wondering...' She pauses for a brief, tactical second until she thinks she's got his interest. 'There may be something in your dataset about my galaxies. The connected ones.'

He raises his eyebrows, thinking. He is definitely interested. 'Well, you could look at the images here in this office, I suppose. No harm in that. As long as you don't print them out or put them in your paper.'

'Of course not,' she smiles kindly.

It's quite easy to find what she needs, even under Richard's eye. Her connected galaxies have indeed also been imaged by the consortium, and as she suspected, because they have so much data they haven't got around to actually looking at these images properly. She shakes her head at the thought of all that lovely data lying unseen. But the consortium's image of the galaxies also shows a connection. Although it's much fainter, and could easily not be noticed unless you'd already seen something similar on another image. Bingo.

She doesn't realise that she's spoken out loud until Richard looks up. 'What?'

'It's there. It's in your data too.'

He comes over to look at the screen and she's aware of his physical presence, the mass of him, just behind her.

'Really? You think that that proves it?' He sounds incredulous.

'Not by itself. But in combination with our data.'

'But you can't actually use this in your paper.'

She feels trapped between him and the screen. 'I know, but it's still helpful to know that this exists.'

His reflection shrugs in the dark screen. 'If you say so.' And he goes back to his own work. She tries not to sigh, she knows why he's being so deliberately casual about this; he's trying to play it down. It's the only way he can convince himself that his own work is just as important.

No matter how hard she tries to move the telescope to another part of the sky, it's locked onto the connected galaxies and won't shift. Its glass lenses are radiant with the dazzle of far away stars. Photons have filled up the length of the tube and are splashing out onto the floor. In the control room, the computer screen glows pure white until a small dark patch appears, and smoke starts to waft up. The screen has caught fire from the light of the galaxies.

Jeanette is astonished when the paper is accepted for publication. The journal's editors make it clear that they don't like the inference that the two galaxies are connected, but they can't spot anything wrong with the data.

Now she knows the paper is going to be published, she starts worrying about it. The image of the galaxies has now been replicated in scores of pictures on the internet, popped up in forums all over the place, been discussed by astronomers in Beijing, Moscow and California. Paradoxically, because it's been approved by other people, she doubts it more. More copies of the picture seem to make it less concrete. It's been cloned everywhere — but are clones real?

She starts waking up at indeterminate times during the night, lying on her back staring at the blankness overhead, worrying; her mind so twisted around the image of the galaxies that it can't seem to pick its way loose. Once, she has the sensation that her body is the telescope dome, and the numbers on her alarm clock are the telescope control panels. There are people observing in her, doing what they want.

The Observatory issues a press release which states that the paper contains 'evidence contradicting the Big Bang theory', even after Jeanette has begged the press officer to tone it down and make the result sound more circumspect. But she suspects that the Death Star has done the exact opposite. He doesn't exactly admit it to her when she asks him, he just says that he has routine contact with the press office.

At the time, they're having lunch with the other post-docs, so she can't really ask him properly.

The others are openly arguing about the link between the galaxies. They've brought a hard copy of her image with them to lunch and have spread it out between the plates to scrutinise it. One of them jabs at the link with his fork.

'It's obvious,' he says to the others. 'There must be something else behind these galaxies that's pushing up the light values on those pixels. A more distant object is mimicking the connection.' A clod of potato drops off his fork onto the picture.

Jeanette winces. She knows she should interrupt, and take control of the conversation. But she's too aware of their jealousy of her paper. It's all any of them want, a chance to write something that other people will read and take account of. She thought she wanted it too, but not like this. Not with all the fear attached to it.

'It's not obvious,' she replies, 'nothing's obvious.'

Later that week, she's interviewed for the lectureship. The interview takes place in the Death Star's office; a thin and dusty room with only one window high up above them all. She sits at one end of a narrow table, and the four interviewers are arranged down either side so that all she can see of them is a series of theatrically diminishing profiles.

She practiced what to say in the bathroom that morning, watching her reflection in the fogged mirror; the boundaries of her body merging into the steam. But in this room she has to be crisp and precise. She doesn't talk about the connecting galaxies; instead she tells them about other, more certain, aspects of her work.

As she talks, she plays with the buttons on her blouse, each one an island stranded in its sea of cotton.

The interviewers' heads nod, and their hands take notes on small pieces of paper. When she peers down the table she can't immediately tell which fingers are connected to which head. Her own fingers continue to grip the buttons.

Finally, the Death Star mentions her and Maggie's paper. He says it's very exciting, and he hopes that they'll follow it up in more detail.

One of the other heads says, 'What do you think it means?'

'Means?'

'Your result. What do you think the physical implication is?' He's looking right at her and she notices that his eyebrows meet above his nose. She has to fight an urge to ask him what this means. She must be serious. She looks away from the joined-up eyebrows and thinks for a moment.

She needs to be careful. She must stand by her result, but not over-identify herself with it. It may be published but it's still very likely to be wrong. She repeats what she said earlier to Richard, 'It'd take more than this to bring down the Big Bang model!' half expecting them to laugh, but there is just silence, and the questioner cocks an eyebrow, waiting for her to say more.

She places her hands on the table where everyone can see them and stretches out her fingers, before she continues, 'What we have is an apparent link between two galaxies at different redshifts, which as you know is not possible in the standard Big Bang model. We worked out the likelihood of something else mimicking that link, and whilst that formal likelihood is not zero, it is small. We've tried to be circumspect in the paper, not to over-interpret the actual data. I think we all — the whole community — just need to wait and see what other data show, before anyone does any more interpretation.'

Someone else, further down the table, states that they've been too hasty in publishing the images and that they should have waited for more data. But Jeanette knows how to defend herself. 'It was a good opportunity. Our data would have been in the public domain next month, so even if we had decided not to go ahead, someone else would have spotted this and published it. We felt it was worth publishing, along with a responsible commentary on it.' The heads nod and the fingers scribble.

The Death Star comments, 'You're walking a tight-rope,' and she can't do anything else but silently agree.

Afterwards, the Death Star comes to see her in her office. 'Well done. Too early to say anything definite of course, but that was a good performance.'

She decides to risk asking him, 'How important is the paper?'

'Can't say, really. It's just one of many considerations.'

After he leaves, she prints off yet another image of the galaxies.

Her office is full of these paper prints. They lie on the floor like dead leaves and rustle against her feet when she moves. She picks up a handful of them, but lets them flutter back down.

Then she walks over to the blackboard to re-examine 'GAG', and touches it gently before tasting the chalk. There's a noise behind her. Her finger still in her mouth, she turns around. Richard.

'How fetching,' he says. 'You look so innocent, sucking on your finger.'

She hastily wipes her finger on her skirt.

'How was your interview?' he continues.

'Oh, pretty good, they asked me all the right questions.' She smiles, hoping to appear confident. 'It was quite straightforward.'

'I see.'

'When's yours?'

'This afternoon at three.'

Silence.

'Any tips?' he asks finally. It's clear he hates asking her for help.

'Not really. Just be yourself!' And she goes back to examining the blackboard. She hears him leave the room and she knows without seeing that his face is focused inwardly on himself and what he has to do.

The next day, when she arrives at her office, she's surprised to see a copy of her paper about the connected galaxies lying on her desk. When she gets closer she sees that it's been left open at the page where she's mentioned the corroboration from the consortium's data. A sentence has been ringed in red and there's an exclamation mark scrawled next to it.

It must have been Richard. But why? He let her look at the data, and she didn't actually use it in the paper, she just mentioned it. It must have been ok. She's still standing there, the paper in her hand, when he comes crashing into her office.

'What the hell...' He's so angry he's out of breath. She stares at him, waiting. He actually looks rather magnificent; hair everywhere, eyes flashing. 'Why the hell did you refer to it? The data's embargoed, you silly bitch!'

'I only mentioned it!' They glare at each other. 'I didn't show the image! I didn't release any information!'

'You said...' and now he scrabbles at the paper, trying to find the right sentence. 'You said, "the consortium also has an image of this pair of galaxies and this image also shows a link, although at a lesser statistical significance".' His voice is deliberately high-pitched, perhaps in some desperate parody of hers.

'So?'

'So...' he's pulling at his hair now. 'You — just — cannot — do — that. Not without getting my permission.'

'But you let me look at the data, what did you think I was going to do once I found the link in it? Just ignore it? Of course I was going to mention it.'

'Do you know what they said they'd do, Jeanette? They're threatening to boot me out of the consortium.'

'Oh.'

He sits down in her chair and puts his head in his hands. She reaches out and pats his shoulder. 'Richard, I'm sorry. Perhaps if I explain to them that it wasn't your fault...'

She can't see his face. They both stay like that for some time, in silence, before he eventually gets up and leaves, still without speaking to her. The paper's fallen to the floor and she leaves it there.

It's still there the next day when the Death Star comes in to tell her she's got the job.

Something else is present in the studio. It's taken up residence since the last sitting. It's touching Jeanette, stroking along the inside of her arms, whispering around the nape of her neck. She feels hyper-sensitive to everything; every movement made by Paula is transmitted to her skin through the dusty air. Perhaps she's so aware of how Paula is moving because she herself has to remain immobile. She feels like she's waiting for something, but she's not sure what. The base of her spine prickles with energy but it can go nowhere. All she can do is watch Paula paint.

As at the last sitting, Paula isn't wearing any make-up, and her skin seems at the same time more ordinary and more interesting than usual. She has the same hollows and bumps and shadows as other people. Her eyes are small, her lips are faded pink, not bright red. She looks more human. And as she works, she is quieter, more concentrated. Jeanette cannot imagine the usual Paula knowing how to mix paints together to create different colours, knowing how to lay one colour underneath another.

There is another session and then the portrait is finished.

'Come and have a look at yourself.' Paula takes a step back from it, and Jeanette suddenly realises how tired she looks.

She walks over to the canvas and is astonished. Against the dark, shadowy background of the telescope dome, her own face looms disproportionately large and pale compared to her body, which looks small and overwhelmed by the scribbled in space around it. She's reminded of the nights she used to spend as a child, standing and staring out of her bedroom window at the sky. In this painting her body is that of a child again.

Sometimes, when she's around other people, she gets the feeling that someone has just left, that there is an absence so palpable it becomes a shape, a presence. She looks at this painting, and sees that Paula has painted the absence, and she's afraid.

'What do you think?' Paula asks.

'Why did you paint my body so small?'

Paula tilts her head and considers her work, before replying. 'I'm drawing attention to it. The smaller it is the more people will notice it. I kind of like that paradox.'

Jeanette wants to ask more. How have you created an absence with paint and colour? What did you think when you looked at my body? How did your mind change it so that you could paint it like this? But she is silent. Paula doesn't say anything either, and the silence settles on them, as they stand side by side in front of the painting.

As the two of them look at the image of Jeanette, it makes her very aware of the three dimensional nature of her surroundings, the feel of denim against her legs, her socks hugging her feet, the pinch of her bra against her chest. And beyond that, in the wider room, everything now seems very complicated to understand. The way the chairs are precariously leaning against each other, each with only two legs on the floor, in an apparent demonstration of Newton's third law; every action has an equal and opposite reaction. If you push something it pushes back. That is in the nature of matter.

When Paula moves, it recalibrates the space between them. All she does is brush her hair away from her face but Jeanette is now aware, as she's never been aware before, of exactly how near Paula is. The presence in the room transforms every mundane movement. Paula rolls her sleeves up and Jeanette feels a feathery touch on her own skin, as if someone is slowly stroking her.

But when it finally happens later that day, there's nothing tentative about it. They're back in the flat and everything feels normal again. The only reminder of the afternoon is the paint caked around Paula's fingernails, highlighting the landscape of creases in her fingers. How complicated the human body is, thinks Jeanette. Galaxies are much simpler.

Paula notices her looking. 'Don't veins make you think of underwater creatures?' she says. 'Like eels. Something slippery.' And she holds out her hand, as if for inspection. Jeanette reaches out and they both contemplate their hands side by side. The hands shift together fractionally. Still, there is space between them. Jeanette looks at where Paula's arm disappears inside her rolled shirt sleeves, and it's as if a switch is flicked inside her, and she's taken back to the studio.

She suddenly realises that Paula has a body hidden under these old paint-stained clothes. She's seen Paula's body of course, it's regularly on display. That's not the point. It was never interesting then.

Now its very hiddenness is for her to discover. She looks closer at tiny dark hairs lying neatly on the white skin. She wants to understand how the hairs fade away into nothing on the soft underside of Paula's arms. She watches as her index finger traces along the length of Paula's arm. Paula doesn't move. Neither of them speaks. Jeanette doesn't look up at her face, that is for later. Her arm is enough for now. She follows the pattern of veins up into the crook of the arm and beyond.

One of them sighs quietly, and Paula lets her arm flop back against the sofa, so Jeanette can reach into the loose shirtsleeve, up to the shoulder and feel the warmth of the skin around Paula's armpit.

It's almost clinical, this fascination with Paula's skin, her body. She simply wants to know it. But then Paula reaches over and touches Jeanette's exploring hand.

'Hey,' Paula murmurs. Only then does Jeanette look at her face, at her half-shut eyes, at the way her lips curve around her teeth.

She strokes Paula along her neck, tracing the gold chain around it, discovering the small ornament hanging from the chain between her breasts. She's never seen this before, and the piece of metal is almost a distraction from the softness of Paula's breasts against her fingertips, and then her lips.

There's so much of Paula to understand that she's almost surprised when Paula reaches forward to undo the zip on her jeans.

To start with, this was an exploration that was equivalent to Paula's painting of her portrait. But now Paula kneels in front of her, the upside-down v of her legs silhouetted by the fire, offering herself to Jeanette at the same time as taking something from her.

She has time to notice the perfect symmetry of their bodies, the simultaneous reaching out and connecting. After that, all she's aware of is how her body buckles in on itself, then someone cries out.

Some time later they're still lying on the floor. Jeanette sees Paula's hand and stretches out to it, stopping just short of touching it. Now she can enjoy the sense of Paula next to her. She's reminded of a phenomenon in physics called the Casimir effect, in which two separated metal plates move together. This is because there is quantum energy in the gap between the plates, drawing them inexorably closer. She tries not to make an analogy with her and Paula lying there. Science can't always provide a description of her reality.

Paula's hand suddenly tumbles towards hers and Jeanette realises she has fallen asleep. Quietly, she gets up and goes to her own bed, where she sleeps soundly.

She's been invited to speak at a conference. This is the first time she's actually been invited, rather than having to apply. She hugs herself with excitement.

It's a big conference, an international three day event on cosmology in Brighton, and when she arrives there, she finds it's being held in an appropriately vast public hall where the ceiling is so far away it's permanently in shadow, and she feels like they're all at the bottom of some endless void.

She's speaking later that afternoon, so now she hunches in her chair and waits, but it's difficult to concentrate on the current talk. The room stretches too far back, and from where Jeanette is sitting, the speaker looks like a puppet. He's using a microphone but this only works intermittently, so that much of what he says is inaudible.

It's an odd experience going to conferences. People, who are only familiar to Jeanette through their names on scientific papers, suddenly come to life. They become three-dimensional, grow faces, and sprout hair. When she finally meets someone, such as Jim Wilson, who's sitting next to her, their knees almost touching, it seems almost obscene; this intrusion of the physical into her mental construction of him. To her, 'Wilson J.' represents a paper on galaxy dynamics, not a short man with a bushy ginger beard and a disconcerting habit of allowing his hand to rest on his right knee too close to her.

All around her people are coming to life off the pages of the journals, acknowledging other people, holding whispered conversations in the corners of the huge towering space, going back and forth for more coffee. She keeps her head down, pretending to study the programme. The entrance door is banging, a staccato noise that bumps through her thoughts.

Now the door bangs again. She looks up, irritated, but it's Hawking in his wheelchair being manoeuvred into the auditorium. Far above, crammed right up close against the ceiling so that it's only just visible in the shadows, is a helium balloon. One of the earlier talks that morning was about the universal proportion of helium; one of the primordial chemical elements, created in the first moments after the Big Bang. The balloon has a cartoon face printed on it, with a manic, toothy grin that beams down on everyone below. She wonders if anyone else has noticed it.

She's nervous. She knows that she won't get an easy time of it here. The work is too controversial. If it's true, then it's fascinating, it changes everything. But she doesn't particularly want to demolish the connection in the Big Bang theory between redshift and distance. She and Maggie never set out to do that. The theory gives a coherence to the past. It imposes epochs on the history of the universe in a way that doesn't exist in the steady state model, which is simply an unending stew of galaxies all jumbled up together.

When it's finally her turn to speak, the auditorium falls silent. And now the vastness of the space seems appropriate for her discoveries. As she stands in front of them all, she's silhouetted against the image of the galaxies behind her. She may be invisible again, but she knows everyone is listening to her.

The image remains there throughout her talk. Occasionally she turns around to face it, to indicate the link between the galaxies.

From up here, she can't tell what sort of silence she is facing, whether it's interested, neutral or hostile. All she can do is talk, describe the sequence of steps that she and Maggie took, to test and quantify the veracity of their claim. The words form a chain that leads from one idea about the universe to another. If the audience grasps hold of it, they will end up, like her and Maggie, doubting what they have believed for the past half a century. She almost feels sorry for them.

She's done the difficult bit about the testing of the data to make sure the link wasn't an artefact of the telescope or the night sky and she's almost finished when, unthinkingly, she starts to talk about the verification of the result from the consortium's data. From up here, Richard's outburst seems small, even faintly ridiculous. She and Maggie didn't publish the consortium's data in their paper. And plenty of scientific papers refer to 'private communications' between people; conversations that aren't documented, or informal sharing of data. There's really nothing unusual in what she did. Apart from Richard's reaction to it.

So she's not prepared for what happens. As she mentions the consortium, she's aware of a man sitting near the front, staring at her. He's wearing glasses and all she can see of him are two oval lenses mirroring light at her.

Then he jumps up and points at her. 'How did you get access to that data?' he shouts. People turn to look at him.

Jeanette says quickly, 'Private communication.'

'But who exactly showed it to you?' He's still pointing at her, his finger seems to be accusing her.

She doesn't want to mention Richard by name in public. She owes him, she's aware of that. So she remains silent, until the man sits down, slowly, and clearly reluctantly. She sees him whispering something to his neighbour who also stares at her.

Somehow she manages to finish the talk. The questions are almost a relief after the interruption. Many of the questions are technical; people are puzzled, they are trying to work out what could have caused this result. There is less scepticism than she anticipated. A lot of people want to discuss the Orion instrument and its ability to decide whether or not the link exists.

An older man stands up, leaning on a stick. By now she knows it's always the older ones who ask the awkward questions. They've got nothing left to prove and they don't give a damn.

'Do you believe it?'

Ah, that word again. It sounds odd in this space. They are all used to statistical odds, experiment, proof, even uncertainty, but they rarely talk about belief. It sounds too human. And they like to pretend that what they do is beyond human.

She looks at this man, whom she doesn't know, and wonders what he thinks. She pauses before she speaks, because she knows this is important. It's one thing to present an odd result, a peculiar image. It's another thing entirely to have to explain your worldview. And she wants to get this right.

'I think we are too used to the current model. Things are too comfortable now. In the 1920s, when Einstein was working on models of the Universe, nobody even knew then whether there were other galaxies outside the Milky Way. They didn't know that the Universe was expanding until Hubble's observations. Einstein thought it was static. And then, only twenty or thirty years after that, we had the great debate between Hoyle and Ryle over the steady state theory versus the Big Bang.'

The man looks at her, questioningly. She hasn't answered him yet. But she will do. She carries on, 'So there was a lot of uncertainty around. Even relatively recently we didn't know what the Hubble constant was, or Omega. All we had were toy models. It never felt very... concrete.

'But recently, we've all become rather used to result after amazing result from telescopes, from satellites. Better maps of the microwave background. Pinpointing the Hubble constant. A precise determination of the age of the Universe.

'Perhaps we're too used to it. It's a wonderful thing that cosmology has finally become a science, but perhaps we've become rather complacent. Perhaps we don't properly question things anymore. We accept too much. It's easy to mock the steady state theory, but philosophically it makes sense. A world without end. Or beginning.'

He looks at her for a moment, and she can't tell at all what he's thinking, what he makes of her speech, until he speaks. 'We don't do philosophy. We do science.' And then he sits down heavily, and the man next to him pats him on the arm, as if to say well done.

She's brought up short. That 'We' seems designed to exclude her.

That evening when she goes for a drink, in a corner of the conference centre that is dolled up as a traditional pub, the man from the consortium is already there, propped up against the bar and sipping a glass of wine. She doesn't want to confront him, she couldn't stand another row about their wretched proprietary data, so she sits down at a table some distance away, trying to act as if she is waiting for someone to join her. She watches him out of the corner of her eye; she knows he can see her too.

She feels a bit daft sitting here in the bar without a drink but she can't go near the bar. And now because she can't get one, she really wants a drink, a lovely cold glass of white wine. Perhaps he's standing there deliberately to prevent her getting what she wants. His wine is finished, and he doesn't look like he's leaving.

Jim Wilson comes into the bar. Jeanette smiles at him brightly so he wanders over to where she's sitting, looking a little uncertain.

'Hi, Jim!'

'Um, hi.' He blinks at her then looks away.

'Jim, could you do me a favour? Could you buy me a drink? A large glass of white wine?'

'Um, sure.' The blink rate increases. 'You deserve it after your talk.'

'No! Don't worry, I'll pay for it.' But it's too late, he's already on his way across the Tudor rose patterned carpet to the bar — much too close now to the consortium man for her to go running after and explain. Shit. Now she'll have to buy him a drink and he'll talk to her about galaxy dynamics for the entire evening.

He returns, carrying her wine and a pint of something dark, and sits down on the stool next to her, far too close, so that their knees are touching.

The man from the consortium walks towards them. 'Enjoy the rest of your evening,' he whispers to Jeanette as he leaves the bar.

'Now,' says Jim, 'Could you explain to me exactly how you took that image of the connected galaxies?'

It starts slowly. A hairline crack appears in the sky. A splinter of light where there should be darkness. Jeanette fails to notice, she's too busy gazing at her galaxies.

Distant stars flicker like failed lightbulbs. Subatomic particles zooming straight along world-lines get lost, spiral into side streets, dawdle down disused train tracks. Jeanette stares at the sky, wonders why the world is winding down.

The link between the connected galaxies blinks and stutters, even as she continues to write about it. Her universe is no longer explainable; she's destroyed its story. She doesn't know what Kate is dreaming any more.

THEN

Kate reading comics in the tent, covered in orange light, as if she were on fire. Kate breaking her tooth on an apple, like something out of a fairy story. Kate dancing round the kitchen after she got her first medal, and the rest of them following her, trying to keep up. Kate flashes into her mind, one memory followed by another, fast and weightless.

They were all in the car driving to yet another of Kate's competitions in some distant grey town. This happened nearly every weekend. But this weekend they were lost.

The heat made the car seat stick to her thighs, and sweat trickle down her neck. Kate was looking out of the window. They were on a narrow road, surrounded by high hedges on either side.

The car had stopped moving. Her parents were silent, still. They all waited in the car. She didn't know why they were just waiting, why her parents weren't doing anything. Kate played with her shoelaces, and then her hair. Although she didn't speak either, she was impatient. She never was any good at waiting.

On the floor at Jeanette's feet was a piece of paper. She picked it up. It was a map of a foreign country. She couldn't understand the way the letters were arranged, but she could follow the pale roads with her fingers, and work out routes between places, imagining herself driving between the straight black lines on the map. Even the green patches on the map were uniform and flat, unlike the ragged branches and hidden depths of the hedges outside the car. The map must be a guide to a toy country where plastic people lived. She let it drop back to the floor, and kicked it under the front seat.

Resting her head against the window, she noticed that even the apparently smooth glass had a tiny city of scratches etched into it. On the other side, a butterfly landed, inches from her nose, and folded itself up into a vertical line.

Still no movement in the car. Her parents remained motionless, speechless. But, finally, the silence was broken by a thin hum that gradually got louder. Another car was driving towards them. And as it got nearer, Kate took charge. She got out and waited, resting against the hot bonnet. The other car stopped and she went over to the driver's window.

Jeanette watched Kate talk to the shadowy head of the other driver, before she came back. As she hopped in, she said, 'I know where we are now.'

Another memory. They were at a family party in some cousin's house. Jeanette and Kate were supposed to be playing with the other children, but they'd given up and wandered back into the living room where all the adults are. Everyone seemed to be clutching a glass. Some of the glasses had slops of wine making red-purple stains in the bottom, like liquid bruises.

The adults were all laughing, throwing their heads back. Jeanette couldn't figure out what was so funny, as one person stopped and another started. Their mother was tipping her glass to one side as she leant back and her throat was stretched out, flat and white. She was all angles in different directions, and she was wearing a dress that Jeanette hadn't seen before, something shiny and dark, a bit like Kate's swimsuits. It slithered around her as she laughed. You couldn't imagine it would be much good in a swimming pool though. It would cling, black fabric seaweed pulling you under the water.

Jeanette and Kate found themselves surrounded by the adults.

'Darlings,' their mother said, for some reason. Jeanette couldn't think what to say and she wasn't even sure why they'd come in here, but it seemed better than staying with the children and their needle-sharp eyes. She stood a bit behind Kate, because it was usually Kate they were interested in.

'How's your swimming coming along? Still the county champion?' said a cousin. He was staring down at them, moving his head back and forward like the crumpled old tortoise they saw at the zoo.

Kate stared back. Jeanette looked around. People were perched everywhere. On the sofas, on the edge of the dining table, on the window sills. They were all focused on Kate, waiting for her to answer. Jeanette could have slipped away unnoticed, as usual, but she decided to stay. Kate didn't seem to care that they were all waiting for her. In any case, she was used to being around lots of adults; swimming coaches and all the hundred and one officials at the championships.

The cousin continued, 'Leaving all the others behind in your wake?' and his eyes flickered at Jeanette as he spoke. Just a flicker but she saw it. She knew Kate did too.

When Kate finally spoke it was in response to this silent gesture, this dismissal of Jeanette's apparent slowness, her inability to be noticed. 'Jeanette's the clever one.'

Clever? At school, she could do the sums without thinking, her reading age was years older than her actual age, she already knew all the things the teacher told them. In fact she was fed up with being taught things she remembered; she wanted the new stuff. She wondered when she would be surprised.

But nobody had ever commented on this before. Was this what it meant to be clever? To know that the moon goes round the earth and they both go round the sun and to be able to see them in her mind, making a corkscrew dance in the sky?

'Clever' sounded like the silence in the classroom as she waited for the others to catch up. But the other kids were still better than her at the important things; the random jokes, thinking up nicknames for their teachers, making each other laugh. She stuck to silence.

The adults looked from Kate to Jeanette and their mother smiled at her, 'Yes, she gets glowing reports from her teachers, she's the brains of the family!'

'Clever' just became visible, then. It didn't make a splash in the pool, or race to be first in the playground. But it belonged to Jeanette. She hugged herself and went off to lean against her mum.

Jeanette starts secondary school, pleased that she can leave behind her and Kate's old school where people stared at her in the corridors, and where some of the teachers avoided talking to her because they didn't know what to say. She doesn't blame them, because she didn't know what to say either.

So it's easier now, in this new school. It's like starting again. Also, there are new lessons, different things to think about. In science, she learns how to push the ticker-tape trolley down the wooden incline, making black dots appear on the paper tape spooling out behind the trolley. She measures the gaps between the black dots and works out how fast the trolley is accelerating. She drops scrunched up paper, apples and stones from the top of a ladder, and watches them all hit the ground at the same time. She loves doing things and figuring out what will happen as a result.

Whenever she gets home from school, her mother is always sitting on the sofa in a nest of newspapers, cigarette boxes, dirty mugs and ashtrays, watching television with the sound turned down.

The school is nearby, about a twenty minute walk away, and when she walks home after school, she starts off light and floaty. But as she gets nearer to home, she gets heavier. Something makes her drag her feet along the pavement. She spends time kicking the dead leaves into the air or looking for conkers, even though she's not that interested in conkers. She arrives home later and later, but her mother doesn't notice. Or at least she doesn't say anything. She never says anything.

There should be two of us, Jeanette thinks. And now that there's just one, that's not half as good or real. It's nothing.

She makes her route home curved rather than straight, so that it takes longer. She walks along unseen roads, past shops she never goes in and through new green spaces and strange parks.

She's aware of the sea off to one side of the town, always visible from the top of the bus. Finally one day she walks down the long narrow hill with the sea waiting at the bottom like a promise.

The road along the coast feels lop-sided, with houses on one side and just the low level water on the other. The houses could rise up and tilt over and fall into the sea, and nothing could stop them drowning.

But she likes this road. It takes a long time to walk along it and turn back home. This becomes her routine. Each day she notices stripes of seaweed and pebbles deposited by the tide at different levels on the beach.

One day she sees a car parked on one side of the road, the side nearest the sea. It's their car, the one her father drives to work each day. But he doesn't work here. His office is outside town in some sort of estate, which she always thought meant parks and big old stone houses, until she visited it and saw that it was white huts huddled together in a field. She doesn't know what happens in the huts, and when she asks him he says it's too boring to explain. Perhaps that's why he's here. When she goes up to the car and peers in, all she can see is the usual stuff on the floor; crisp packets and crumpled maps.

It's odd, seeing their car here. She looks up and down the road, but she can't see him. As she walks home she wonders why he goes there. Does he also think it's separate from home? Somewhere secret?

The next day the car's parked in the same spot. She glances at the house opposite, wondering if he's inside. Some curtains are hanging half off their rail in the downstairs window. Or perhaps he's walking on the beach. Sure enough there are a few stick figures a long way off, two grown-ups tucked into each other. She ducks down so she can't be seen, and watches them. Is it her dad? But the man is silhouetted against the sky and she can't make him out.

The next day, the curtains are pulled shut against the late, low afternoon sun. She blinks as it shines in her eyes. That's the one problem with walking home this way; she has to squint into the yellow distance for over a mile.

After a few weeks it has turned into a habit. Walk along the road, glance at their car, and keep walking. She hasn't seen the people on the beach since the first time, and the curtains are nearly always shut. This time when she looks at the car, it has been parked really badly and one end is practically sticking out into the road. Her dad must have been in a hurry. She can imagine him swerving into the parking space and leaping out of the car. Inside the car, on the passenger seat, is a bag she's never seen before. It looks like a lady's handbag, but it's not her mum's. She gazes at it for a bit, it's smart and black and shiny. It doesn't seem to go with the owner of the curtains.

When she first starts at this school, she tries to tell her parents things. One night, as they're all sawing away at their dinner, she says, 'I got an A in my maths test.' Nothing. If anything the silence gets deeper. The next night she says, 'I failed my French.' Again, nothing. This is what it's like if you're an astronaut in space, she thinks, floating in the blackness beyond the curve of the Earth.

Her mother has that glassy, faraway look. Unfocused. Jeanette knows, because she can do it herself; deliberately make her eyes go out of focus, so she sees two blurred images of everything instead of one sharp one. Perhaps when her mother does it, she sees two daughters instead of one.

The next night; 'Some chemical elements are so unstable they only last for a tiny bit of a second. You can't detect them directly, only what they've left behind.' She's thinking of the imprint of fireworks on the night sky, the swimsuits left around the house, the pale scar of wallpaper where Kate's photo used to be.

After that she gives up on the truth, and she just tells them anything she likes;

'One plus one is one.'

'The moon is a bubble.'

'We cut up a dead elephant today.'

Even so, her voice is thin and scratchy, barely making an impression on the dull silence.

Her father starts smiling a lot. He smiles when he comes home in the evenings, but the smile isn't directed at anyone. To Jeanette, the smile looks like the sort of after-glow you get when you glance at something bright like the lightbulb or the sun, and the image is imprinted in darkness inside your eyes. Her father's smile is a negative smile and his eyes are looking at something that's not in front of him, something they can't see. Perhaps he can see Kate.

One evening, fed up with the silence, she says to her father, 'Why do you go to the beach in the afternoons?'

It's not anything like as interesting as all the outlandish stuff she's told them in the past, but for some reason it works. They both look up from their plates, and straight at her.

'The beach?' Her father places his knife and fork quietly side by side on the plate, so that although they're close, they're not touching. 'I'm at work in the afternoons, nowhere near the beach.'

'I've seen our car there, it's always there. When I walk home from school.'

'But the beach isn't anywhere near the way home from school. What on earth are you doing there?'

Her mother has the glassy look, but now it's tinged with fear.

'I walk home that way.' She knows it's not really about her, in spite of what he says. 'And every day there's our car. Once I thought I saw you, walking on the beach, but I wasn't sure. It's a bit difficult to see things properly when the sun's in your eyes.'

'It's not our car. You must have got it wrong.'

She hasn't got it wrong. She doesn't get things wrong. She bends her head over her plate before making herself look up again.

Her mother says, 'Is that why you're always home so late?' It isn't clear which one of them she's asking.

After a long pause that feels cluttered with silent words, Jeanette decides to answer. 'I go there after school sometimes. I like it, it's — empty.' Empty of all the invisible rubbish here at home.

'You're not supposed to go home that way…' Her father is swerving back to where he thinks this conversation should be headed. But suddenly her mother smacks the table with her hand so that the plates jump and jitter and everything tinkles. 'It's not about her! It's about you! What the hell is going on!'

So there are things they don't tell each other, as well as not telling her. She's relieved she doesn't have to justify the meandering walks, the attempts to avoid coming home. Her mother looks different, she's lost the grey veil that seemed to settle over her after Kate died.

In contrast, her father shrinks slightly into his chair. 'Nothing, nothing… I just go there for some fresh air in the afternoon, occasionally. Not often.'

He's lying. Why? She watches him closely, interested in what he will say or do next. He's crying now, tears running down his cheeks. They look fresh and new, and make the rest of him look even more tired than usual.

Her mother's eyes snap open, they're brighter and rounder than they have been for months. 'What's going on?' she shouts. There is a horrible moment when she stares at Jeanette and Jeanette knows that she isn't really seeing her at all, before she bolts from the table, fiddles with the back door and runs into the garden.

It's the first time she's been in the garden since the fire. Or maybe she goes there all the time, Jeanette thinks, the way her father goes to the beach, secretly when she thinks nobody can see her. But he goes there because it's different, and not like home. The garden is like the inside of their house except it is even worse, it's like the inside of their minds, all burnt out with nothing there.

Their phone is on the landing and some evenings, when Jeanette goes upstairs after tea, she can hear him whispering into it;

'When?'

'Please...'

She tries not to imagine that it's Kate he's talking to, asking her to come back. If her mother comes out onto the landing when he's on the phone he puts the receiver down, very quietly so it doesn't make that clicking sound, and turns round to face her with the smile. It doesn't work though. Her mother usually starts crying. As Jeanette recedes up the stairs she can hear her voice, sliding around even more than usual;

'Why her?'

'Why not me?'

But she can't hear her father's reply.

It's what Jeanette sometimes imagine her parents saying to her; 'Why Kate?' or 'Why not you?'

If she had died instead of Kate, she can't see how they would have noticed. After all, they don't seem to notice her now, when she is alive and here. So they probably won't notice if she isn't here. It was always Kate, not her, at the centre. She was on the edge. Watching. But now there's nothing for any of them to watch.

Her mother stops eating dinner with her and her father. She takes a tray into the living room and sits with it on her lap as she watches TV. When she eats, her eyes stay focused on the television screen. If you look closely, you can see reflections glowing tiny and blue in each of her eyes, like two radioactive daughters.

Sometimes when Jeanette comes home from school and stands between the sofa and the TV, she wonders what her mother actually sees. A girl slouched, her school bag at her feet. Waiting. She's aware that sometimes her mother can hardly stand to look at her, that she prefers to look at her made-up world beyond the glass. That world doesn't have the power to hurt her.

At night, after Jeanette finishes her homework, she watches the sky. She realises that the stars rise in the east and set in the west, and that different stars can be seen at different times of the year. The planets are more complicated. Venus is erratic, sometimes visible just after sunset, sometimes not. Mars can move around the sky, and then stop, before changing direction.

She steals her father's binoculars from the sideboard in the dining room and learns how to adjust and focus them, to make objects contract from fuzz to sharpness, and reveal the true nature of themselves. Things in the sky have a clarity that is lacking down here. Jupiter has small moons surrounding it, Venus changes shape from a crescent to a full disk and back again. The Milky Way roars across the centre of the sky. The Andromeda galaxy is just a pale thumbprint off to one side.

Stars and planets are solid. They make her feel solid too. They don't look through her as if she's transparent.

NOW

The next morning Jeanette leaves the conference building in search of daylight. The wind is a slap in the face, but it wakes her up as she mooches along the seafront. She's debating whether to go back inside when she sees a group of people from Edinburgh. They're silhouetted against the sky, so she can't pick out their faces until they stop right in front of her. Mark is there and she smiles at him but she can't see if he's smiling back. There's silence and she wonders why they've all stopped like this, as though they've been choreographed. Mark steps out so he's in front of the rest of them, only a foot away from Jeanette. He clears his throat. Ridiculously, she feels nervous. Is there going to be a showdown?

'Mark?'

'Why did you publish it?' he asks her, straight out. It makes her want to laugh. Have they followed her from the conference building in order to meet her out here, and challenge her?

'Why shouldn't I have?'

The rest of them are silent, looking at her and Mark. The sun goes behind a cloud, and now she can see all their faces in the dull grey light. They're so young. She feels ancient in comparison. They've never known anything else. Neither has she, but at least she knows that she will die, and at some point become uncoupled from this smooth trajectory that has carried her through school and university to this. They don't know that yet. They're still on the upper part of the trajectory. They haven't figured out that they have to land somewhere, that they might yet fail.

Someone else chips in, 'The press are beginning to say that the whole Big Bang model is wrong. The research councils might think that too. It might affect our grants.'

'I don't think my work's that important!' she laughs, but they do not. 'Seriously,' she continues, 'Are you saying I shouldn't have published this?'

'No one believes it,' says Mark. 'No one but the nutters.'

'So what's the big deal?'

'Because it helps them. There'll be stuff in the media giving credibility to all sorts of nutty theories.'

Someone's phone starts ringing, and the noise is a tinny simulation of some famous bit of classical music, but she can't put a name to it.

'It can cope, you know,' she carries on. 'It won't all crumble and fade away just because of a couple of peculiar galaxies. What about the microwave background? Nothing else can explain that, apart from the Big Bang.'

But they don't say anything, and as she turns her back on them and walks back to the conference, she can hear them shuffling behind her, mumbling to each other. Her shadows.

Later that week, when she gets back to the Observatory, she finds out that an application for grant money has been successful. Because she is now a permanent lecturer, she is able to apply for money from the research council to support more junior researchers, and she has been awarded enough money to support someone for three years. This is part of what she is now expected to do, build up her own team of people. She already has some ideas about who she wants, who would be suitable for her work. She sits at her desk and drafts an advert to be placed on the astronomical job website. Just to make sure the right people know that she has them in mind, she emails it to them as well. Now all she has to do is wait.

She makes a visit to her parents to tell them about the new job. From the window of the train the landscape looks brilliant, sparkling blue and green. The morning is cold, and her breath is visible.

She takes the short cut from the station to the house, to avoid the long and tedious hill. But when she arrives, her father isn't home, so she and her mother have to sit and wait. She wasn't expecting this, but she should have remembered that her father works late most evenings. Or at least he doesn't come home until late.

She searches round for something to talk about. It's as quiet and empty as ever in here.

'How's work?' she asks her mother.

'Busy.'

But she can't imagine her mother being busy. 'What do you do? I mean, how do you encourage people to throw their stuff away?'

'Oh, they're always pleased, even if they think they can't bear to get rid of their things. They're always grateful afterwards.'

Jeanette can't stop thinking of all the things taken away, like some sort of surgical procedure performed by her mother. People amputated from their favourite belongings.

'Are you sure it's good for them?'

'They write to me afterwards and tell me that they can breathe better. They feel freer.'

Jeanette gazes round at the living room with its sofa, TV, armchair and dresser. On the dresser is a mathematical formation of crystal glasses. There is one picture on the wall, a photo of a wooden jetty leading out into a vast expanse of water surrounded by mountains. There are no people in the photo.

The clock ticks on. Her father seems to be even later than usual, or perhaps time has slowed down. She resists the urge to keep looking at her watch.

'Perhaps I should take my things to my room,' she suggests, after about ten silent minutes, and gets up before her mother can reply.

Upstairs she walks quickly past the locked door. She hasn't been in that room since she went in there as a teenager, with Alice. It's a stage set, a faked history. Her own bedroom is a relief, as it always was when she lived there. Somehow it's survived her mother's relentless decluttering and its walls are so covered in her photos that they're a patchwork of black and white images. A small one of Alice, near her pillow. Larger ones of planets, a smudged Jupiter with its rings all out of focus, one of the Moon looking like a still from an old movie. She doesn't think her mother ever comes in here. But she's not sure. Perhaps her mother comes in here and lies down on the bed and cries into the pillow. Crying for lost girls. Surreptitiously she feels the pillow, but it's not damp.

She sits down heavily on the bed and waits as long as she dares, before getting up again. Even so, when she gets to the top of the stairs her mother is already hovering at the bottom, peering up.

Her father arrives just before dinner, when she's already sitting at the table, trying not to drink the wine too quickly.

'Hello!' He smells cheerful and beery as he hugs her. Perhaps he went to the pub on the way home.

'Hi, Dad,' she grins, watching as he pours himself a glass of wine and then one for her mother.

'So, I think we've got something to celebrate?' he winks at her. 'Has our ridiculously clever daughter found out something amazing about the Universe?'

Her mother spills casserole onto their plates and smiles.

'Kind of. But there's something else as well.'

'Something else? Even better than that?'

She likes him in this mood. 'Yep. I've got a job. A proper job. A lectureship.'

He punches the air, and she realises that he is a bit drunk.

'But you had a job anyway,' says her mother.

'Yes, but...' She's half proud, half fed up, with explaining the minutiae of the University's hierarchy and the endless gradations of jobs. 'It's the next level up. It's a big jump. If everything goes ok, I'll be permanent in a year.'

'Do you hear that?' Her father swivels round to face her mother. 'Permanent!'

'How did you get it?' asks her mother.

'Because she's so blooming clever!' says her father.

'No, Mum's right. It's because I found something, at least I think that's why I got it.' She still isn't sure and that's what makes her worry that it might yet disappear in a puff of smoke.

'Did you discover something new? A new planet?' Her mother has finished and has cleared her plate away, even though she and her father are still eating.

'No, I don't do planets.' She's not that interested in planets. They're little more than fluff around stars. 'I do bigger things, galaxies, stuff in the early Universe.'

'A new galaxy, then? Presumably that would be more important than just a planet.'

She has to admire her mother's logic. 'Well yes, but it's much easier to discover galaxies than planets, because they're much bigger and brighter. I've probably discovered thousands of galaxies.' For the first time she realises how topsy-turvy her work is. What does it mean to 'discover' something like a distant galaxy in the early Universe, which probably doesn't even exist now? Is it like discovering the grave of someone who's been dead for centuries? 'I found something odd between two galaxies, something that shouldn't have been there. It's caused a bit of a stir.'

'Well, let's drink to it,' says her father, but her mother's already washed and dried her own glass.

Later, when they're watching television, her father says he has to go upstairs for a bit. She doesn't think anything of this, until she glances at her mother and sees her expressionless face, like a mask. And she remembers all those childhood evenings with her father upstairs, whispering into the phone, and she realises that he's still having an affair. He's here but he's not here.

She can hear him walking around. 'What's Dad up to?' The news is on. Something to do with floods in some distant country.

Her mother shrugs, not looking away from the TV.

She wishes she could think up some other chat to distract her mother; perhaps she should tell her about her new flatmate. But she doesn't trust herself not to betray her feelings about Paula; she's not that good an actor. And to her parents she is always single, always neuter. She has never told them about any other women, they have never met any of her girlfriends, never heard her happiness at meeting someone new, or sadness at the end of a relationship. When she split up with the ice woman she was abrupt with them on the phone, to avoid any of the misery leaking out. This is the way it's always been, but now she realises that she's made a large chunk of her life invisible to them. She's made herself invisible.

The news is showing pictures of people sitting on rooftops. Each roof has one person sitting on it and waiting for help, surrounded by dirty water which, according to the news reporter, is still rising. Each person is isolated, silent.

The next morning she lies in bed looking up at the photos. They rustle gently, and it looks like they're breathing. She wonders where Alice is now. She never heard from her again, not after she reached out to stroke Alice's face and Alice went away.

After she's dressed and ready to go downstairs for breakfast she walks into her parents' room. Their double bed is neat with the cover pulled taut. It doesn't look like anyone ever sleeps in it. Perhaps they don't sleep there, perhaps each night on the stroke of midnight her father goes back to his lover and her mother folds herself up like a sad lost umbrella, and waits in the corner of the room until morning.

There's nothing else in here, no other signs of life. It's as clean as downstairs, and as empty. Emptier, because there's nothing on the walls. No clothes heaped on the laundry hamper, no knick-knacks gathering dust on the chest of drawers. But as she glances around the room something snags at her vision. There is something here, ruffling the smooth absence of things. A tiny bit of texture. There. She's spotted it — she moves closer to the chest of drawers. Laid flat against the surface is a photo.

It's a photo of Kate. Kate in school uniform and her face all smiling. Jeanette's eyes fill. She hasn't seen this for years. It was the very last photo to disappear, when all the other things that Kate owned, or that were associated with her, receded one by one beyond the horizon where they couldn't be seen anymore. Why did her parents keep this to themselves? Why couldn't they have shared it with her?

She tilts the photo, gazes at it from different angles, even holds it up to the window. But it can't share its secrets with her.

She watches as her hand sneaks out, picks up the photo and slips it into her pocket. The photo's snug against the curve of her body now, not left out in the cold of her parents' bedroom.

She walks downstairs for breakfast and doesn't tell her parents about her secret stowaway.

Jeanette finds it difficult to remember the first time with Paula. There are gaps in the timeline, things her brain has not registered. So the second time is slower, more deliberate; she wants to record this physical phenomenon in her memory.

Paula is lying naked on the bedroom carpet, with Jeanette kneeling between her legs. She wonders what she looks like from this angle and for a moment it saddens her that she will never know, never be able to see and truly understand herself. She only knows her own body from studying other women, and their bodies can only be an imperfect mirror of her own. It occurs to her, as Paula trembles slightly against her fingers, that she spends her life looking at images of reality without ever being able to reach reality itself.

Even as Paula shudders, Jeanette has to observe her, noticing the way her face flushes pink, her hips arch up away from the floor. Information to be stored for analysis later.

Afterwards, when they're both lying on the carpet, Jeanette thinks about her first girl and remembers that brief moment when she thought she understood it all.

The first girl was a girl in a blue shirt. Jeanette was a student, going to a club off Grassmarket each week, hanging round the dark, damp space, trying to notice other girls and get noticed.

The girl came over to talk, but it was too loud so they just smiled at each other. Jeanette couldn't stop looking at the girl's shirt, where the soft fabric met her skin.

They walked home together and stopped at the edge of the Meadows. The girl turned to Jeanette. She still didn't know her name, but now she could see that her eyes matched her shirt.

'Please touch me,' the girl whispered as she clung to Jeanette. They were still upright but the girl had backed Jeanette against the wall. She said it again; 'Touch me.' More insistent this time, less pleading.

Touch me. As if that was what she was. She was her body. And when Jeanette reached out the girl had already unzipped her jeans, so there was smooth skin, then coarse hair, then she was at the limit of the girl's body and the edge of her cunt, before she found what she'd been looking for all these years. Similar to herself, and yet so different.

This is what women did, then. To each other.

The girl had her own hand in Jeanette's jeans now. 'I want to touch you,' she sighed in Jeanette's ear.

You. You are this. All this is you.

Jeanette was still vaguely worried about being seen by passers-by. They were only a few metres from the nearest streetlight and the people in the tenements opposite could have just looked out of the windows and seen the two of them doing this to each other.

She was too wound up and tense to come herself, even though the girl was pushing inside her, stretching her wider. But as her finger slid and bumped around on the girl's clit, she could feel the girl gasp and clutch at her, not able to do anything but ride her orgasm until it broke and they were both stranded, slumped against the wall.

The girl took a step back, and they looked at each other. The girl's skin was moon-pale in the streetlight. Jeanette's cunt ached and there was a thump in her belly because she wanted more, but at least she had the smooth slick of the girl on her fingers.

The girl slowly ran a glistening finger around Jeanette's mouth. 'Thanks for that. You're lovely,' she said.

She had never been lovely to anyone before, she was made lovely for the first time that night. She kissed the girl again, wanting to feel the stickiness between their mouths. But the girl pulled away. 'I'd better go,' she said. She lived with someone, that was why they were out here in the cold, trying to hide from other people. And Jeanette couldn't imagine bringing a woman back to the flat. To her male flatmates she was the sensible one, the one who didn't shag random people or have dating disasters. They asked her for advice about women, probably not realising what she thought about these women.

'See you at the club again, maybe?' Jeanette offered.

'Yeah. Maybe.' The girl walked off down the street, waving goodbye behind her, past the row of shiny-eyed windows. Jeanette was still leaning against the high stone wall, her own jeans wide open, not wanting to move away from that moment. She no longer cared if anyone had seen them together.

Now, on the carpet with Paula, Jeanette thinks she's fallen asleep so she glances at her. But Paula's eyes are wide open and she's staring at the ceiling.

Jeanette's see-through. She's swimming, slipping through the water as easily and quickly as Kate used to. She's gliding up and down the pool, effortlessly. But she's translucent, a jellyfish girl. As she pauses and then falters, alone in the water, she looks down at her body, fascinated by the structure of her bones and veins. Just like the branches of a naked tree in winter. Even her swimming suit is pale. Only her heart is the wrong colour. It's dark red. It looks bruised, vulnerable.

Other astronomers are repeating the experiment. They're taking more images of the galaxies to see if they too can spot the link. Almost an entire volume of one of the leading academic journals is taken up with these repeat observations. The good news is that everyone can see this link, although nobody can see it very clearly. The bad news is that no other galaxies show anything similar. There appears to be only one pair of linked galaxies at different redshifts in the observed Universe. People trawl through old datasets, rummage around in their office through forgotten computer tapes, get their students to re-check their results. Nothing.

The consortium publishes a paper in *Nature* showing an analysis of all their thousands of galaxies. They are scathing about Jeanette's and Maggie's work, and claim that their own image of these galaxies shows a very low statistical significance and should not be used in support. But Jon writes a letter to *Nature* the following week, reminding people about Orion and encouraging them to keep an open mind, at least until then.

The problem is, thinks Jeanette as she reads Jon's letter, that we're stuck on Earth with only one point of view. Never has she felt so frustrated by the essential passivity of the way that they work. If only she could reach into the sky and grab hold of the galaxies, turn them around in her hands, examine them from every direction.

It's Becca's birthday and there is a cake with candles, because Becca always does things properly. She would have been the sort of little girl to have birthday parties with other little girls in nice dresses, and fairy cakes, and sandwiches cut into triangles. After Kate died, Jeanette's mother stopped doing those sorts of parties. Watching the candles on Becca's cake makes Jeanette's eyes fill.

'Are you ok?' Paula whispers. She nods. They're in a restaurant in town, surrounded by Becca's friends from work, who are all as well dressed as Becca. Jeanette has made an effort with her smartest jeans, but still feels like a slob. She surreptitiously tries to tidy up her nails by pushing back her cuticles, and draws blood.

She's sitting next to Paula but they don't touch, and they don't even talk much to each other. But she's so aware of Paula; it's as if her body has turned into some sort of precision instrument whose sole purpose is to detect Paula's. The hairs on her arms have turned to needles on the scale of the instrument and they're trembling. All the information she's received is overwhelming her; the way the shoulder straps on Paula's dress keep slipping down on her arms so that she has to pull them up again. Each time she does this, Jeanette gets a glimpse of the paler skin at the top of her breasts. Her hands resting so close to Jeanette's on the table keep reminding her of the way those hands touched her just before they left for the restaurant. She can't concentrate on anything else, not on making polite conversation to Becca's boring boss, not even on talking to Becca herself.

Becca doesn't know. Jeanette wants to tell her, but Paula is more cautious.

'She doesn't have to be "told", does she? We don't have to "come out" to her, do we?'

'She'll be upset if she finds out from someone else.'

'But nobody else knows either.'

'They may guess.' To Jeanette it is inconceivable that people won't guess when they see her and Paula together. Surely it's obvious. 'She'll guess. She knows both of us so well. She's bound to notice something's changed.'

Becca is sitting further down the table, cutting the cake. Wedges of it are passed around the table, tiny cliffs of chocolate earth. Jeanette has to stop herself from staring at Paula's mouth as she licks her lips to get the last of the icing.

'Hey, Paula,' Becca calls down the table, 'You still with that bloke you met at your party?'

'Of course not,' Paula calls back, easy.

'Of course not,' Becca echoes her, knowingly, and laughs.

'What bloke?' she mutters at Paula.

'Just a bloke.' Paula gives her a small sideways smile, 'Don't worry. It was quick and painless. He didn't suffer much.'

She remembers seeing Paula talk to Richard, and there was another man asking for her. She can remember too much, and it's all the more painful because it meant nothing then. Why didn't she anticipate the future, then? Why didn't she notice more?

'Who?' she has to ask again.

Becca looks down the table at them. 'I suppose your style is a bit cramped in Jeanette's flat.' It sounds to Jeanette as if this is a question. She wants to answer it, wants to share her knowledge of Paula's style, but she stays silent. Paula stays silent too.

She likes explaining things to Paula, likes talking about her work. Perhaps she's worried that without it she's not so interesting. What is it that differentiates her from any other smallish not-so-youngish mousey-hairedish woman in Edinburgh? So, like Scheherazade, she spins out the story of the Universe to keep Paula intrigued. Fortunately, in many versions of this story there is no end. But she doesn't know what will happen as the Universe continues to expand, and everything travels further away and all the stars die out one by one. Will Paula still be interested then?

Paula seems to like the mistakes best, so today Jeanette is telling her about galaxies. The great astronomer Hubble thought he'd solved the problem of why there are different types of galaxies. Some are featureless elliptical blobs, and others are spirals; great Catherine wheels of stars that it's easy to imagine spinning across the sky.

Hubble set out images of different types of galaxies in a diagram that resembles a tuning fork, and convinced other astronomers that elliptical and spiral galaxies both evolved from a more primeval form and that at a certain point, the evolution bifurcated to give the two different shapes.

It was simple, clever — and wrong. The idea fell apart in the sixties when astronomers started getting better, more detailed data on the different types of stars in the galaxies. But Jeanette still likes the idea because it articulates the desire of transforming yourself into something else. Even if it does take billions of years.

'How extraordinary,' murmurs Paula. 'What happens here?' She gently touches the point where the long legs sprout from the body on the tuning fork diagram.

She and Paula are lying in the garden, grass bunched beneath them, waiting for a predicted meteorite shower.

They are quiet together. She likes this new aspect of Paula. She never imagined it would be peaceful, being with her. She can't remember Paula being quiet, staring at the night sky, when they last lived together.

Tonight, the sky is obligingly clear and dark, and there is no moon to get in their way. They wait. At the peak of this meteorite shower, there should be one meteor every minute, but they haven't noticed any yet.

'What's that?' Paula points at a thin, steady dot of light making its way overhead.

'A satellite.' Satellites are a nuisance for astronomers, their tracks polluting the sky, like fast cars bombing along country lanes.

'You should be called Stella,' Paula says.

'Hmm?' Jeanette can't always keep up with Paula's twists and turns.

'The starry woman.'

'Oh. Stellar. I see.' She reaches out to touch Paula's hand and they continue to lie there, watching occasional flashes of light in the surrounding darkness.

Pau-la Pau-la Pau-la. Jeanette walks down the street to work, her feet tapping out an easy one-two rhythm. The name brings its own joy, independent of the association with its owner.

It's still early on in their relationship, it's still simple and straightforward to understand. She's aware that at some point, other elements will have to be included, and the model will get more complicated. There will be aspects she won't fully understand, probably related to other, earlier, interactions. There are things you simply have to accept, in any models of the physical universe. When she was young, her teachers thought she'd go on and do maths at university, but it was always physics that drew her. Trying to describe the reality, the complexity of what you see around you.

But right now it's just Pau-la. When Jeanette strokes her stomach, it quivers like a small animal. Pau-la rests her head on Jeanette's shoulder when they watch telly together. Paula used to wear contact lenses that made her eyes an improbable but definite shade of sky blue; Pau-la's eyes are a more tentative and changeable greenish-brown.

But there is a vague sense of unease, because she still can't figure out the exact chain of events, the cause and effect that brought them together. They've been friends for years, after all, so why didn't it happen earlier? What made it happen when it did? She can't even remember, although she tries so hard, the first time they met. She conjures up an image of Paula haloed by light, garlanded with flowers, but knows this is a fiction. Most likely it would have been in a pub. She can't even remember what she thought, or felt, about Paula. But there was one incident shortly after they met, which now seems prescient.

They were walking along the beach at Musselburgh, one pale evening in summertime. She can't recall why they were there, but her memory places them on the beach, walking away from the low sun and towards their own long shadows, as they picked their way along the stretches of shells and pebbles.

'They find all sorts of things here. Things get washed up from the past,' Jeanette said.

'Like what?'

'Old bottles. Bullet cases. Clay pipes.'

Paula looked down. 'All I can see are pebbles and stones.'

'Most of the interesting things are submerged. You have to dig for them,' suggested Jeanette.

So Paula obediently crouched down and picked up a stone. 'Eurgh! It's filthy!' she shrieked, and burst out laughing. There was a man watching them further along the beach. Jeanette could see him looking at Paula as she laughed. She nudged Paula, but Paula didn't seem to notice or care, until it was too late and the man was walking towards them. He stood there in his ratty little jacket and wiped his mouth on the back of his hand before speaking.

'Found anything?' he asked Paula, smiling. Jeanette guessed he was smiling at his own audacity in speaking to her.

'Only dirt,' Paula replied, 'Nothing interesting.'

'Oh, I don't know. You can find all sorts along here.'

'Yes, so my friend said.'

He turned to Jeanette and winked before Paula continued, 'She also said everything's usually old and past it round here.'

Jeanette winked back as the man stumbled past, hissing under his breath, 'Bloody lezzers.'

Paula burst out laughing, delighted. 'Lezzers!' she screamed. 'We're lezzers!'

Jeanette smiled, but felt shaken. Was her sexuality so obvious? Could people tell? 'Ssshhh,' she said, 'He'll hear.'

'Good!'

Paula clutched onto her, still laughing, their shadows merging together.

Her memory finishes there, leaving them laughing on the beach. She savours it in its innocence, and her present self feels almost jealous of her past self for not knowing what would happen, the unexpected happiness that was waiting in the future.

But she still can't attach a clear meaning to this. Did it matter? Was it a foretaste of what was to happen between them? Or was it essentially random? And if she can't even figure out the past, how can she hope to navigate the future?

One morning she switches on her computer and finds an email from Richard. He's applied for her grant. She can't believe it. He was not one of the people she ever had in mind. Even apart from their personal differences, she doesn't rate his work. He's too much of a follower, a data processor. She needs someone who can think for themselves, who can take her initial ideas and create something of their own. She's never seen any evidence of Richard doing that. He spent his entire PhD churning the handle of his programmes and spewing out data. She doesn't think he ever actually analysed it.

But. She needs to tell him that he's not going to be successful, and tell him nicely. There's space for him somewhere, on someone's project. But hers is not the right one. She doesn't have enough data for a start. He'd flounder.

It's coffee time. Before she gets up from her desk, she watches the smooth progression of the second hand on the wall clock, suddenly aware of how time can only be represented by spatial movement. How odd it is to rely on clocks, with their proxy measurement of the passage of time. The real thing is so much more difficult to grasp and understand.

She walks down the curved stone steps to get some coffee, as she has done hundreds of times before, thinking about her history always intersecting at this place.

Richard's sitting in the far corner of the canteen, surrounded by pieces of paper scattered all over the floor. She ignores the other lecturers where they are gathered together and walks over to him. As she gets closer he glances up at her, from beneath his eyelashes. Almost a flirtatious glance, but she notices the pouched, dark skin around his eyes, and guesses that he hasn't been sleeping well. She needs to speak to him so she perches on the arm of a nearby chair. Now she notices that the pieces of paper are identical to what he sent her, they're all job applications.

'Richard.'

He glances at her again and then back at the paper, as if he's too busy to talk to her.

'Thanks for your application.' She remembers being told about an apocryphal rejection letter that an Oxford professor is rumoured to use; 'Thank you for your application. Lots of good people applied for this post and you were not one of them.' She grins, before realising that this is rather inappropriate. But Richard seems to take heart from this and smiles back, almost shyly, as if he can expect some good news.

A few weeks ago he told her how many jobs he'd applied for and she'd been secretly shocked at the high number. It was the opposite of bragging about sexual conquests, an admission of how many times you'd tried and failed to seduce would-be employers. She feels for him, but she has to tell him. 'I'm sorry.'

There is a silence, before he asks, 'Have you already done the sift, then?'

Oh, shit. 'Sort of.' She's not followed the proper process, but it won't make any difference. He still won't make it onto her shortlist.

'I thought I'd be in with a chance because of the data... There may be more data in the future, other projects that we could work on together...'

Is he trying to bribe her or blackmail her? Is there a difference?

'The point of my grant is to work on new projects, get new data, write new papers.'

'Your paper relied on the consortium's data.' His voice is almost dreamy now, as if he's reminiscing about good old days. He's staring down into his coffee mug now, perhaps to avoid looking at her. She's quite irritated now, the paper was helped by her reference to the consortium's data, but it didn't exactly rely on it. She knows enough not to contradict him directly, though.

'You can't read your future in instant coffee,' she tries to joke. Again, completely inappropriate. She should be professional about this. Clear and brisk, but helpful. 'Do you want me to help?' She gestures at the piles of paper.

He squints up at her. 'Help?'

'I could read what you've written.'

'Just because you're a step above me in the food chain doesn't mean you're better than me.' He starts scrabbling around to pick up the papers.

She steps back. 'I'm only offering because I've been through it too.'

'Well, good for you.' He starts to read something and then looks at her again. 'Shouldn't you be at one of your very important meetings?'

That's too much. 'You're right, I should go.' As she walks away, she calls out, 'Good luck with all your other applications!' and she hopes it sounds bitchy.

That afternoon the college press officer phones to ask if she can be interviewed at the BBC. Yes, she can. Does she need any help in getting ready? Jeanette knows that the subtext to this question is; does she look recognisably female? Jeanette says that she's wearing a skirt, and the press officer purrs with gratitude.

'Just like all the other stories that have been hyped up and then sank without trace,' Jon says when she tells him. 'A rotating universe, a neutrino-filled universe, anti-matter galaxies.' He ticks them off one by one on his fingers. 'Enjoy your fifteen minutes of fame.'

Silently, she agrees with him.

Now, as she stands waiting in the BBC office, she looks at the reflection of the sky in the water of the Clyde. Every time a boat goes past, the sky breaks up into little chunks.

When the news researcher finally appears, she has to unclench her hands, and she's surprised to see crescents of dark red on her palms.

The researcher glances over her, making her feel shabby. Her skirt seemed smart in her own office but here, under the sharp lights, it looks dull and used. The researcher's wearing something so black and shiny that she appears to have been dipped in plastic.

Jeanette talks about the tenuousness of the results and how it's really too early to make any grandiose claims. The woman stares down at her notes. 'But if it's right now, how can it be wrong in the future?'

'We don't know if it's definitely right. All we can say is how likely it is to be right — or wrong.'

'I thought science was about definite answers.' The woman's lips form a sad little pout and for a moment Jeanette feels bad about letting her down.

'That's exactly what science isn't about,' she says gently. 'Usually it's about quantifying uncertainty.'

The woman perks up again. 'The uncertainty principle? Like, nothing's really there until you observe it?'

Jeanette tries not to sigh. But the next thing that the researcher says gives her a shock. 'We're really pleased because we've managed to get David Grant here today. We're going to interview him alongside you.'

David Grant? A tinny noise starts up in Jeanette's head. She can't immediately remember who David Grant is, but she associates the name with something unpleasant, something wrong.

'He's come up here all the way from Manchester specially to take part.'

Ah. She remembers. David Grant is what is politely known as a maverick astronomer, or if you want to be less polite, a loony.

'He's very excited about your work.' The researcher is actually smiling now. She thinks she's doing Jeanette a favour, interviewing her alongside someone who agrees with her. But the researcher doesn't know what Jeanette knows, that David Grant is the kiss of death for any real astronomer. She's never actually met him before, but she's seen him in the distance at conferences, standing by the dirty coffee cups, trying to talk to people. Come to think of it, he was at the Brighton conference. She remembers how she veered away when she almost sat next to him by accident. She didn't even want to sit next to him then. And now she has to talk to him. On national television.

In the green room he comes bustling up to her and the researcher introduces them. Jeanette has to shake his hand and only realises how much she's been sweating, when he wipes his hand theatrically on his trousers.

'Oh, my dear,' he booms at her. 'It's all going to be alright. Don't worry. We're going to have fun out there!'

He takes a step back then and regards her as if she's on display. Perhaps she is. Too soon, they're both in the studio, in front of the lights and cameras.

The interviewer is one of those BBC types who regards science as a joke, done by 'boffins'. He actually uses this word in his introduction, as he glances at both Jeanette and Grant, over his half-moon glasses.

'The world of astronomy boffins has been turned upside down by the latest discovery that the Big Bang never happened. With me here to explain it all — in simple language for all of us ignoramuses who never got beyond Maths O-grade, haha! — is Dr. Jeanette Smith, from the University of Edinburgh, and David Grant, an amateur astronomer from England.' He turns to Jeanette and beams at her, 'Dr. Smith, can you explain to us what it is you found and why it's so important.'

Jeanette knows what she has to say, before she gets cut off. She has to bring this down, back to the reality of what she and Maggie actually did find, and away from all this hyperbole. 'To start with, we haven't found evidence that the Big Bang is wrong. We've just found a couple of peculiar galaxies that appear to be connected.'

'In a way that can't be possible in the Big Bang theory,' David Grant chips in and already she wants to hit him. But she manages to carry on.

'As I said, they only appear to be connected. But there's a lot of uncertainty about this result. The image is very faint. To be really sure of what we've found we need to get some more detailed observations of the stuff that appears to connect the galaxies. Only then can we say more definitely whether the galaxies are connected — or not.'

'Isn't there going to be a satellite?' The interviewer looks very pleased with himself.

'Yes. Orion will be able to make a much more definitive study of these galaxies and hopefully answer all our questions.' She feels her stomach muscles relax slightly. The interviewer turns to Grant and she sneaks a glance around the studio. She catches sight of her image in one of the camera lenses, tiny and glittering and far away. The row of black lenses regarding the three of them as they perch on their chairs in the ersatz room makes her feel as if someone's at the other end of some microscopes, observing her.

'But just one result can change a theory,' Grant is saying to the interviewer. 'Galileo looked at moons orbiting Jupiter and what he saw there shattered the old Earth-centred model of the universe. I think this observation is as important as Galileo's.'

'Really?' The interviewer looks sceptical. But Grant isn't deterred.

'Yes. This could be a turning point in cosmology, one that finally breaks the hegemony of the Big Bang theory and marks a new era.'

Hegemony? Jeanette is baffled. Don't they just get data and interpret it according to the model that best fits it? She knows there are standard models, but these are standard for a reason, they're the ones that best explain the observations.

'So if the Big Bang can't explain it, then what can?' Fortunately, the interviewer is still focused on Grant.

'Oh, there are all sorts of possibilities. The plasma universe is one. In this model everything is connected by twisted magnetic fields...' He's off. Not even the interviewer can stop him spouting an incontinent stream of alternative theories. Jeanette feels polluted just listening to him. It's all words. He's not making any attempt to explain these madcap ideas, they're just spilling out all over the studio, most likely confirming the interviewer's prejudice that science is long words and jargon, designed to exclude ordinary people.

'...C fields.' He finishes. The interviewer turns to Jeanette, his spectacles have slipped slightly down his nose, giving his face a twisted appearance.

'What are you doing to test all these other...' he pauses, 'possibilities?'

'Nothing,' she says crisply. There is a small pause.

'Nothing?' repeats the interviewer.

'You see, that's the problem with the institutionalised approach to science.' Grant's face is purple with the effort of getting his views across. 'Only certain ideas can get accepted, and no one else can get funding.'

Jeanette carries on as if Grant hasn't spoken. We already know they're wrong. The Big Bang model isn't perfect, but it explains more observations than any other idea, and it makes predictions that can be tested. All we're doing here is testing one aspect of it. That testing isn't complete yet.'

'Ah,' says Grant, and the interviewer's head bobs back to him. 'Aaaah, but I know you scientists, you won't stop looking until you get the result you want.' He's actually wagging a finger at her now. 'You should read your Popper, Dr. Smith...'

'I know all about Popper, Mr. Grant,' she hisses at him. 'If you try to use one result to falsify an entire theory, you'd better be pretty damn certain that the result is correct.'

'And that's all we've got time for right now! We'll have more on this story when the satellite launches.' There's no mistaking the look of relief on the interviewer's face. The camera swings away and the studio goes dark. She and Grant are led off back to the green room, where she goes straight over to the table of drinks. She wants a whisky, but makes do with some water. Fortunately, Grant is standing just slightly too far away for any sort of pretence that they're going to have a post-interview chummy chat. Her hands are trembling so much that she slops some water onto the table.

'You shouldn't be so modest, my dear.' He is going to try and speak to her after all. But modest? She thinks she probably came across as rather arrogant. He continues, 'You've found something extraordinary. Take the credit. It could be the making of you.'

'You don't understand.' She's trying to keep her voice down, trying to stay calm and quiet. 'I meant what I said. This observation is just that — one observation. You can't bring down an entire theory on the basis of a few fuzzy pixels. Especially when you don't have anything else...'

But he doesn't appear to be listening. He's leaning back against the table now, gazing at the ceiling. Water is dripping off the table and splashing onto his shoes but he doesn't notice. 'It's always a failing of female scientists in the end. The lack of any sort of killer instinct. The apparent contentment to let others get the glory for their work.' He looks quite happy about this. She glares at his horrible face and walks off.

In the women's toilet, her own face looks back at her out of the mirror, as if it fails to recognise her. She tries to smile and her reflection twitches like a fish hooked on a line. Failing? Is she failing? She doesn't feel like she has any sort of choice right now. There seems to be no free will in her universe, now that she and Maggie have found these wretched galaxies. Events just happen to her.

Outside, in the corridor, the researcher is waiting. 'Why did you play down your results?' she asks.

'Because that's my job,' answers Jeanette. 'To be realistic. Like I told you before, we just don't know yet.'

'Why did you agree to come and do the interview, then?'

'Because you asked me. Because people need to understand how science works.'

'It doesn't seem to work very well, does it?' snaps the woman and she walks off, her black plastic legs creaking down the corridor.

The tube journey back to Queen Street, with its rhythmic stops, feels as restful as a heartbeat. She wonders what will happen next with the galaxies. Down here, so far from the sky, it's easy not to care. In fact, she's tempted to stay in this enclosed space, insulated from everything up there on the surface.

When she goes to the Observatory the next day she wishes she had stayed on the tube, going round and round underneath Glasgow. Because they're waiting for her. She was never bullied at school, always felt a worm of contempt for the kids who had dog shit smeared on their books. Now she wishes she'd been more compassionate. Because they're all waiting, all in a line, propped against the wall outside the canteen. She feels her stomach turn over. But she knows she did the right thing. What else could she have done?

'We saw you on the news,' one of them says. Turner, a post-grad in his final year, with a generally unwashed appearance and currently writing up his thesis.

She nods to acknowledge this, and opens the door to go inside. Apart from anything else, it's cold. The wall is the only thing between them and the hills south of Edinburgh, and at this time of year the wind skirls up the slopes before blasting people foolish enough to stop outside. She needs hot coffee. She needs peace and quiet.

But before she can escape someone else says, 'You shouldn't have done it.' The words are made physical in the cold air, little puffs of emotion.

'Why not?' She pauses, the door half open.

'Because...' Silence. They're not good at expressing themselves, this lot. Ask them how to derive the Friedmann-Lemaitre equations, or plot data on the Hertzsprung-Russell diagram and they can be fluent, graceful even. Ask them if they prefer sausages to bacon, or what their hopes or fears or dreams are, and they're silent. She can articulate it for them, but she doesn't see why she should. She waits.

Mark steps in. 'The phone's been ringing off the hook, Jeanette.

None of us are getting any work done.'

'Is that all? Well, I'm here now. Just put the calls through to me.' But she knows that isn't all. She can see Richard out of the corner of her eye, standing a few metres away on the grass. He can probably hear what they're saying.

Mark shakes his head, almost sorrowfully. 'Why are you talking on the news? What do you think that will achieve?'

'It's our duty to explain, to communicate. What's the point of doing science if you don't tell people about it?' But she knows this sounds pompous.

'And David Grant! F'Chrissakes!'

She winces. 'Well, that wasn't my idea. I didn't even know he was going to be there until the last minute.'

'You should have refused.'

She remembers what Grant said yesterday, about female scientists being too modest and doing what they're told.

'Fuck off, Mark.' And she goes inside to get her coffee.

THEN

One day, when Jeanette gets home from school, there's a large white envelope on the coffee table in the lounge, addressed to her.

'Aren't you going to open it?' Her mother seems expectant, as if she knows something Jeanette doesn't.

She picks the envelope up. Its whiteness and freshness seem alien in this environment. She slowly peels open one corner. There seems to be a certificate inside. Something to do with Kate's swimming? Kate used to get stacks of certificates. But when she removes the stiff piece of paper from its envelope she notices a drawing of a five-pointed star and a crescent moon. Underneath this drawing are the words, 'You are the proud owner of a star named...' and then there's a series of dashes where someone has written 'Katherine Agnes Smith' in red biro. Below that is a series of numbers which she recognises as stellar coordinates.

'I've bought a star for you,' Her mother says.

'What?' She finds it difficult to speak. She clears her throat. 'Why?' It comes out louder this time.

'I thought you'd like it. You seem to like the stars...' Her mother's voice dies away. And why doesn't she like it? In fact, she's horrified. She fingers the piece of paper, and realises from the coordinates that the star is in the southern hemisphere. It doesn't say how bright it is. So she won't able to see it from here, and she may never be able to see it at all, if it's too faint.

'When you do your astronomy...'

She looks at her mother on the sofa, wearing the same skirt that she wore yesterday and hugging a cushion, squashing it tight against her stomach.

But she thinks about the sky, the cold, clean, hygienic starlight that she looks forward to watching each night, the light that's uncluttered by anything in the rest of her life.

'It's nonsense,' she bursts out.

'What is?' Her mother is still cradling the cushion, still obviously hoping that she's done the right thing.

'Buying a star. Giving it a name.'

'But I paid for it. It's entered into a catalogue.' Her mother holds out her hand and Jeanette passes her the certificate, pleased to get rid of it.

'Stars are usually only ever given numbers, depending on where they are in the sky. They're just coordinates, like latitude and longitude.'

'But I thought you said that some of them have names too.'

Jeanette puts her head in her hands. 'Bright stars, the ones that have been known about for ever, they have names. And if you discover something extraordinary, it may get named after you. You can't just buy it and name it.'

'But now when you look up in the sky, there's a star named after... I thought you'd like that. To have a connection.'

It's too much. 'The star's in the wrong hemisphere! I can't even see it from here!' She grabs the paper out of her mother's hand and rips it in two. 'And I don't want to! Why bother naming a star after her? She's not there. She's nowhere!'

She's holding a piece of jagged paper in each hand. Her mother cowers against the back of the sofa, as if the pieces of paper are dangerous.

As she leaves the room, she can hear the click of the TV being turned on.

Another day after school, she finds her mother lying on the sofa, her face buried in the cushions. The TV is on but the sound is turned off, and the silence in the room is like a thick shell surrounding them.

Jeanette is afraid to speak in case she breaks it and something bad spills out. So she just puts her hand on her mother's shoulder, gently, her fingertips barely touching the smooth cotton of the blouse. But her mother twitches and leaps round, her face distorted and wet.

Since the explosion her parents have been wearing masks, white and rigid. This is why they're not able to speak very often, because the masks won't let them. Only their eyes aren't covered by the masks, but their eyes are a long way away, staring down at the world like frightened gods.

Now her mother's mask has gone, and her face is naked. Jeanette thinks she prefers the mask.

One evening, picking over the remains of dinner, her mother says, 'I went into the garden today.'

Jeanette blinks, surprised, at her father. As if she can read their minds, her mother says, 'Actually, I go out there regularly. It helps me think.'

'What do you think about, Mum?' Jeanette is genuinely curious.

'Things. All sorts.' She jabs her food. 'It's very neat isn't it? Everything's in its place.'

'Thanks,' says her father, but Jeanette doesn't see why this is a compliment.

'But there seem to be lots of cut stems on the rosebushes. Where do the flowers go?'

Jeanette knows where they go. One day when she was walking home from school along the sea road, she saw a large vase of flowers in the window of the house. From the pavement she could only see vague red splodges, and she couldn't tell what sort of flowers they were. But now she knows they were roses.

She walked away from the house, across the road and down the beach, right to the water's edge. The wet sand gleamed in the late afternoon sun, the tide was coming in and as she wandered along the edge of the sea, she looked over her shoulder and watched the water drown her footprints.

'Jeanette,' her father says, 'Are you going to look at the stars tonight?'

'I might do.' It's a clear night and she hasn't got much homework.

'How far away is the nearest star?'

'You mean the Sun? Ninety-three million miles.'

'And the next nearest? The first proper star. The Sun's not really a proper star, is it?'

She stares at him. 'Yes it is. Of course it is. It's just that it's much nearer than all the others so you see it differently.' She's well aware that he's deflecting attention onto her, and away from himself and the disappearing flowers. But at least for once they're actually listening to her.

NOW

On the phone, Jeanette's mother says that she's coming to visit her in Edinburgh because she 'needs a break'. She doesn't say what she needs a break from.

Since Jeanette's last visit to her parents, there has been no mention of the disappearing photo. It's joined the list of things that aren't talked about. When she first brought it back with her, she displayed it on her bedside cabinet. But its visibility is too disturbing. To see Kate's face every morning compresses time and takes her back to the era of grief and silence. So she hides the photo in a drawer of scarves where it stays wrapped up in something delicate that she hardly ever wears.

But if her mother is coming, surely they will have to talk about it. Before she goes to pick her mother up from the station, Jeanette unwraps the photo from its silky shroud and props it up against the lamp on the bedside table.

'Hello, Kate.'

Kate's too silent, her gaze is too steady.

The rest of the flat is silent too. Paula's been packed off for the weekend because there's not enough room in the flat for all three of them. At least, not if they sleep separately. She would like to be in a parallel universe where her mother sleeps on the sofa bed and she can share her double bed with Paula.

It starts to rain on the way to the station. She wonders if her mother will mention the photo.

Her mother kisses her cheek. They wait at the bus stop, huddled together under her umbrella, and the noise of the rain on it is like static on the radio drowning out all the words. They don't say much. Her mother doesn't mention the photo.

The flat has been hastily tidied, and Paula's things are scattered in the corner of the living room. Her clothes look as if she has only just stepped out of them and run away naked. Jeanette slips her hand into a mound of underwear, feeling the fabric slide against her fingers and imagines Paula hiding in the garden, her skin smooth against the rough bark of the trees, waiting to be found.

She doesn't invite her mother into the bedroom. They will have a nice afternoon first.

'Where's your flatmate?' asks her mother.

'Staying with friends.' Her mother will have her bed and she'll sleep on the sofa bed. That way at least she can wrap herself in Paula's sheets, and smuggle herself into Paula's dreams.

She tries to see her flat through her mother's eyes. There's stuff everywhere; she can sense her mother itching to tidy it up and hide it all away.

'What do you want...' she pauses to sip her tea for maybe too long, '...to do?'

Her mother looks around at the books, the papers, the clothes. 'Some fresh air would be nice.'

So they head back towards the bus stop, Arthur's Seat behind them. Once in town, they take a meandering route through the streets.

'I love glimpsing bits of the sea from up here, right in the centre of the city,' Jeanette says and her mother nods in agreement. But Jeanette knows that the sea is problematic. The sea also means a seaside house with her father's car parked outside, the curtains pulled tight shut so that it's dark in the room with only a small amount of sunlight creeping along the carpet. A woman stretched out on the bed, waiting. She swallows.

But walking around town isn't a bad thing to do, and the silence between them is almost pleasant. When the rain starts again they have to go back home. Families, she thinks, are like black holes. They're inescapable, because no matter how hard you try, they will suck you in.

At home, she still doesn't take her mother into the bedroom. Is she making her mother wait on purpose? Delaying the confrontation?

'Do you want to help me cook dinner?' she asks, and they make a curry together. She takes care to add in all the spices and flavourings her mother wouldn't normally bother with.

And when her mother says, between forkfuls, 'This tastes nice,' she's mean enough to think of that as a victory. But there was the macaroni cheese. Perhaps that justifies it?

Not long after Kate died, Jeanette asked her mother to cook macaroni cheese. It was Kate's favourite meal, and they hadn't had it since.

'Why?' Her mother looked round from where she was sitting on the sofa, watching TV.

'Because.' The TV was on too quietly, Jeanette thought. Her mother couldn't possibly hear it properly.

'But you don't like it. You always say it's too gloopy!'

'What are you watching?' Jeanette pointed at the screen.

Her mother sighed. 'I don't know, I'm just waiting for something better.'

When they had the macaroni cheese that night, it was as awful as ever and Jeanette wondered what Kate liked about it. She tried to swallow, but there was too much of it, lying heavy in her mouth, weighing down her tongue, like soil packed into a garden pot. Perhaps it would suffocate her.

She pushed the remains of it around her plate with her fork, scooped it into mountains, plains, valleys, all the time wondering what to do with the stuff in her mouth.

Her mother noticed her plate. 'You're too old to play with your food, Jeanette.'

Her father looked at her properly for the first time that night.

'You asked for it, missy. Just eat it.'

If she swallowed it, she knew she would be sick. Finally, she opened her mouth and let it spill out, almost fascinated by the pale slime.

'Jeanette!' Her father hit the table, and the salt and pepper shakers rattled against each other, like chattering teeth. She was afraid to look at him so she stared down at the plate, at the horror.

'Leave her be,' her mother muttered.

She was still connected to it by a line of drool. Her mother leaned over with a napkin, and dabbed at her face.

'Eat your dinner!' her father roared again. But when she dared to look at him, she realised she was angry too.

'Why! What's going to happen if I don't?' And she ran out of the room, managing to knock her plate onto the floor.

So they were all angry and there was nowhere for it to go. And now with her mother here, she's still angry. Angry at the silence they always settle into, like train tracks leading to the same destination that they never want to visit. So she drinks a lot of wine with dinner, and talks about work. This is a safer topic.

'The students have all gone nuts over my peculiar linked galaxies. They think it's an excuse not to have to learn the usual stuff. The Big Bang theory.'

Her mother laughs a little. 'It always sounds odd when you say that. It's as if it's just normal.'

'It is normal to me,' she smiles. 'What else would be normal if you didn't have the Big Bang? It would just be — chaos. No structure at all.' And she realises, maybe for the first time, that most people don't have this structure to their lives. This cosmic scaffolding to cling onto. Perhaps that's why they go for religion.

'But doesn't it make you feel so inconsequential? The enormity of it? The numbers with strings of zeros after them just to measure the distance to the nearest star?'

No. No, she doesn't really feel that. She feels like she can grasp it all in her hands when she writes down the correct equations to work out those distances. Smaller things in life are more capable of cutting her down, making her feel as small as them.

'If you understand it, you don't feel overwhelmed by it.' She takes another gulp of wine. Her mother hasn't drunk that much, but they seem to have got through a bottle.

'If you understand it all perfectly, that means there can't be anything else left to discover.'

'No...' She's surprised by her mother's grasp of the balance between what is known and what isn't. 'You're right, there's always more to find out. Anyway,' she says, pouring another glass of wine, 'I got a job out of it.' And she holds the glass up to her mother, as if making a toast.

'Well, that's great,' says her mother. 'Dad and I were saying the other night, how great it was. But what will you do if they don't make it permanent?'

When she's finished the wine she offers to take her mother's case into the bedroom.

'Yes,' says her mother. 'Thanks.' And as Jeanette leads the way, she feels a small flourish of triumph deep within her. She is in control of this situation, she has led her mother blindfold along this path. Her mother walks in, looks around her and sees the photo. Walks over to it in silence, and picks it up, still silent. She's turned away from Jeanette and all Jeanette can see in the stoop of her shoulders is an absolute concentration, or intenseness of purpose. Is this why her mother came here? To reclaim the photo? She's almost afraid of her mother turning around, of having to face her.

When her mother does turn round, her expression is unreadable. 'Why did you take it?' she asks.

Because I wanted it. Because you hid it away from me. Because I hadn't seen Kate for so many years.

Don't you think I have a right to see it?

'I don't know, I just did. I saw it and I took it.' She's trying not to sound apologetic. She doesn't even want to explain this to her mother, to give spurious reasons for her actions. Who knows why she took it? Why anyone does anything at all?

'You should have asked me,' says her mother. Jeanette notices the absence of her father from this statement.

'Why? Why should I have to ask if I can see a photo of my own sister? Why do you get to control everything?'

'You took it from our room without saying anything. I would have given it to you, if you'd asked.'

'You took it from *me*! When you hid it away. I was just — liberating it.'

Her mother is holding the photo in both hands. Jeanette can't see it properly now. 'You can see it at home any time you like, Jeanette. Don't you think this is a bit childish?'

'It's not my home!' But she's aware that she does sound like a child. In a minute she'll start crying and bawling. 'And I don't see why never talking about things is especially grown up!'

'What things.' Her mother slips the photo into the dark pouch of her handbag and clicks the metal clasp shut.

'Dad. Where he goes every day. Why he's always late home.' She's finally named the unnamable, given voice to the silence. 'The other woman.'

Her mother's face seems to sag and slip, as if its structure has just been removed. Jeanette catches her breath. She gazes out of the window at the garden and remembers burnt grass glistening in the moonlight. The ghost of a white bottle in the distance. The scorched smell of leaves.

'Shall we have a cup of tea?' her mother suggests and Jeanette is grateful for a breather. They stand side by side in the kitchen in front of the kettle. It doesn't click off the way it usually does, so they watch steam rising for some time.

As Jeanette pours out the sputtering water, her mother finally speaks. 'Some things are better off not talked about. I know about Dad, and where he goes.'

Jeanette concentrates on stirring tea. 'Doesn't it make you angry? How can you stand it?'

'It's how he copes. He has another life. If it's just the two of us, we fuel each other's sadness. The marriage generates sadness, it's an engine for it. I'm almost grateful to the — to her.'

They sip their tea. Why don't you leave, thinks Jeanette. Live another life. But perhaps the sadness is a prop. Perhaps her mother wouldn't know what to do without it.

'You can have your own copy of the photo. I'll make one for you.'

They go back to the living room.

Later when her mother's in bed and she's picking her way to the sofa bed, she hears a noise at the front door. Paula.

Paula's drunk and she's forgotten she's not supposed to be coming back here. Just as Jeanette reaches the sofa bed the light snaps on and she's in the doorway, grinning.

'Hey,' she says as she reaches down to remove her stilettos. 'What are you doing in my bed, Goldilocks?'

'My mother's here, remember?' hisses Jeanette, watching Paula slide her tights down over her smooth white legs.

'Oh. Shit. I'm not supposed to be here, am I?' and she giggles unevenly, lurching against the wall as she tries to pull her dress off.

'Just try to be quiet,' Jeanette sighs as she moves over to the edge of the bed. It isn't really big enough for two and she's worried it may collapse under their combined weight.

'Don't want your mum knowing what we do, do we?' Paula giggles again.

Jeanette doesn't reply. There is a world of unspoken actions here, going all the way back to Alice Airy. Her parents don't know about her. Or at least they don't talk about it, and for the first time she wonders how much they do know about her and don't mention. Is she jammed into the same Pandora's box as her father's affair?

Paula's in the bed now. 'Jesus, you smell of smoke,' Jeanette mutters as the bedsprings twang under them. But Paula doesn't have anything on apart from knickers and Jeanette can't stop herself from running her hands over Paula's skin, burying her face in her neck.

The bed rattles uneasily beneath them as they tremble and sigh against each other's bodies. Afterwards she says, 'You'll have to leave first thing, before my mum gets up.'

'Why? We're flatmates. Nothing wrong with that.'

Jeanette is silent. There's nothing wrong with any of it, she wants to say. But she's said enough to her mother this weekend. She can't cope with any more secrets being exposed. So, at seven o'clock in the morning, when it's still dark outside, she makes Paula get up and get dressed.

'When can I come back, then?' Paula's astonishingly obedient as she tries to put on her thin tights, in some inept time reversal of last night. But perhaps she's used to being bundled out of people's beds, being a secret in their lives.

'This evening. She's getting the four o'clock train.'

'Toodle pip, then.' Paula smiles but her eyes are half shut and she still smells of smoke.

Later, before her mother appears, she gets up and tries to tidy the room. She doesn't think there's any visual evidence of Paula having been there during the night. But she worries about the noise. What could her mother have heard?

Over coffee her mother says, 'I slept well.'

'Good.' She tries not to smile.

'It's very quiet here, isn't it?'

'Yes.' She moves to shut the window which has been open all morning to let out the smell of Paula.

'Were you talking to someone on the phone last night? I thought

I heard voices at about midnight.'

She looks down at her hands, trying not to think about her childhood, her father coming home late each evening, before the silent family dinners. Why should she be the same as her father?

'Dad...' she starts.

'Yes?' Her mother looks surprised, wary. 'What about him?'

He was always with someone else, another woman. Invisible, unseen sex. She feels sick. Why can't she be different?

'Yes,' she says, 'my flatmate came back last night. Unexpectedly.' Because everything Paula does is unexpected, her tongue flicking softly between Jeanette's legs. Her desire for Jeanette is unexpected.

'Your flatmate,' says her mother, staring into her coffee. 'So why isn't she here now? Did she have to go to work or something?'

'We didn't want to disturb you.' All she can hear is *we - disturb*. Paula disturbs her, to her core. But it's not the same as her dad. It's only them for a start. Nobody else is involved. 'She's gone...' But she doesn't even know where Paula's actually gone so she stops abruptly.

'Oh. Well, it's alright, you know. She can come back, I promise I won't bite.' But her mother shifts slightly on the sofa, now neatly folded back into place with all the night time activity tucked away. She looks around her. 'It's a bit small for two people.'

'It's fine.'

'I suppose it's only temporary? She can't sleep on a sofa bed for ever.'

But Jeanette doesn't want to think about Paula moving out. She cleans up the empty coffee cups in silence.

Jeanette's in the darkroom, teaching Alice how to print photos. They slip the pieces of paper into the tray of developer and watch as the hidden images emerge.

But the last piece of paper already has a picture on it before it is placed in the tray. Jeanette sees her own face fade under the liquid. Her eyes and lips are washed away and the paper turns white.

Alice takes the empty photo out of the bath and pins it to the wall. 'See?' she says, 'that's you. Don't you look lovely?'

Paula hasn't been in the flat for some time. She seems to be out working, or just out. Jeanette isn't sure where.

What is happening between her and Paula doesn't seem connected to their past. It makes her nervous that she can't determine the cause of it. If it's bubbled up out of nothing perhaps it could just as easily disappear again, leaving no trace. But she knows that this is wrong; that what is happening will leave some physical evidence on her. Her skin feels marked, and she can remember the precise detail of what Paula has done to her, where she has touched her. When she's dead and her bones are being examined by archaeologists, they will see the effects of Paula.

Jeanette sits in the living room waiting for her, but then she gives up and goes to bed, lying in the dark. Some time later the door opens and Paula slips in. Jeanette watches her as she peels off her clothes, her breasts visible in the lighthouse beams from the cars outside. She gets into the bed, and for a moment they just lie there side by side, not touching. Then there is a soft sigh as Paula turns to her.

Afterwards Paula slips away again. Nothing has been said by either of them. Jeanette surprises herself by falling asleep easily and waking up, feeling refreshed. But when she wanders into the living room Paula is gone, the sofa bed tidied away. The only external evidence of her recent presence there is her wet toothbrush in the bathroom.

One evening, they're both at home. Jeanette is making notes for her next lecture on special relativity for the undergraduates, and Paula is studying for an essay. The phone rings.

'I'll get it.' Paula lunges for the phone. Jeanette carries on writing, but can't help listening.

'Where do you work?' Paula writes something down. 'Oh yes, that's good, that's interesting.'

A pause. Jeanette watches her twist her hair around her fingers. She does this when she's in the pub, talking to someone new.

'Can I meet you there tomorrow, at five, say?'

Who is she meeting? Jeanette stares at her, but even after the conversation is finished, she doesn't offer any explanation.

'Who are you meeting?' Too abrupt. Paula looks at her, startled, before Jeanette sees her narrow her eyes slightly, as if focusing on something a long way away.

'I mean...' Jeanette flounders, 'Was that a friend from college?'

'No.' Paula picks up her pen and carries on writing, the pen scarcely leaving the page as words flow smoothly from it. In contrast, Jeanette's breathing feels jagged. She tries to write an explanation of the equivalence between different frames of reference. On a train, it is impossible to tell if you are actually moving at constant speed, or stationary. You may end up in different places, but the experiences are physically equivalent.

'It's another sitter,' Paula says out of nowhere, just when Jeanette has finally managed to think her way back into her lecture. 'I put up an advert. After I painted that portrait of you, I realised I wanted to do some more, of real people doing real jobs. Not just students.'

Jealousy shoots its barbs into Jeanette. Paula's painting someone else? 'What does this — person — do?'

'He's a butcher, which is going to be fantastic. Great bloody sides of cow and entrails. But I can't decide whether to keep him in his white coat, which would be a brilliant contrast with the meat, or have him naked. Life flesh and dead flesh, next to each other.'

Naked. Jeanette squeezes her hands together, until the blood disappears from her fingers and they turn blue-white.

'Oh, come here.' There is a note of exasperated affection in Paula's voice. Obediently, Jeanette gets up and stands in front of her. Paula runs her hand up Jeanette's leg as far as her hip. A precise, minimal movement. 'You're not jealous?'

'No,' Jeanette lies. She puts her hand on top of Paula's and stays there standing, motionless for a moment before Paula pulls her down.

Afterwards they carry on working.

So the relationship becomes more efficient, stripped away to its essentials. They don't waste time sitting on the sofa, or lying in the garden. They don't talk so much. There doesn't seem to be time for Jeanette's stories. Jeanette tells herself it's because Paula is busy. She has to prepare for a new show, she's at the art school most evenings. This is the way it's got to be. Paula's absences make Jeanette feel guilty, she should also be working hard, but she's been neglectful lately.

Paula appears in Jeanette's room about one night each week, but Jeanette never knows in advance when it's going to happen. She learns that to stop herself thinking about it at work, she has to maroon it in her mind, cut it off from the rest of her. Paula's only visible at night, her head on the pillow next to Jeanette. She doesn't exist in the daytime; she's swamped by all the other information that Jeanette has to process. She's too faint and delicate to compete with the demands of work.

Jeanette hasn't felt this seriously about anyone since the ice woman. She's managed to stop thinking about her recently, but now she finds herself remembering more and more of that summer.

The first time they met, she appeared without warning in the Observatory canteen and sat down next to Jeanette. She didn't slouch down in the low slung chairs like everyone else; she sat upright with her back straight, her hair so glossy in the sunlight that Jeanette couldn't see what colour it was.

The woman explained to Jeanette that she'd come to work at the Observatory for a few months, to finish writing a book on the cosmic microwave background. Jeanette always pictured this remnant of the Big Bang hanging through the whole universe like smoke from a fired gun.

The woman told Jeanette about her plans to release a detector on a balloon high into the thin air above the South Pole. The balloon would fly for three weeks, pointing at the sky and collecting information before sinking back down to earth.

As they drank coffee out of the Observatory's chipped mugs, the woman talked about life in the Antarctic, and the thousand variations of white in the snow. 'The only colours you see are artificial. Human life is artificial there. It's like living in outer space.'

'How long have you spent there?' asked Jeanette.

'Six months.'

It was summer now in Edinburgh. The woman would be going back to the Antarctic in the autumn to fly her balloon.

'Where do people here go in the evening?' The woman wore an ivory-coloured scarf tied around her neck, and Jeanette watched her skin pulse as she spoke.

'There's a pub nearby, at the bottom of the hill.' Jeanette felt shy, as if this might be inadequate. The pub was a grotty students' drinking den with bad beer. But Jeanette didn't think the woman drank beer.

'Good. I'll see you there at seven?'

Jeanette nodded, and the woman turned around to talk to someone else. Jeanette's supervisor waved at her from across the room; he had some feedback on her thesis. He also wanted her to proofread the exam paper for the undergraduates. When she went back to her office, she realised she didn't know the woman's name.

Jeanette sat waiting in the pub, her whisky and water reduced to a slick on the bottom of the glass. Finally, the woman arrived and bought a glass of red wine.

'Cheers,' Jeanette said, but the woman didn't reply.

Silence. Jeanette wiped her sweaty hands on her jeans and imagined herself somewhere dry, still, safe; on the moon.

The woman inspected her wine. 'So,' she said, finally looking at Jeanette, 'You want to fuck?'

The sex wasn't particularly interesting that first time. The woman's body was oddly anonymous; her skin seemed exactly the same colour and texture all over. She behaved as if she were used to being naked with strangers, as if they were doing this in public.

It was very dark in the woman's hotel room; the curtains were pulled tight shut against the rest of the city. The woman said she couldn't sleep when it was light. In the Antarctic summer, days crashed up against each other with no gaps in between. She said there was nothing to do but work. Everyone worked night and day.

At coffee time the next day Jeanette saw the woman on the other side of the canteen. She felt the woman glance at her, once or twice, before she left. She had a lot of work to do on her thesis.

Later, the woman appeared in her office. 'So this is where you're hidden away,' she smiled. 'I'll see you this evening?'

Jeanette nodded and continued reading her supervisor's feedback. He had found gaps in her analysis; she had made too many assumptions. The last chapter was going to have to be completely reworked.

This time Jeanette found a cluster of freckles at the base of the woman's spine, only fractionally darker than the rest of her skin. This time the neatness of her body was admirable.

'You are so fair,' the woman kept saying as she stroked Jeanette's breasts. 'Like ice, like snow.'

It was nearly Midsummer's Eve, and sunlight managed to slide its way into the room in spite of the curtains. Throughout the night, the woman kicked at the sheets and sighed, as Jeanette tried to sleep.

The next day she found it difficult to concentrate, so she went to find the woman. But her office, a clean, bare box of a room with whitewashed walls, high up in one of the Observatory's towers, was empty. Just an abandoned academic paper idly flapping in a draft near the window.

It was the same all through the summer, the woman was never in the office. Sometimes Jeanette would find evidence of her; the pattern of the room would be disturbed by her jacket flung over the chair. A rich dark plum coloured jacket that made the rest of the room seem even paler in contrast.

One night just before the equinox, when day and night were almost equally balanced, they lay parallel on the bed, tracing the edges of each other's bodies and Jeanette dared to ask, 'Will you email me from the South Pole?'

But the woman didn't reply and Jeanette felt almost dizzy surrounded by the black space, her head floating near the ceiling. The woman's hand in hers was the only thing that tethered her to the bed, to the surface of the earth.

The next day the woman said, 'I couldn't sleep last night,' but Jeanette knew she had. Jeanette was trying to work, her fingers lying inert on the computer keyboard. The woman stood behind her and kissed the nape of her neck very lightly, so that all Jeanette felt was dry lips on her skin. Or perhaps the woman didn't kiss her at all. Perhaps she only touched Jeanette with her fingertips; Jeanette wasn't sure exactly. On the screen, the woman's distorted image walked away.

Back in her office, she printed out the revised version of her last chapter. But when she went to the printer, something was wrong. The pages were blank. There were faint scratchy marks on a few of them, but most were pure white. No warning lights flashed on the machine, no indication of what had happened, or where her work had gone. Her supervisor refused to read the electronic version. She didn't know what to do. She just wanted to sleep so she climbed the stairs, knowing the woman's office would be empty, and her supervisor wouldn't look for her there. She wandered over to the chair and sat staring at the blank screen before she reached out and jiggled the mouse, bringing the screen back to life. She looked closer, there was an email;

```
Darling, have missed you so much this summer.
Can't wait to see you again.
```

That night, Jeanette pretended to fall asleep straight away. The woman was sprawled in the middle of the bed, snoring gently. Jeanette opened her eyes and stared into the darkness, as thick as black coffee, for the rest of the night.

A few days later, the woman gave a seminar. It was the last week of her stay in Edinburgh. Jeanette arrived late at the lecture theatre and had to squeeze into one of the few remaining seats.

The woman started talking about her last balloon experiment, two years before. Jeanette didn't know about this previous experiment. She'd only been told about the future one. But here, in front of everyone else, the woman talked about the balloon lurching out of the sky and tumbling to the ground. She showed a photo of the balloon's skin slumped on the ice. It reminded Jeanette of crumpled bed sheets. The data collected during the balloon's flight was lost somewhere on the vast expanse of the Antarctic, and would never be found. The audience sighed as the woman told them that years of work had depended on this one short flight.

Jeanette's eyes filled. She looked down and a tear splashed onto her left shoe, exploding into dark water. She waited until the spot faded away before she dared look up again.

The woman left the next day. It took some time before Jeanette started to sleep better.

Now, Jeanette knows what the link is between Paula and the ice woman. She is going to get hurt again. It's strange how she knows this, there is no direct evidence of what Paula will do, or not do. But Jeanette can tell that it will go wrong. The only thing she can't predict is how this will happen.

From the undergraduates' exam paper:

1) What is the observational evidence for the expansion of the Universe?
(50 points)

2) Explain how we can see galaxies at distances of more than 20 billion lightyears, when the age of the Universe is only 14 billion years.
(50 points)

3) In 1964 Penzias and Wilson discovered the cosmic microwave background radiation; experimental proof of the Big Bang theory. They initially thought this radiation was caused by bird shit. Which one of them shot the pigeons nesting in the telescope?
(50 points)

4) Draw a Minkowski space-time diagram. Now plot on it the precise points showing when and where you first met your ex-lover, had sex with her and then cried yourself to sleep over her.
(1 point)

One night, Paula doesn't come home at all. Jeanette knows this because she lies awake, waiting. At some point everything becomes a jumble in her mind. Paula is in the observer's cage with her and they're wheeling through the sky, not connected to anything.

It's still dark when she gets up and goes through to the living room where the undisturbed sofa bed mocks her. She gets into it and buries her head in the pillow, trying to convince herself she can smell Paula, before she gives up and starts to cry.

The next day she has to get up early; it's nearly the end of term and time for the ritual of the examiners' meeting. She teaches the undergrads a few lectures each term and then she contributes a couple of questions to their end of term test.

She has to go to the examiners' meeting, to discuss the results of the test and resolve how to deal with borderline cases. This is the first time she's been invited to any examiners' meeting, and she's quite excited. It feels like she's crossed another invisible barrier, become adult in another way.

That morning she puts on some lipstick before she leaves the house. Increasingly the bathroom feels like a place of refuge to her, even though every surface in it is covered with containers of Paula's make-up and perfume. But her reflection looks reassuringly solid and as she stretches her mouth before applying dark red colour to it, she feels like a proper person. Then she leaves the bathroom and has to face the empty sofa bed yet again. The absence of Paula is beginning to feel more and more like a leaden presence. The flat feels unnaturally silent without her, even though it never felt particularly quiet before she moved in.

Jeanette's grateful to escape outside, to walk up the hill to the Observatory. It's another windy day, making it difficult to walk quickly, and her hair blowing across her face gets caught on her lipsticked mouth, an odd sensation and one that's she not used to. How do women like Paula cope with lipstick in Edinburgh? And she sighs as she realises something else has brought her back to Paula.

The others are already seated around the table when she arrives. It's the same room where she was interviewed for the job and arriving like this, slightly late, makes her feel as if she is the one who will be examined here today. But she sits down and builds a professional little pile of papers in front of her, and then smiles at the Death Star. He stares back at her, motionless, impassive.

She presumes this meeting will be very boring in a nice, peaceful, monotonous way. A bit of arguing between some of the older and crustier lecturers, the ones who actually enjoy teaching. She's hoping for just enough distraction to take her mind off Paula. She's not expecting to have to do any work.

She devised two questions out of the twelve in the test, and her two are near the beginning. Before they get to these questions, there's an unnecessarily lengthy discussion about a particularly inept student who's under the impression that the cosmic microwave background can only be observed in one part of the sky.

The Death Star hands round some of the students' scripts. 'Turn to questions three and four.' Her questions. He nods at them all. 'You'll see what I was talking about earlier.'

Earlier? Were they talking about her before she got here? What was he saying about her questions? They must have been alright because they were reviewed by the faculty panel. But perhaps none of her students could answer them, because she hasn't taught them properly. Her stomach turns over. She flips to her questions in the script in front of her.

But there are no answers to her questions, just the words, 'THIS THEORY HAS JUST BEEN PROVED WRONG SO WHY ARE WE BEING TESTED ON IT.' The letters are slightly wobbly, perhaps due to nerves or excitement. She glances at her neighbour's script. It says the same thing, with a similar wobble to the letters.

'Jeanette, did you tell the students about your result?' His voice is so quiet she can barely hear him.

'No. No, of course not.' Why does she feel as if she's the one being examined here? Opened up and inspected? She sits on her hands in case their trembling betrays her.

The Death Star looks around the room. 'Has anyone else noticed the students questioning what we've been teaching them?'

The professor of optics, a crumpled looking bloke in tweed at the end of the table pipes up, 'They never question anything at all in *my* lectures,' to general laughter.

'So it's just you then.' The Death Star turns his death ray on her.

'At least they've been paying attention to something,' another crumpled bloke says quietly. This is Stone, emeritus professor of theoretical cosmology. He's never really spoken directly to her at all.

'Can hardly avoid it, can they? It's everywhere.' She can't tell who said this.

This must be what it's like when you're ill and facing a roomful of doctors, she thinks. There is no privacy and they all talk about you as if you aren't there. Perhaps she isn't there. Perhaps she's still in the bathroom piling on the lipstick, or better, in bed with Paula. Perhaps right now Paula is whispering in her ear, trying to wake her up, so they can make love again. She sighs without thinking, and realises Death Star is staring at her.

'It's probably just an excuse,' Stone says. 'Perhaps they just couldn't be bothered to do the work. It's only an end of term test after all, it doesn't count towards their formal marks.'

She glances at Jon, but he's staring at the wall in front of him. Is he trying to avoid her?

'I've a good mind to fail the bloody lot of them,' says the Death Star.

'How many are we actually talking about?' asks Stone. She wonders why he's helping her.

'Four. I wonder who the ringleader is? There must be a ringleader.'

Four? Is that all? There are twenty in that class. She sits back in her chair and relaxes slightly. What a hoo-hah over nothing. But the Death Star is pointing his pen at her. 'You need to do all you can to correct this misunderstanding.'

'I haven't done anything to *cause* this misunderstanding.' Paula has evaporated now. She's no longer in bed waiting for Paula to appear. She's in this room glaring at the Death Star. 'I taught them the standard stuff! A bit of general rel, Hubble's observations, the Friedman-Lemaitre equations, radio source counts, abundances of primordial elements, the microwave background...'

He cuts her off with a swipe of his pen through the air, like a conductor controlling an orchestra, 'Yes, yes, alright. That's enough.'

Stone starts tapping the table with one finger. 'Actually it could be quite helpful, in some ways.' Jeanette notices Jon looking at Stone, the first time he's shown any signs of engagement.

'How?' The Death Star's voice is acerbic.

'If nothing else, it teaches them about uncertainty. They learn all this stuff like it's the catechism. Perhaps they need to think a bit more about the limitations.'

'We do that in the second year.' The Death Star still won't give any ground. 'The flatness problem, the horizon problem and so on.'

'Exactly. All the dogma. And by then it's no good, it's too late. All these first years are straight out of school, they need to be shown how to think differently. Not to regurgitate the same old stuff.' Stone glances at Jeanette. 'No offence.'

She wants to smile at him but can't quite summon the energy. 'Perhaps everything will become a bit clearer once we get the results from Orion.'

'Orion?'

'Jon's satellite instrument. It's going to provide a proper test.'

He looks tired for some reason. 'A proper test indeed. In the meantime we're all being shaken up.'

They are being shaken up. There's no avoiding it now. Not since her appearance on the news. Googling the phrase 'Downfall of Big Bang theory' brings up more than half a million hits, #bigbangwrong is one of the most popular hashtags on Twitter. It feels like almost every time she turns on the radio someone's commenting on what the discovery means for cosmology, for astronomy, for science, for humanity. The last time she heard it being talked about on the radio they'd dredged up one of Hoyle's old students to reminisce about the good old days. When there were fights outside Cambridge pubs between different factions of astronomers, over the merits of the Big Bang theory versus the steady state. Hoyle had a mean left hook, apparently, but Ryle could topple him with a swift kick to the shins. She wishes this could be settled as easily as a pub fight.

That afternoon she goes to visit Jon in his lab. Orion has been completed and shipped to the European rocket launch site in French Guyana. The lab feels a lot larger and emptier without the instrument, a bit like the way Jeanette's flat feels when Paula isn't there.

Jon is still rather quiet. He's tidying up some drawers full of different types and thicknesses of wire. They look a bit like frozen pieces of sewing thread. She likes watching him methodically extract each loop of wire and wind it round a pencil before returning to its home. Clara is sitting nearby, doodling on a pad of paper. Everyone here seems to have more time and less purpose, now that the instrument's gone.

'What's the chance of it blowing up?' she says suddenly. Her words take her by surprise, she didn't know that's what she was thinking. But Jon nods as if he were expecting it.

'Blowing up?' Clara's voice rises incredulously. But Jeanette knows it's not that unlikely. About one in a hundred, maybe?

'Well?' Perhaps she's angry with him for not speaking up on her behalf this morning. Is that why she's trying to force a response out of him?

But Jon doesn't reply.

When she gets back to her office, she has an email from Maggie, containing an image of the cover of a book just published by some religious college in America. The cover shows a picture of their galaxies, but the book isn't about astronomy, it's about intelligent design. Their galaxies are being used as the scientific equivalent of Michelangelo's God and Man connecting on the ceiling of the Sistine chapel. According to the book, the image of the linked galaxies is so unlikely it proves God must have had a hand in it, somehow. Maggie hasn't provided any comment, and Jeanette just stares in silence at the book cover.

That evening, Paula's in the flat when Jeanette arrives home. Jeanette doesn't ask her where she was last night. She's chopping onions in the kitchen and the radio is on. Things may be normal.

They eat dinner and Jeanette talks about the examiners' meeting. Paula sips her wine and nods at regular intervals, she's obviously making an effort. Jeanette tries not to look at her too much, tries not to notice how tired her eyes are, tries not to wonder how little she slept the night before.

'Becca says hello,' Paula announces in a gap between Jeanette's words.

Becca? 'When did you see — ?'

'Last night.'

Silence. Jeanette doesn't know what this means.

Paula holds out the bottle of wine. 'A refill?'

Jeanette studies the way her fingers curve around the bottle. Since they became lovers, Paula exists in several dimensions, in a way that no one else does. Other people are just collections of clothes and faces and hands. They might be interesting to look at, but they don't overwhelm her with information and memories in the way that Paula does. She can't look at Paula's arms without being reminded of the first time she stroked them, and felt the texture of the skin. Only Paula fully inhabits space and time.

'Do you want a refill or not?' Her impatience is only just audible.

'Sorry. No.'

More silence. Perhaps they can go back, rewind to earlier times.

'You should be called Urania.' This occurred to her weeks ago but now, spoken out loud into the heavy silence, it sounds absurd.

'Urania?' Understandably, Paula looks baffled. She stares at Jeanette for the first time that evening, and Jeanette knows that she doesn't hear the echo of that earlier night under the stars, of starry girl.

'Yes.' She feels obliged to explain, even though she knows that it won't help. You can't induce feelings in other people at will. 'She was one of the nine muses in classical times. The astronomical muse.'

To her credit, Paula is still making an effort to understand. 'You mean I'm your muse?'

Jeanette doesn't know how to reply. When she first thought of saying this to Paula, the imagined conversation ended with Paula's burbling laughter, with them kissing. Not with this dull, inert air blocking up the space between them.

Paula clatters the plates together and disappears into the kitchen. Then Jeanette hears the back door slam and knows that Paula has gone into the garden to have a cigarette. To get away from her.

Maggie comes to Edinburgh on a short visit. She's moving from Heidelberg to a new post in California and she's stopping off to see Jeanette on the way. When she gets a cab to the Observatory from Waverley, Jeanette runs out to meet her.

'Is this all your worldly belongings?'

Maggie's standing on the lawn by the east tower, gazing around her. She's wearing one of her jackets covered in functional zips. It's the colour of dirt, presumably to hide any actual dirt. A large rucksack and a small suitcase are parked at her feet.

'Mostly. My books have been shipped separately. Wow. I'd forgotten how amazing this view is.'

No wonder she's able to move around so easily. Jeanette suddenly feels very heavy, weighed down by her emotions.

'Oh, the view... you get used to that.' She grabs hold of the small suitcase. 'Come on, I want to show you some new images. Simulated images of the link.'

But Maggie's still motionless, staring at the hills in the distance, the wind whipping up her hair, until Jeanette prods her gently with the suitcase, 'Come on!'

The images are mock-ups, simulations of what Orion should be able to see if the link is real.

'Looks impressive.' There's a precision to Maggie's voice that Jeanette hasn't noticed before. Perhaps it's because she's not used to speaking English? 'How long will it take for Orion to resolve this detail?'

'The same as a large ground based telescope. About half an hour.'

'That's really good.'

They go for coffee in the canteen. As Jeanette opens the door she sees Richard sitting in a far corner, and she realises she hasn't spoken to him since the last time she saw him in here, surrounded by job applications. She's able to steer Maggie to a seat some way from Richard. She doesn't want to speak to him now, there might be awkwardness. There's something else too, another reason that she can't quite put her finger on, for keeping him away from Maggie.

She sits facing him so she can keep an eye on him. Maggie's telling her about California and what she's expecting to do out there.

'I'll be able to apply for time on the Lick Observatory telescopes, as well as Mauna Kea. You can come and visit me, I'm sure there's money for visiting fellows. If you have the time, now that you're a lecturer!' Maggie laughs, and Jeanette tries to laugh too. But she doesn't like the thought of going to California. How could she leave Edinburgh for any length of time, as long as Paula is in her life? There's already so much psychological distance between them, any physical separation could be lethal.

Richard gets up and starts walking to the exit. Jeanette watches him but he doesn't look at her. She thinks she can hear him humming. As he passes by, he swerves smartly and walks towards them. He has wrongfooted me, Jeanette thinks, quite literally. I didn't predict that movement.

'Maggie,' he nods at her. He's looking ragged, not as smooth as usual. The shiny hair hasn't been brushed as well as it should be, she can see clumps of dandruff. He even has a spot on his chin.

'Oh... Richard.' Maggie knows about his failed job application. She manages to smile at him, but she's not a good actor and Jeanette can see pity taint the curve of her lips. But then she smiles properly. 'Hey. Now that I'm here, can I see something?'

He nods again, more uncertainly this time. 'What?'

'Well, because we were able to refer to the consortium's piccie of the link in our paper, after you showed it to Jeanette, I was wondering if I could see it too?'

After the lightning strike, a moment of silence. Then, 'You've got a nerve.'

'Sorry?' Maggie glances at Jeanette, confused.

'Or hasn't she told you?'

'Told me what?'

They're both looking at her now. For some reason they seem larger than her, and it feels like they're her parents and she's a naughty child. Of course she hasn't told Maggie about the problem with the reference to the consortium's data. It was her problem, not Maggie's. There was no reason to tell Maggie.

Richard smoothes a hand over his hair, restoring it to something like its past glory. 'Well, I'll leave it to Jeanette to explain it all to you. She's so good at explaining things, isn't she?' And he walks off.

'Well?' The word sounds compressed, as if Maggie doesn't want to say anything more than the minimum.

Jeanette stares at the floor. 'He let me look at the galaxies. And of course I found the link, but it wasn't as obvious in their data so they'd missed it.'

'Yes, I know that...'

'He told me not to use the data, so I didn't use it. I just mentioned it. That's not actually using it. There was no information about it in our paper.'

'For heaven's sake!'

'No information at all — apart from the fact it showed the link...'

'Why didn't you explain all this to me?'

'Explain?'

'Don't you think I had a right to know? I was the other author on that paper, remember? Yes, I know you like to forget that, and just swan off and talk about it all over the place and get all the credit, but I was there too, remember?'

Jeanette does remember, all too clearly, the cold control room at four o'clock in the morning, and Maggie was angry with her then, too. For doing something she shouldn't have, something that other astronomers, other people, didn't do.

'I'm sorry.'

'You always are sorry, after the event, aren't you? When it's too late. When you've already buggered things up!'

'I haven't buggered things up...'

Maggie's mouth looks too small to be able to squeeze any words out. 'You're supposed to be such a good observer, but you just can't see what you've done. You never can.'

Maggie leaves the next day, after spending the rest of her time at the Observatory chatting to other people. Jeanette doesn't see her again, after the row. She supposes things might settle down, once Maggie moves to California. She'll email her in a few weeks. They've got another observing trip soon. They'll have to patch things up. They've had rows before. It'll be ok.

One day during the next week, the Death Star phones her, and asks her to see him in his office. She's annoyed at being summoned like this, and also at having to interrupt her work on a new project, examining regions of the Universe that have less than the average density of galaxies in them. Not much is known about these regions, because by definition, not much happens in them. But she's curious. She thinks she might try and map one. It might be her *terra nova*. She can do this by herself, she doesn't need Maggie.

Before she goes to see the Death Star, perhaps as a gesture of defiance, she phones Paula. To her surprise, Paula answers the phone and suggests that they meet in the pub later. She allows herself to feel joy for a moment, before realising this arrangement is ambiguous, they've always gone to the pub. It can't be used as a proxy for Paula's feelings.

As she leaves her office she notices the shadow chalk-marks for the first time in ages. 'GAG' is still visible.

When she reaches the Death Star's office, she supposes he's in there somewhere, although it's difficult to tell. There could be bodies buried in here and nobody would be able to find them under the dry mountains of papers, or the metallic rubble of computer tapes.

He really isn't here. She stands in the small patch of clear floor, trying not to think about why she's there, and why he's making her wait. She stands very upright. She will not be cowed by him.

She can hear him rustling along the corridor like an inescapable avalanche, so she pulls her shoulders back. But then the rustling stops. Silence. Perhaps she is reprieved. She sticks her head out of the office and sees that he's standing still, staring at the photos of the faculty and students like an officer inspecting his troops. Why?

He doesn't seem to notice her, but just carries on scrutinising the shrunken heads. There are about fifty photos, and she knows that if you're standing that close to them they lose their human qualities. It's a bit like looking at pictures of galaxies.

'You've been elevated.' He flicks one of the photos. 'Up to the top row, with the rest of the lecturers.' He flicks the photo again, harder this time, and it falls off the wall. She watches herself spin through the air and land face down, so all she can see is the white cardboard reverse of the image. She wants to pick it up, but he moves towards her.

'Come along,' he says crossly, as if she is the one distracting him, and he herds her into his office. She's worried about her photo now. It'll get dirty, she needs to rescue it.

Wisps of his hair stand out from his head, like the Sun's corona. Every wall in here is insulated by old books with dark bindings. There's only one bit of space that isn't taken up by bookshelves, and on this brief part of the wall is a small plaster statue of a face. The expression on it is wrenched and taut, the eyes twisted up, the mouth a narrow line.

'What's that?' she asks.

He turns to see what she's looking at. 'That? Newton's death mask.'

'His... death mask?'

He doesn't seem surprised, as if this is the reason she is there. 'Yes. Quite common in those days, to preserve the moment of death. Do you want to have a look at it?' He unhooks it from the wall and holds it out to her, as if making some sort of offering. Even under its shroud of dust, the thing is dreadful. She won't touch it.

'What on Earth's it doing here?'

'The Earl of Crawford gave it to the Observatory, when he bequeathed all his astronomical books and tools to this place at the end of the nineteenth century.'

'But what's it doing here in your office?' Why does he have it? Does he use it to weave secret spells? She can imagine him muttering incantations over it. Newton was a strange man.

He doesn't answer her, but instead replaces the mask on the wall and removes a stack of papers of one of the piles, to reveal a secret chair which he lowers himself into. There is nowhere for her to sit.

This is the reverse of Maggie and Richard in the canteen. The Death Star will keep her standing to prove he is in charge here. Why is she never in control with anyone? But she will see Paula in a few hours, and perhaps it really will be alright this time.

He makes a little telescope dome out of his fingers and stares at her over it with his pale, rotund eyes. 'You know why you're here.'

'No. No, I don't.'

He doesn't seem disconcerted by that. He knows she doesn't have a clue. He just wanted to demonstrate, yet again, how little she understands.

'You'll recall that your lectureship is temporary. For one year only, until and unless you can demonstrate that it should be made permanent.'

'Yes.' But nobody's ever lost a lectureship like this before. Not when they've published as many papers as she has. She stares at the top of his head without moving an inch. If she's got to be a soldier, she'll go down fighting.

'I understand Richard was lucky not to be forced out of the consortium because of your unilateral reference to their data. This is not a safe way to work, Jeanette. Not if you want to keep on good terms with your colleagues. And you need collaborators. You can't do everything all by yourself.'

Too late for that, she thinks, remembering Maggie's angry face. She sighs, 'I know. It just seemed so exciting at the time. What the data were showing seemed so much more important than remembering who was allowed to see what, and when.' It still does, she thinks, but does not say this out loud.

'I'm not even sure it made any difference to your paper, to be honest. The consortium estimated a far lower statistical significance for the link between the galaxies than you claimed.'

Claimed. He sounds like he doesn't believe her any more. Perhaps he never did.

'What about Orion?'

'Let's see about Orion. Let's just wait and see.' He looks old and tired. For the first time she wonders how many times he's been through this in the past, warned younger colleagues to be careful. 'What are you working on now?' He's clearly keen to move away from the whole messy subject of connected galaxies.

'I'm thinking of something to do with less than averagely dense regions.'

'Good. That sounds a bit more mainstream.' The edges of his mouth twitch upwards in what might be a smile. 'We'll be making a decision about the lectureship next month. I have to warn you it's in the balance. Can you get another paper out before then? That may help bury the — ah — other stuff.'

As usual, she can't work him out. Is he being a complete bastard, or just trying to be kind? Outside, she picks up her photo, but the pin that held it to the wall has vanished. There's a gap on the wall now, a blank where she used to be.

In the pub, she wishes she'd brought some lipstick with her, even though she knows it's pointless. She looks down at her clothes, suddenly hating them, hating herself in them, even at the same time realising that it's not about the way she looks. Something is going wrong, but she can't work out what it is.

Her past relationships have ended in one of two ways; they have either faded away, or, far less often, they have exploded into a fireworks display of sadness and misery. She knows that what she feels for Paula is not going to go away, they are not headed for a quiet talk in the pub followed in the future by occasional but affectionate reminiscences. It will have to be the fireworks, then. Unless she is wrong, and Paula does care. Perhaps she's just preoccupied with her work, her art.

Sometimes Jeanette feels like she spends half her life waiting for Paula in the pub. She has a drink, and then another. She refuses to phone her; Paula knows where she is, knows she's waiting. But even now, as Jeanette swirls her wine around her glass and shovels crisps into her mouth, she knows she still wants Paula. Wants to push her up against a wall and fuck her.

Paula is an hour late. And when she does arrive, Jeanette can't speak to her. Not because she's angry, although she is, but because she doesn't know what to say that won't shatter what remains between them. She tries to choose some words but can't find the right ones. And she knows that she's not always good with words. She spends her life studying physical things, so when she has to manipulate the names for those things, or even worse, the symbols for less palpable aspects of life, she feels at a disadvantage.

Paula sits down. Jeanette notices that she's not wearing lipstick either. This is Paula naked. But it's too difficult to look at her face, she's frightened of what she might see there. So she looks down, studies Paula's hands instead. Hands are more neutral. Paula's are slightly crossed, the fingers of one covering the other. It is an oddly old-fashioned pose, more suited to a nun in quiet contemplation. But the skin around the nails is stained with paint, as if Paula has been digging in blue earth. There is more blue further up her arms. It makes her skin look even paler than usual.

'Sorry I'm late,' she says finally, and pauses, waiting for Jeanette to speak. After a bit she carries on, 'I forgot about the time because I was working so hard. I've still got to paint ten more paintings before the show.'

'When is the show?' Jeanette asks. What else can she say? She supposes it could be true.

As she sits there and listens to Paula, she realises they will never be able to communicate. They are facing each other across a scarred wooden table, across battle trenches, across the entire universe.

Later, Jeanette does just what she imagined earlier. She does it in silence, with nothing but the sound of both their breathing loud in her ears. As soon as the front door is shut, and before the light's turned on, she puts her hands on Paula's shoulders and kisses her hard. As their lips smash together, Paula pulls her tight so that their bodies slam into each other. There is still this, then. They still have this. Paula undoes Jeanette's shirt buttons, then tries to tug her jeans down, but Jeanette pushes her hands away. She only wants to get at Paula, get inside her where she's tender. Make her feel something.

But even as Paula gasps and her cunt sucks at Jeanette's fingers, it doesn't seem like much of a victory. And as soon as she gets her breath back, Paula moves away and straightens her clothes as if trying to hide any evidence of what's happened, before reaching out and snapping the light switch. Jeanette would rather hide in the dark, she doesn't want this scene to be illuminated. The light strikes her in the face like a blow. She tries to touch Paula's arm, aware as she does so that this is the first physical act by either of them all evening that shows any affection, but Paula moves towards the door. She's closed off again. In fact, in spite of its post-coital flush, her face looks angry. Her lips are pulled tight, and she won't look at Jeanette.

'See you later,' she announces. 'I've got to get back to the studio.'

'When...' but Paula is gone. The sound of the slamming door makes her wonder if this night has connected with an earlier one, like a snake eating its own tail. She is Paula's invisible woman.

The next day, she gets up mechanically. In the shower it's an effort to drag the soap over her body. Food seems too complicated to negotiate. Walking to the Observatory is more straightforward, one foot in front of another until she arrives at her desk where she can watch the smooth progression of the second hand on the wall clock, suddenly aware of how time can only be represented by spatial movement. How odd it is to rely on clocks with their proxy measurement of the passage of time. The real thing is so much more difficult to grasp and understand. She is beginning to feel a sense of distance from the events of last night, much more than she did when she woke up this morning, when it still seemed so immediate. Perhaps the passage of time is linked to a change of place. Now that she's not in the flat, it's easier to think rationally about Paula, and easier to understand where Paula's coming from. Perhaps there is something to salvage. They did have sex, after all.

THEN

When Jeanette is thirteen, her parents buy her a camera. It's a proper SLR, and it makes a satisfying thunk when the shutter is released. She spends hours outside, taking photos with different settings. She learns that when she increases the f-stop to reduce the size of the aperture, the resulting photo is darker, but more of it is in focus. There is a tension between clarity and light.

She's able to bolt the camera onto the back of her telescope and she takes time-lapse photos of the sky. Her father buys a second hand enlarger and they use it in the bathroom, with duct tape stuck around the door to stop any light getting in. The resulting photos are pinned onto the washing line to dry. They're black and white; they look like photos in an old textbook.

She takes photos of starlings perched on telegraph poles, and of fish lying on slabs in fishmongers.

'Very nice,' says her mother. 'Why don't you try taking some photos of people?'

So she offers to take photos of the school play. That year the play is 'Mother Courage'. Jeanette doesn't know the story before she goes to the dress rehearsal. As she sits watching in the school auditorium, she realises it's about death. Mother Courage drags her cart and her three kids through battle zones to make money, but she can't protect them, and they all die. The two sons' deaths are pointless, but the silent daughter, Kattrin, dies saving the lives of a family caught in a fire.

The rehearsal proceeds in fits and starts. Lights go on and off at random, regardless of whether anyone is on the stage. People appear in the wrong places and have to disappear. The two sons have to die over and over again because neither of them can remember their lines. The Universe is supposed to go like clockwork, but this one is flawed. Eventually it reaches its conclusion, and Mother Courage shackles herself to her cart yet again, and goes off to another war.

At the beginning, Jeanette takes loads of photos, but by the end she is simply holding the camera up, to stop people from seeing the tears running down her face. Death by water and now fire. She wonders how her parents can stand watching all those TV programmes full of dead bodies.

'You've been working hard!' Her teacher, Miss Nightingale, silhouetted in front of the stage.

She nods.

'Are you going to develop them now?'

She nods again, and stumbles off.

The school darkroom is in the basement of the science block. When she tries to open the door, it's locked. Someone else is in there.

When she rattles the door handle again, a voice squawks from inside, 'Hang on!' And the door opens slightly, just enough for a cross face to peer out, flushed red from the safety light. 'I haven't finished actually.'

'But I booked it. This afternoon.'

'Oh,' and the face looks a bit doubtful now. Jeanette recognises it; Alice Airy from the year above. 'Sorry.'

'Is there room enough for both of us?' she asks.

The door opens a bit wider. 'Suppose so. Come on.'

The most difficult part of the process is at the beginning; getting the film out of the camera and onto the developing reel. That has to be done in complete darkness without even the safety light. As Jeanette slowly and carefully guides the tip of the film into the reel, she's aware of Alice, silent and invisible, on the other side of the room.

'Won't be long.'

'Doesn't matter,' says Alice. 'I'm not in a hurry.'

But something goes wrong, the film tightens itself into a knot and won't wind on properly. Jeanette has to start all over again. It's like learning to see with your fingers. Everything you do has to be guided by what you can feel.

'What are your photos of?' asks Alice, out of the darkness.

Finally she gets the film into the developing tank and is able to turn the safety light back on. Alice is sitting on one of the benches, perilously close to the sink, swinging her legs. She has short tufty hair and large eyes, with lots of black eyeliner crayoned on, making her look younger than she is.

'Why are you staring at me?'

'I'm not.' Jeanette concentrates on shaking the developing tank. It's important to keep the liquid moving. She looks around but she can't see what Alice is working on. 'Where are your photos?'

'They didn't come out properly. I threw them away.'

Jeanette waits for her film to dry and wonders why Alice is still there.

'I don't want to go home yet,' Alice says. 'Do you ever feel like that? Home is piss, really, since my mum had my baby brother. It's just baby baby baby. It's really embarrassing too. Fancy having sex at that age.'

As she sets up the enlarger, Jeanette watches Alice out of the corner of her eye. 'Yes.'

'Yes what?' Alice is still swinging her legs.

'Yes, I feel like that too.'

She holds the negatives up to the light, and squints at them. Impossible to see, at this stage, whether they will make good photos. But she likes looking at negatives, at the world transformed into bone-white and coal-dark. She offers one of the strips of film to Alice. 'Careful. Don't touch the surface.'

Then she notices that the bin is empty, 'Thought you said you'd thrown your photos away.'

Alice swings her legs and doesn't reply. Jeanette lies the wet contact sheets on the counter and inspects them. This time she doesn't get emotional. It's more about the arrangement of the bodies in the frame of the photo. The world seems more manageable in shades of grey. She can even examine the photo of Kattrin standing on the roof of the burning building, just before the plunge to her death.

Finally the contact sheets are done, the tanks are all cleaned and stacked against the wall, the enlarger is back in its box. Jeanette's ready to leave.

'You coming?' she says to Alice.

Alice slowly eases herself off the counter. 'Suppose so.'

When they leave the darkroom, Jeanette's eyes are so used to the monochrome red safety light that everything seems larger, lighter. Through the windows the sky looks bluer than she ever thought possible. She laughs and so does Alice.

'Wow,' says Alice, 'It's like technicolour. Like a cartoon.'

It's late now and all the other kids went home ages ago. As they walk down the long corridor, Jeanette says to her, 'You never developed any photos, did you?'

And Alice shakes her head, not looking at Jeanette. 'It's nice and quiet. No one would look for me there.'

Jeanette feels a small splutter of annoyance. 'If you're going to hide in a darkroom, you might as well learn how to use it.'

Alice grins. 'Are you going to teach me, then?'

Jeanette brings Alice home for tea.

'What's in there?' Alice asks as they go past the locked door on their way to Jeanette's room.

'Nothing.'

At teatime, the two of them sit waiting at the dining table. It's sausages, they could smell them upstairs before tea. But when her mother brings them in, on the old tin baking tray that's always used for this meal, Alice says, 'Oh.' A small sad sound.

'Oh?' her mother echoes.

'I don't eat meat. I'm really sorry.' She looks it too. Her eyeliner is smudged, as usual. It makes her look like she's been crying, even though she hasn't.

'Why didn't you tell me?' Jeanette's mother turns to her, exasperated.

'I didn't know.'

Her mother sighs. 'How about an omelette, then?'

'That would be lovely. I'm so sorry! Thank you!' Alice smiles, hugely, brilliantly.

Her mother smiles back. 'More sausages for Jeanette, then. Lucky her.'

But Jeanette remembers that Alice ate a chicken sandwich for lunch. 'You do eat meat,' she hisses, when her mother is back in the kitchen.

'Not sausages,' says Alice. 'Not processed meat.' She looks sad again.

Her father arrives home halfway through their meal. 'Well, well,' he says. 'Hello.'

'Hello,' says Alice. She's only been picking at her omelette and Jeanette's mother is looking exasperated again. 'I'm Alice.'

'Very nice to meet you, Alice. I'm Derek.' And he leans forward to shake her hand. Jeanette stares at her father. He doesn't usually talk like that.

He's wearing a short sleeved shirt and Jeanette can see the old burn scars on his arms, where the skin is gouged and contoured. She wonders how visible the scars are to other people; if you didn't know about them, would you be able to see them? She wishes she could undo the knowledge of them.

'Sausages!' he says, and smiles at Alice. Jeanette watches Alice smile back.

'I once knew a dog who could say 'sausages'.' Alice says. 'It was a poodle.' Jeanette's father laughs.

When Jeanette returns to the table, after helping her mother clear away the first course, she realises there are four of them. Two to the power of two. The family has been lopsided for so long, like a broken chair, that she's forgotten what it looked like when it was whole.

She pauses at the doorway to look. If she squints her eyes — but Alice doesn't look anything like Kate. Kate had been solid, she'd shovelled in food efficiently and cleanly as if she were stoking a fire inside. Alice is too fragile, all eyes and skinny legs and leftover food. Even though she's three years older than Kate ever was, she's probably still smaller.

Her mother passes round the dessert bowls and her father starts telling a story. It's long and rambling, and Jeanette can't really get the gist of it, but she isn't used to her father talking this much.

Every now and then he pauses, and Alice laughs politely. Jeanette eats her pudding in silence. When she finishes eating, she gets up immediately, as she always does, but her mother frowns. She sits down again, not used to not having a reason to be there, the usual alibi of food. Her father is still talking, and Alice has hardly started her ice cream.

Later, Alice says, 'Your dad's childhood sounds amazing.'

Childhood? Was that what he was talking about?

'In the country, with all those brothers and sisters.'

They're walking upstairs now, past the room she never goes into, to her own bedroom. Something has happened to the room behind the door, nobody has seen it for so long. There could be anything behind it. A whole new world. A vast dark space. A narrow bed where no one ever sleeps.

Downstairs, the TV is switched on, the TV voices knit together, and life goes back to normal.

As she promised, Jeanette teaches Alice how to use a darkroom. She gets Alice to practice winding film onto the spool with the safety light on. Even in the light, Alice keeps dropping things. 'Sorry,' she says as the spool hits the floor yet again.

'What's wrong with having a baby brother, anyway?' Jeanette's been to Alice's house and seen the baby, who sat in a mound of cushions on the floor, grabbing at people passing by. When Jeanette picked him up for a cuddle, he gurgled and smiled at her. They had chips for tea and the whole of the small house was filled with noise. It seemed pretty good to her.

As if Alice could read her mind, she says, 'We have chips all the time. Mum never has time to cook anything else. And she shouts. I wish she'd stop shouting at me.'

'At least she notices you.'

Alice has finally wound the film onto the spool.

'Now you have to do it again, this time with the light off.'

'You are bossy,' Alice murmurs, as Jeanette snaps the switch off. She's used to the way darkness makes the room feel larger, makes you forget the edges of your own body so that you seem to swell into the surrounding air. There is the regular creak of the spool as Alice winds the film onto it. It sounds as though she's got the hang of it now.

'Ready!' she sings out, so Jeanette turns on the light again. But something has happened to the geometry of the room; Alice is much closer than she thought, close enough for Jeanette to reach out and touch her.

'What's the next step?'

'Sorry,' and Jeanette blinks.

In bed that night, she imagines reaching out in the dark and stroking Alice's cheek, just making contact with the skin, and something takes up residence in her mind. Something whispers, *you want this*.

She invites Alice back to her house again. This time Alice eats all her omelette, and Jeanette stays in her place after the end of the meal, listening to her father. She isn't used to so much talk. She's never heard him say all this stuff before. He's talking to Alice about gardening, and Alice smiles and nods and only occasionally glances at Jeanette. Her mother seems to spend a lot of time in the kitchen, perhaps more time than is necessary.

Afterwards, when they go upstairs to Jeanette's room, Alice pauses outside the shut door again.

'What's in there?' she asks, the same question she asked the first time.

'Nothing,' Jeanette answers. She finds it impossible to imagine anything in that room, for that room to exist at all as a collection of walls and carpet and windows. There can't be anything behind the door but blackness, space, vacuum. If it was meant for Kate and Kate doesn't exist, then what is the point of it?

It becomes a habit for Alice to come back for tea at Jeanette's at least once a week.

'Poor thing,' says Jeanette's mother. 'Not a scrap on her. You do wonder what goes on in other people's houses.'

'It's alright. They eat plenty,' says Jeanette, but her mother just shakes her head. 'At least she gets a decent meal here.'

One evening she says to her mother, 'Alice is coming over next Friday.'

'Next Friday?' repeats her mother, and Jeanette notices something in her eyes, the translucent grey veil settling between her mother and the rest of the world. And then Jeanette remembers. Next Friday is Kate's birthday. One of the days of the year that dumps them back in the past. No matter how many times the Earth orbits the Sun it has to go through this same bit of bruised space, exposing them to the same pain. But it also reminds them how much has changed. The only thing worse than the sharp pain of grief is its numbing with time, because that dullness reminds you that the death, and the life it owned, is being swept away into the past, and you yourself are being swept into the future.

That Friday evening, as they all sit round the table, the air is thick with sadness. Jeanette has not warned Alice in advance, has not been able to think of how to explain to her the significance of this date. Jeanette knows that Alice thinks of her as a lucky only child, in a blessedly quiet house with no noise or mess. This house is Alice's haven.

When Jeanette first started secondary school, she learnt to answer the standard question, 'Have you got any brothers or sisters?' with a quick shake of her head. No words were needed. No explanations were given. It was true, after all. Some other kids knew about her sister, most didn't. Because Alice is in the year above Jeanette and didn't know her at primary school, she doesn't know. It's better that way, Jeanette thinks, and it's beyond explaining now.

But on this Friday, Jeanette is worried. Silent words buzz around between her and her parents, words that have never been spoken. Words such as 'Why did she have to die?', 'Why her?', and sometimes Jeanette thinks she can even hear 'Why not you?'

The words manage to attract energy to themselves as they fly through the air. Some of them are bound to crash into Alice, as she sits in the fourth chair, chattering about her baby brother learning to talk. The three of them seem to be staring at Alice, as if astonished that she can be so ordinary on a day like today.

They finish their main course, and Jeanette's mother clears the plates. Jeanette, Alice and Jeanette's dad wait. Sometimes this day is a relief, Jeanette has found over the years, the days and weeks beforehand getting more and more strung out, taut as a wire before the final release of energy on the day itself. This year it isn't like that, the tension hasn't dissipated. Something else has to happen but she can't imagine what, so she has to wait.

Ice cream appears. When Jeanette glances at Alice, she sees her running her left hand along the arm of her chair. Kate used to do something similar, and Jeanette blinks.

'Who used to sit here?' Alice mumbles through a mouthful of ice cream.

The three of them look at Alice and the silent words crash to the floor. Now they have to deal with reality.

Alice continues, 'It's all worn away here.' And she touches the patch of fabric made smooth by Kate's fingers.

Someone has to say it. 'Kate,' mutters Jeanette. Her parents just sit there.

'Who's Kate?' says Alice. But Jeanette has run out of words. She stares down into her bowl, not wanting to look at Alice's bright innocent face. Suddenly, Jeanette hates her. How dare she ask questions like that? How dare she use the present tense? Doesn't she realise you can't just say things in this house? How dare she not know?

Jeanette gets up, still not looking at Alice, and slams her chair into the table. Her parents seemed to have turned into ice. Perhaps they always were. 'I've finished,' she says much too loudly and walks out of the room not bothering to wait for anyone's response.

As she bangs upstairs, she hears Alice behind her, 'Wait for me,' and there's a sudden scraping noise as Alice falls over. 'Ow!' Good. Pain is good, especially physical pain, but Jeanette would rather feel it herself. There's no point in Alice getting hurt. So she stops to wait for her.

Upstairs, safely away from her parents, Jeanette tries to breathe deeply. Grief is the same as gravity, the same word, and the same heaviness. Grief crouches on her chest and stops her breathing properly. She pauses in the hallway; Alice is right behind her, so they bump into each other.

'Sorry,' says Jeanette.

'What's going on?' Alice whispers. She seems to have realised that today is not normal. Their house is not normal.

They are standing outside the room, and it's finally possible to open the door. Alice waits, not moving, until Jeanette tugs her arm and pulls her across the threshold.

Inside. Superficially the room looks like Kate's old room, in their old house. There is her bed, covered with her favourite duvet cover, the one with wavy blue and green stripes. Her swimming medals are hanging in a shiny jangle off her bookshelves. Swimming certificates are pinned to the wall, and Jeanette knows without looking inside, that the cupboard will be full of her clothes. She has an urge to open the cupboard door and rub her face in them, to smell the last of Kate.

Schoolbooks are piled on the desk by the window. Jeanette can remember her clear, round handwriting. The books will be full of it, but she isn't sure she wants to see it. She's beginning to feel sick now. People aren't like houses, or cities. They're not just collections of their own belongings. She could stroke the strands of hair in Kate's hairbrush, sitting on Kate's dressing table, and it would be no nearer to Kate than peeling a dead animal off the road.

It is utterly silent. Alice's eyes are even wider than usual as she watches Jeanette walk over to the window. The view here is slightly different to the view from Jeanette's bedroom, although you can only tell the difference over short distances. And Kate never saw this view at all. Jeanette thinks of her lying in bed, waiting for the morning when she would get up, and go to the pool for her daily practice, and die.

She wonders when her mother carried out this recreation of the past, and whether it worked for her, whether she is able to get any comfort from it. Does she come in here during the day when no one else is around, and pretend that she has two daughters? Is that why she always looks so unhappy when Jeanette returns from school and she has to return to reality?

But it is false.

Standing by the window, she looks down and sees something dark lodged between the wall and the radiator. One of the swimming suits. She tugs it out, and it flops onto the floor at their feet. A pelt the colour of a starless sky, it lies separate from them, a portal leading down into the world of death. Jeanette is afraid now. She has disturbed the pattern of the room. She is even more scared when Alice bends down and picks the thing off the floor, scrunching it in her hands.

Jeanette touches Alice on the arm again, this time steeling herself for the feel of soft skin against her fingertips, and they leave. As they shut the door, Jeanette realises that the room is like an event horizon showing the last remaining bit of ordinary life clinging to Kate, surrounding the black hole of Kate's death. Like death, a black hole is unknowable, shut off and unseen from the rest of the known Universe.

Back in the present, Alice sits hunched up with her chin resting on her knees, listening to Jeanette as she talks about her father setting fire to the garden, her mother's anger. About the emptiness, the unspoken words, the 'Why her' and 'Why not you'.

Jeanette thinks she's never talked so much in her life. She looks down at her hands as she talks and she studies their surface, noticing how the skin seems to become more detailed, until she can see every individual freckle, and even the pores seem magnified. It's as if she's growing larger. Perhaps her talking has expanded her, made her occupy more space.

She stops speaking and lets a silence take over, but it's a nice silence. Nothing like the silences between her parents over dinner. Jeanette listens to Alice breathing, soft little puffs that dissipate into the air surrounding the two of them.

'What was she like?' Alice finally says.

It's difficult to distil Kate down into words. She didn't have to describe Kate when she was here, and nobody has asked her about Kate since. Kate simply was, and isn't any more. She's too large to be boxed into words.

Finally she says, 'She swam fast in straight lines and was proud of it, but she never looked down on me because I couldn't,' and Alice nods to show that she understands.

Jeanette takes a photo of Alice. She has planned the taking of this photo for some time, rehearsed the way she'd casually touch Alice on the arm, and suggest that since she had some film left in her camera, she might as well use it up on Alice.

And Alice doesn't appear to notice that in fact there seems to be a lot of film left in the camera, enough for at least twenty shots as she stands just outside the school gates, her hair flipped up by the breeze, her face slightly turned to one side, but her eyes still looking at the camera. At Jeanette. It takes some time for Jeanette to steady the camera, with her trembling hands.

The next day she develops the film in the darkroom, easing it out of the camera and onto the carousel, hoping it's worked. Once the negatives are developed, she can turn on the safety light and see what she's caught.

Alice in reverse has white eyes and white hair against ghost-grey skin. Alice is so tiny, she can shelter in one hand. She's delicate too, and Jeanette is afraid of damaging the surface of the film. It can only be held by its edges, by her fingertips.

She lies the negatives onto the paper and makes a contact strip. Now, twenty versions of Alice flutter in the fixing tank. But she's still too small. So Jeanette selects a photo and enlarges it as far as she can, to make Alice cover the entire base of the enlarger and spill over onto the table.

It feels luxurious to be able to stare into her eyes, touch a finger to her lips and have Alice stare back. Jeanette can look as long as she wants. She doesn't have to worry about betraying herself. And she sees things she's never had the opportunity to notice before. A freckle on Alice's chin, just fractionally darker than the surrounding skin.

An asymmetry to her lips, giving a slight twist to her mouth. Jeanette longs to push her own mouth against Alice's, to smooth out its pale puckered surface.

Jeanette finds a pair of scissors and cuts the contact strip into its constituents. She really wants to take home the large photo, but it's too large to hide anywhere. The small ones are ideal, she can carry them in her purse everywhere she goes.

Alice is always blind to Jeanette's glances. Jeanette has to ration herself to avoid staring at her. It doesn't matter, she's used to reconstructing Alice from jigsaw pieces of memory; a curl of hair quivering against the base of her neck, the downwards sweep of her eyelashes.

But she's all movement. The photos are too inert, too static. Alice never stays still. And that's the joy of watching her, and all her fluttery trembly motion. No wonder she is so skinny. Jeanette has seen the skin pulse at the base of her throat, can imagine her heart beating away, pushing the blood around her body.

Jeanette never touches her beyond an occasional pat on the arm. She gets used to calibrating the distance between their two bodies, working out what is acceptable closeness.

Once she has the photos, she memorises them, and gets to know them so well she doesn't need to refer to them any more. She spends more time with the two dimensional black and white image than she does with the real Alice.

Alice is getting ready to leave school. She has plans to travel for a bit before she decides what to do with her life. She isn't sure where she's going to go, exactly, perhaps Thailand or Australia. Perhaps she will work in a bar, hang out on a beach. These generic descriptions of her future life make Jeanette so anxious she can hardly breathe. Where will Alice be? What will she be doing? And who with?

So Jeanette panics. It's late Spring and she knows their days together are numbered, once the exam season is finished there will be nothing to stop Alice taking off and escaping. She listens to Alice talk about all the possible future beaches and bars, and she panics and reaches out. She doesn't know why she's doing it, doesn't know what she expects Alice to do in response. All she knows is that the photo of Alice is no longer enough. She needs the body behind the image. So used for so long to touching Alice's paper hair, it feels easy to simply reach forward and stroke the reality of it.

She has time to feel the strands of hair soft on her fingertips before Alice jerks her head back. 'What are you doing?'

She could lie, pretend she's removing some fluff, pretend her action is innocent. But she's not capable of lying. She stares at Alice, watching her work it out.

'I have to go now.' Alice stands up. She doesn't look at Jeanette as she gets ready to go, and Jeanette knows she will never look at her again. This is the first time she has ever risked anything in her life, betted on something and lost. Perhaps it's better to remain invisible, unseen. But even that night, as she lies awake staring at the space above, she can't stop thinking of the brief moment when she reached out, full of hope.

And then Alice leaves, properly this time, and all Jeanette has is the image.

NOW

On the day of the launch, Jon announces that there will be a party in the lab to celebrate.

When Jeanette goes along to the lab, people are gathering round a computer which is linked to the website showing the launch. They all watch the technicians at the European Space Agency launch site in French Guyana milling about, the rocket high up on its gantry a mile or so behind them.

Jon's bouncing around the lab, looking like a wound up spring, as if he might burst with energy. She's never seen him look like this before, but it is one of the defining moments of his life. He's worked on this instrument for ten years.

The countdown starts. Jeanette is aware of a different sort of tension now in the lab. It feels like a thin gas permeating them all. They're gathered around the computer which is now focused in on the rocket.

The countdown reaches zero and the rocket starts its swoop into the sky above the crowd of spectators, blasting upwards through the air, leaving a thick grey funnel of smoke in its wake. But suddenly it flops over to the left until it's horizontal. There's a general murmur in the room. This is not expected. Rockets are not supposed to lean over like this, so near the beginning of their launch. Then two horns of smoke spiral across the sky, followed by a shower of sparks in all directions. The rocket has exploded. The satellite and its instruments are destroyed.

Jeanette doesn't realise she is holding her breath until the view on the screen cuts away from the explosion to show the people at the launch site gasping and pointing at the sky. In the lab, Jon is clutching his head, pulling at his hair, as if he too is about to explode. His glasses fall off and bounce onto the floor. Everyone's just staring at the screen, watching the heavy grey clouds. Jeanette knows that those clouds are full of smashed up bits of metal, plastic and glass all mixed together with the acid fuel, all of it tumbling to the ground.

Again the view cuts away to show the people at the site, and this time they're running for cover, in case they get hit by the debris and fuel. Here in the lab they remain motionless. They continue watching even when there is nothing to watch, apart from the people's stunned faces mirroring their own. They don't know what to do now.

Finally, Jeanette goes over to Jon and puts an arm around him, but he doesn't seem to notice. He's leaning over a bench, his arms hunched protectively around his head as if to ward off the debris falling out of the sky. She can't see his face. His glasses are still on the floor, so she picks them up. One of the lenses is cracked, a vertical fissure the length of the glass. She tries to hand them to him, but he can't seem to grab hold of them so she just stands and waits.

The others start to wander around the lab. Some of them go to look out of the window, at a sky that doesn't have a catastrophe happening in it, as if to remind themselves that the sky is not always a harbinger of doom. Still, nobody's said anything yet.

One of the students is trying to open a bottle of champagne, but then realises too late that the cork will come firing out. The noise is a relief, though. It allows people to start talking. Finally Jon moves, he rubs his face with his hands and slowly blinks at Jeanette, who gives him a plastic cup of champagne. He sips it in silence.

Eventually he can speak. 'What happened? What the hell happened?' He starts gulping the rest of his champagne and holds out the cup to be refilled.

'What the hell...' he repeats, quieter this time.

'I don't know,' says Jeanette. None of them know, of course. They'll have to wait for ESA to tell them.

People are leaving the lab now. Jon grabs the half-full bottle of champagne and swigs from it, inaccurately, so that the liquid bubbles up from the narrow opening and gushes over him onto the floor. His glasses lie abandoned on the lab bench.

She watches the launch again on the news that evening, and learns that the explosion was deliberate. Due to a software error, the rocket started veering off course and had to be blown up by ESA as a safety precaution to avoid a potentially worse catastrophe. Better to have a controlled destruction, than risk the unknown. The software error was caused by an information overflow; the rocket's acceleration was so large the onboard computer memory couldn't store it, triggering an inaccurate change to the flight path, which meant the rocket had to be destroyed. It's already being called one of the worst software errors in history.

There is a time-reversed film of the launch on the internet and she watches this too, sees the smoke coalesce, the bits of metal fly together, the rocket sink gracefully to earth. She can't stop watching this reversed film over and over again, with its fake happy ending.

Later, she sits in front of her laptop. She needs to say something to Maggie. Finally, she sends just one line;

`What are we going to do now?`

She can't think of anything more to say. They were waiting for Orion to get more, better quality data, to provide the definitive answer on whether or not the galaxies were really connected. And now they won't get that. There's only the grey fog of uncertainty. The apparent link between the galaxies will probably just remain as an anomalous, peculiar result. Something unexplained and unexplainable in a world where everything has to have an explanation. It's not a comfortable place to be.

Now she wonders what she's done to the universe, to the beautifully written story of its creation. She's taken a pencil rubber and erased an essential part of it, without replacing it. And what does that do to the story of her own life? Now, as she imagines Kate lying dead on the side of the swimming pool, Kate seems to be fading away before her eyes. The square patterns of the tiles are clearly visible through her body. Only her swimming suit is a solid dependable block of colour.

She has clear memories of Kate, ones she relies on like milestones. She and Kate are standing right against the kitchen door frame and their father rests a pencil against the top of each of their heads. When they wriggle away he shows them how much they've grown. There is a succession of wobbly pencil marks with 'J' and 'K' and the dates by their sides all the way up the paintwork, and for each date, 'J' is always slightly lower than 'K'. Like two planets with nicely predictable orbits.

She remembers saying to Kate, 'I'll catch up with you one day,' and Kate just rolling her eyes. Of course, she did catch up with Kate, although she doesn't remember any more pencil marks being made after Kate died.

Now, just as clear as any of the actual memories of these measurements, she sees Kate shrinking down to the kitchen floor until she's no bigger than the pencil itself, before disappearing completely, lost in the dust and dirt on the ground.

She remembers Kate in the pool, swimming up and down as she always did. But now she sees multiple Kates, so many of them that they're getting in the way of each other, and they're accidentally kicking each other. They're still trying to swim up and down, but they're not getting anywhere. All they can do is zigzag randomly around the pool, bumping into each other. Soon, one after the other sinks beneath the water, until there's only a single Kate left. But there's no way of telling if this is the original Kate, or just a copy.

That night in bed she watches car headlights scribble unreadable messages in light across her bedroom walls. I never set out to do this, she thinks. I didn't mean to fall in love with Paula. I didn't mean to disrupt the laws of physics. Things just seem to happen in this Universe. But the car headlights generate light, which travels in predictable lines from the filaments to her bedroom. She must have wondered about Paula years ago, must have fantasised about kissing her. Kissing your straight best friend is the most predictable gay fantasy. And she thinks of Alice.

The name of the rocket which exploded today is called Ariane, the French word for Ariadne; the ancient Greek heroine who gave Theseus a thread to lead him out of the minotaur's maze. She realises now how appropriate this was — right up until the rocket exploded she had hoped it would lead them all out of this mess. Now she's afraid they'll have to remain in the maze.

The next morning she's slogging up the hill to work when she sees Richard ahead of her, stationary at the bend in the road, silhouetted against the sky. If she had a gun she could pick him off quite cleanly. Perhaps he has seen her too, and is waiting for her so they can have yet another argument. She slows down, hoping he'll get bored and give up. But he just stands there, watching her as she struggles up the steep slope. Why does this hill never get any easier? No matter how many times she walks up it, it's still an effort. An awful, accurate metaphor for life.

'Sorry about your satellite,' he drawls as she approaches. She grunts in reply, and they continue walking, almost side by side up the remaining road.

'I'm sorry about the consortium,' she says, finally. She hasn't said this before, not properly. 'About referencing your work in our paper.' Now she's started she has to carry on, 'without asking your permission. I know I should have got permission. I'm sorry.'

The good thing about walking alongside someone else is that you can't see their face. They've almost reached the gate of the Observatory before he replies, 'I suppose we all make mistakes.'

She nods in agreement, and she's just about to open the door to the east tower and head inside to her office when he carries on, 'Some of us are going out for a drink tonight. Do you want to come along?'

Why not? She supposes it might help her forget about things. There seem to be quite a lot of things she wants to forget right now. 'Thanks. See you later.'

When she logs on to her computer, the chatter on the internet is all about the exploding rocket. There's only a bit about Orion and even less about the planned observations of the link between the galaxies. She rummages through various websites, skims through the usual blogs that comment on astronomy. But they're all focused on the software error that brought down the rocket. There is not yet much discussion of what this means for astronomy itself. For her result. She supposes she should be grateful, that she should just sit quietly and wait to see what happens. But she's been invited to speak at another conference soon. The expectation is that she would have the results from Orion, that they would all have some answers to the questions. Without Orion, what on earth is she going to talk about?

No answer from Maggie, even though she's read Jeanette's email. Maggie always replies promptly and the lack of response from her is unsettling.

She remains in her room all morning, until it's time for the weekly staff meeting. She doesn't really want to go and face other people, and speculate with them about what will happen now, and when she finally gets there she's late. Everyone else is already waiting, apart from Jon.

The Death Star shuffles his papers and clears his throat before starting the meeting. 'Jon won't be here today. He's taking a few days off.' He glares at Jeanette as if this is her fault. I didn't make it explode, she thinks. You can't blame me. But she's aware of the other lecturers looking at her too, as if the answers to all their questions are visible on her face. She stares down at her pad of paper.

They get on with the tedious business of the meeting, and nobody mentions Jon again until the end. Just as they're standing up to leave, the Death Star says, 'Has anyone seen Jon's student, Clara? I need to speak to her.'

People shake their heads. Jeanette remembers Clara in her reading group sessions and hanging around the lab.

Back in her office, and still nothing from Maggie. She's wondering what to do, wondering how she can possibly work, when the Death Star sticks his head around her door. 'Jeanette. A word.'

She's fed up with his words, but then he adds, 'No, it's about Jon.'

He comes into her office and tells her the full story. Not just the bit he told everyone at the meeting, about Jon asking for a few days off to recover from the shock of the launch failure. He tells her that just after he spoke to Jon, Jon's wife phoned. She hadn't seen him since the disaster of the launch, which she only knew about when she saw it on TV. Jon had disappeared. Did the Death Star know where he was? No, he didn't.

The Death Star pauses significantly before continuing. The wife phoned again, a few hours later. Jon had contacted her to say he's leaving her. He's having a relationship with one of his students. Clara.

Jeanette is fascinated, horrified. She doesn't remember ever noticing Jon and Clara even talking to each other. She can barely breathe as she tries to put the pieces together in her mind. Jon has always been so upright, so straight. How could he have done something like this? Did he know himself he was capable of it? Jeanette knows his wife was a teacher. They both believed in doing good, in helping people.

How can you understand the world if you can't understand people? If you can't predict the way they're going to behave? She realises she needs to know. Did Jon know in advance what he was going to do? Or was it the shock of the rocket blowing up? If he at least knew that there was the possibility of this happening, then however reprehensible that is, it makes the whole thing more understandable.

Her mind veers towards Paula and away again, as if she's in a car trying to avoid a crash. At least she's always been aware that Paula was capable of betraying her. She's never been under any illusions there.

'And now it seems that Clara has disappeared too.' The Death Star looks at her. 'I know you know Jon. Do you have any idea about where they might be? Presumably they're together.'

'I don't know anything at all. He never mentioned this to me.' Suddenly she's angry.

After the Death Star leaves her office, she escapes the Observatory and stands outside, trying to phone Jon, tapping at her mobile. No signal. She wanders further away, still no signal. She's in the trees now, not really paying attention to where she's going, vaguely aware of a shape, perhaps a dog walker ahead on the path.

Soon the shape is in front of her. It's Jon, looking tired and crumpled. He seems to be alone.

'What are you doing here? Are you coming to work?' But even as she speaks, she realises how daft this is. He's not coming to work. The memory of him in the lab, surrounded by his ordered equipment, belongs to some ancient time. This version of Jon standing in front of her has not shaven, or washed. But it's more than that, he's changed in some more fundamental way. It's as if there have been two Jons leading different lives in parallel universes, and the one that Jeanette has been friends with has been replaced by the other one. Does an affair make that much difference to someone, she wonders. Perhaps.

'How could you just walk out? Just leave everything behind you?'

He rubs a hand over his eyes and she sees that he's crying. 'Jeanette, it was the only thing I could do. Everything else was — gone. There was nothing left.'

'Just because the rocket exploded? You've got other work...'

He doesn't reply and they continue to stand there in the trees, facing each other, until he finally says, 'Look, if you buy me a whisky, I'll try and explain to you. Ok?'

She is a scientist. She needs information. 'Ok.'

They go to the grotty pub at the bottom of the hill. She hates this pub, always associates it with the ice woman. But it seems an appropriate place for Jon to sit and gulp whisky and cry.

She waits until finally he's able to speak. 'I loved my wife. I still do. But we used to sit in the same room and it would be as if we were on top of distant mountains. She'd say something and it was in a foreign language. I didn't understand her. She didn't understand me. It was exhausting. Physically tiring. I'd come home from work, feeling ok, and half an hour later, I'd be shattered. She was too. She'd sit in the bedroom to get away from me. She's fine without me. Much better.

'Clara is...' He looks away as if examining an image of Clara on the wall of the pub before continuing, 'Clara is more real. She makes other people seem two-dimensional, like photos.'

Jeanette winces; this is how she feels about Paula. She waits to find out more, trying not to look at his face. He's aged since yesterday. The creases around his mouth are deeper, his skin is greyer. Time has sped up for him. Perhaps he prefers it like this, after the years of stasis with his wife.

'I remember telling you about my great-grandfather, Crommelyn.'

She nods, a bit surprised.

'I always thought he did the right thing, you know. He performed that experiment to the best of his ability even though he wasn't particularly interested in what it might prove or disprove. He was the proper impartial observer. Unlike Eddington, who wanted a certain result.'

She nods again. Of course.

He carries on, 'There's a saying in our family that comes from

Crommelyn. "The shortest route is not necessarily the quickest." Apparently they were trying to find the best place to position the telescope on Sobral and they were lugging it up this mountain. A local man was guiding them and he warned them, "The shortest route is not necessarily the quickest." '

He shakes his head and they sit there for a bit in silence before he continues, 'All he meant was that they should take the slower, shallower mountain road rather than try to save time by going a steeper route through the jungle. But afterwards, when Crommelyn told this to Eddington, he noticed the analogy with their experiment. Light takes a curved route around a massive star because that's the quickest path, even though it doesn't look like it to an observer. To us.'

Jeanette's not sure what she's supposed to be learning from this, until Jon leans forward and she sees the dried tear tracks on his cheeks. 'I feel like I've crashed off the road, and into the wilderness. And I don't know what the shortest or the longest path is, or even where I'm supposed to be going. She — Clara — crashed into my life. And I thought about what sort of route I was taking, and perhaps it was possible I didn't know what the right one was, anymore.' He wipes his eyes, but somehow this just makes his whole face look blurred. 'I thought I knew the right way to live, but what did I know? I wasn't exactly happy. Neither was my wife.' Saying this last word makes him cry again.

The chronology of events is still not clear to Jeanette. 'So why did you disappear after the rocket blew up?'

He passes a hand over his eyes. 'This is going to sound stupid but it seemed like a sign. You know in medieval times, people used to believe that the sky foretold the future. Well, they still do, I suppose. But things like comets or supernovae were harbingers of doom. That's what the exploding rocket was like for us.'

Us. Jeanette notes how casually he uses that word to refer to himself and Clara. She has never managed to bracket herself and

Paula together in that way.

'It seemed to signal to us that we couldn't carry on in secret. That we had to make a decision. Hell, it even offered us a way out. With no instrument, and no data to analyse, I'm not tied here anymore, not professionally anyway.' His cheeks are flushed now, there's more energy to his voice. For the first time she can actually believe that he and Clara will just go away.

'What are you going to do now?'

He shrugs. 'We'll probably go abroad, Clara can finish her PhD somewhere else. I've been offered posts in the States before now.' But he still looks terrible. His life's been wrenched apart, Jeanette realises. All that talk of being upright and good, and now this. How do you balance rightness against love? Doing what is right for other people as opposed to what is right for you? He's just realised what he's capable of, the hurt he can inflict on other people, and his understanding of the world has been shattered.

He's gripping his empty whisky glass. She has to say something. What do people say in these sorts of situations? 'It will work out, Jon.' But she doesn't think she sounds particularly believable.

He looks at her, 'How do I know what the right route is?'

'You'll figure it out.' She hopes this is true.

Back in her office. Finally a reply from Maggie, but it offers no comfort. It doesn't mention the rocket explosion, it just says:

```
I've started a new project here which will take up
all my time, and so I won't be able to come on our
next observing trip. Take care.
```

She's been professionally dumped. Maggie doesn't want to be associated any more with such a problematic result, and the explosion was the final straw. Professionally, she's on her own, now.

Later that night, and yet another pub. The place where she is meeting Richard is not the usual astronomers' drinking den. As Jeanette walks through the darkening streets towards the evening, she realises she is heading in the direction of the art college. Fear and desire almost make her stumble on the pavement. Paula won't be here, surely? But when she walks into the pub, she sees a familiar leopardskin coat in action by the bar.

She's able to watch Paula surreptitiously for a moment. Her face is powder-white, her lips are jam-sticky red, and she's wearing black leather, the leopardskin coat draped over one shoulder. She's a cliché, and Jeanette almost feels some relief that the woman she made love with so many times seems to have disappeared. Or perhaps she never existed at all.

Jeanette finally walks over and receives an air kiss. 'Darling! What a surprise to see you here!' But Paula doesn't actually look at her. They stand at the bar, and Jeanette's grateful to have the cocktail menu to study. There are too many mirrors in here, she thinks, as she keeps catching sight of her and Paula. Paula looks fine of course, she's designed to look good under artificial light. But Jeanette looks bleached out, even smaller and paler than usual, almost not there at all. They look odd together. They don't match. Certainly nobody would guess they had ever been lovers.

When Richard arrives, with some sort of friend in tow, it turns out not to have been a coincidence after all. Richard's friend wants to go to art college and so Richard phoned Paula to ask her along too.

Richard calls Paula 'Venus in fake furs' which makes her laugh, although she doesn't like the word fake.

'Don't be so pedantic,' she says. 'You just need to use your imagination.'

'I have to be accurate,' Richard replies, 'I'm a scientist.'

'So you never wear rose-tinted glasses?'

'No. Just beer goggles. But I'm not wearing them now.'

Jeanette, unnoticed, watches them smile at each other.

A band starts playing in the pub, and it becomes too noisy to talk. Jeanette knows she should leave, knows that whatever happens that evening won't be good. But she still can't bring herself to walk away from Paula, even if this is not the right version of Paula. At a break between songs, Paula turns to her, and says too loudly, 'Are you enjoying yourself, my love?' There is an exaggerated emphasis on the last two words. Paula isn't above flirting with her as a proxy for flirting with the men.

She can't find the right words to reply, and Paula shrugs. Out of the corner of her eye, Jeanette can see Richard grinning at Paula. She can't stand it anymore. She manages to shove her way between the clumps of people out onto the street. Leaning against the wall of the pub, she breathes in the dank night air and shuts her eyes for a moment. Perfect, peaceful blackness. She can hear faint noises coming from inside, but it's quiet out here.

But it's not enough. She feels something settle next to her and opening her eyes, sees Richard also leaning against the wall.

'I need some air,' he says.

She stays silent. She doesn't have to validate his actions.

'Are you ok?' He's fishing around for his cigarettes and matches. She feels a great weariness. Now that she's leaning against this wall she wants to stay there forever. She can feel the wall supporting her, giving her strength.

'I'm fine. Why?'

'Doesn't look like it.'

'Richard...'

'Is it to do with her?' He's struck his match and the flame burns for a moment like a small piece of hope, before he drops it onto the ground.

'Her?' Has he guessed? How could he?

'Paula.'

When he says her name, it makes a gash in the night. She feels like crying; her eyes prickle when he looks at her, but she stays silent.

Perhaps she should try to tell him about Paula, get it out into the open, drain the poison out of her body. She notices the way he's smoking with his usual precision, the ash forming a neat mound on the pavement. She has a horrible feeling that she does not quite exist in the same way that he does. There is a balloon inside her, filled with helium. Perhaps she should float up into the night sky and disappear, rather than continue with this.

'Yes.' The word is a sigh, not much more than air escaping from her. But he hears it and as they look at each other, she can tell he's feeling something like sympathy for her. They've both had a shit time lately, he with his job applications, she with Paula.

He smiles at her, 'Ah well,' and stubs out his cigarette. 'Think of the future, Jeanette. There'll be others.'

She's spent years studying neat little space-time diagrams in lecture courses on relativity, with particles predictably moving along the time axis from the past to the future, but her own future just feels like a dense black fog. She can't believe in it. Perhaps he sees his future as a sunlit hill dotted here and there with women lying on the grass like daisies waiting to be picked by him.

There's nothing else to do but follow him back into the pub. She's not even that surprised when he flings an arm around Paula and says, 'What a lovely couple the two of you make.' There's just a dull thump of pain inside her, an old bruise being hit yet again. She wonders why he's brought this out into the open. Is it just a desire to see what happens? Does he have an ambition to be the catalyst for some sort of experiment between her and Paula?

Paula laughs, 'What couple?'

'You and Jeanette.'

Paula's eyes flicker over her as if she's an inanimate object before finally replying, 'We're only flatmates, we're not an item.'

Betrayal. The splendour of their past has been kicked into dust. She puts her hand over her mouth, afraid of what she might say, because she knows now that words are dangerous. This can only end in blood.

Richard looks puzzled. 'Oh, I must have misunderstood something Jeanette said.' Only now can she hear the purr of malevolence in his voice. For him, this is payback. How stupid has she been? How many actions has she misinterpreted?

'What.' She can just see a hint of gleaming teeth as Paula speaks. She sounds as if she's biting off a chunk of meat. 'After all, I'm not really Jeanette's type.' She tries to laugh, but the laughter is metallic. 'And she's certainly not mine.'

'Stranger things have happened,' Richard laughs as well, as if a mistake has been made, a small and rather humorous error that they can all joke about. His friend just looks puzzled.

'I'm not seeing anyone just now.' Paula gives great emphasis to each word.

'Really?' says Richard, 'What a coincidence. Neither am I,' and he laughs his easy laugh again.

She manages to leave the pub, knowing what's going to happen, and somehow gets home. There, she sits up for the rest of the night, not bothering to go to bed because she won't be able to sleep, and stares out of the window at the streetlights. Fake stars. If she moves her head quickly, the tears in her eyes blur the lights into great smudgy arcs. There's really no difference between the metal structures emitting light, and the bands of light in front of her eyes. They're both real, or false. She's not sure about the difference.

She no longer believes her memories of Paula, she's not even sure there is anything inside Paula, apart from a set of Russian dolls with identical red lips and black eyelashes. The other version of Paula, the one that belonged to Jeanette, seems to have gone.

She tries not to look at the clock, tries not to think about what they're doing right now in Richard's flat. The whole night is right now, a single moment of time. Perhaps she is stuck in this moment for ever. Outside, cars sweep by rhythmically, the thump of their engines rattling the windows of the flat. She wants to go outside and lie down on the tarmac, be run over again and again. Anything to stop this pain.

Night is replaced by grey dawn and the streetlights are turned off. She can't remember how to move now, so she remains sitting, waiting. Only when the phone rings is she startled out of herself, able to stretch an arm and pick up the receiver. But she still can't speak.

'Paula?' It's a man. She remains silent. 'Are you there? Paula? Damn, sorry, I must have the wrong number.' He rings off, but she carries on holding the receiver to her ear, its incessant whirr like some high-pitched electronic heartbeat.

Later that day, she tries to do some work. She starts to reads a scientific paper;

In an expanding universe all galaxies are receding from each other. In addition to this universal recessional velocity, there will be local gravitational forces due to neighbouring galaxies. This will lead to additional velocity components and corresponding variations in the space density of galaxies. In those parts of the universe with lower than average galaxy space densities, there will be no counter to the recessional velocity, which will therefore increase. So, a part of the universe with fewer galaxies in it will expand at a higher rate than its surroundings, and will get even less dense. This will lead to a runaway situation in which parts of the universe will get cut off, and isolated from the rest of the universe.

In this way it is not clear if Einstein's theory of general relativity is fully consistent with Mach's principle. The latter claims that our movements here on Earth only have meaning with respect to the distant stars, and thus every single object in the universe is connected.

Connections. Does everything have to be about connections? She throws the scientific journal away from her. But then she realises. She has data on galaxies. Are her galaxies moving as they should be with the rest of the Universe, or are they in their own little void, cut off from everything?

She sits and thinks, as the sun advances across the sky into the evening and her shadow grows larger on the wall.

That night she decides she should tidy up Paula's belongings. It may make her seem less physically present in the flat if Jeanette can't see her piles of art books, or nests of underwear, or tottering towers of vintage crockery, or clotted remains of old nail varnish bottles. She feels efficient as she finds a bin bag and carefully places the objects inside. She's not doing this to be vindictive, she's not a clichéd ex-lover chopping the sleeves off clothes. She doesn't want to destroy any of Paula's belongings, she just doesn't want to see them.

Behind the sofa bed she finds Paula's suitcase. Perhaps she could store her belongings in it. But it's already full. Inside are some crumpled clothes; pastel-coloured cashmere sweaters, a polka-dotted dress from the fifties, and yet another one of Paula's blasted kimonos. She burrows beneath them, not sure why she's bothering to look any further. She knows all there is to know about Paula now. She's come to the dead end.

But there is something else underneath the clothes. Something flat and smooth lying at the bottom of the case. She dumps the clothes onto the floor to reveal a white canvas. It's slightly smaller than the suitcase, and about the size of most of Paula's paintings.

She doesn't think she's seen anything so white for a long time. It's remarkable in its smoothness and featurelessness. It could be a depiction of the state of nothing before the universe began. But when she gets the canvas out of the suitcase and holds it closer, she notices faint smudges hidden in the white. She takes it over to the light and scrutinises it.

Yes, there is her own face. Her eyes, nose, and mouth are all drowning under the surface of a white sea. This is the portrait of her that Paula painted, and that she has subsequently destroyed.

She has been whitewashed out of Paula's history. For the second time that day she throws something across her flat.

The balloon inside her has expanded to completely fill her. She is in a bubble of helium. She is cut off.

She still manages to get up every day and go to work. She gives lectures, talks to colleagues, supervises students, goes to meetings. But everywhere she goes, she takes Paula with her. Paula can't speak because she's caught in a single moment of time, her head thrown back, her mouth open in an O of desire, her lips moist and red, her tongue catching at her teeth. Just the way that Jeanette remembers her from all their times together. At first she's grateful for all the detail she's able to recall, the feel and pattern of Paula's body against her own, and then she realises she's damned herself. She is caught in the hell of unrequited longing, which seems to be so strong it has created its own illusion. She could drink to blot it out, but when she tries that, she doesn't even have the energy to work and has to stay at home staring at the white portrait. The death mask.

She's hung the canvas on the wall. She doesn't hate it anymore, because now she thinks that Paula has been rather clever in forecasting how she looks. She doesn't bother looking in real mirrors, she knows there won't be anything there. She has disappeared.

The real Paula has also disappeared. Jeanette hasn't seen her since the night in the club, and guesses that she's staying at friends. She won't still be with Richard. Jeanette sees Richard at work, watches him sit in front of his computer churning out his numbers and feels sorry for him because she knows they're meaningless. But they're all he has.

The first day at work after the night at the pub, Richard came up to her and said, 'How did you get home?'

And she was able to reply that she'd walked home.

'We...' he looked at her all the time he was speaking, hardly blinking, 'We went on to Sneaky Pete's.'

'Did you.'

'And then we drank tequila and Paula lost her phone.'

He seemed stuck in the minutiae of that night. Perhaps she should help him out. 'And then the sun rose and it was a new day.'

He looked at her oddly. 'Yes, that's right. We had breakfast in that caff on Forrest Road.' Was he giving her an alibi? Perhaps he hadn't slept with Paula after all. But nothing else could explain Paula's utter absence. And there were the signs between them in the pub, like semaphore. Their red flags of desire.

It seemed to have cancelled out her refusal to consider him for her grant, because he said to her quite cheerily, 'Loads more job applications to do!' Or perhaps it was simply his revenge. She wasn't able to assess the mixture of the different motivations for what happened, so she walked away. And that has set the pattern for all their subsequent encounters, which is fine by her.

When she does see the real Paula, and not the phantasm created by the engine of her desire, spacetime buckles and warps. She gets home from work one day, about a week after the night in the pub, and finds Paula waiting in the flat.

Jeanette sits down opposite her on a chair that is hardly ever used. She is close enough to reach out and touch Paula, but the space between them has stretched to infinity. Conversely, time has collapsed so that all the layers of their history are present in the room. Jeanette can't look at her without seeing the past and present; Paula lying naked on the sofa, and Paula sitting there in her old paint-stained overalls. Paula with her eyes shut, eyelashes fluttering on her cheeks, and Paula inspecting a patch of paint on her hand, as if she is trying to avoid looking at Jeanette.

She waits for Paula to stop scraping the colour from her skin, and speak.

Paula nods at the white canvas. 'What's that doing there?'

'I found it in your suitcase, when I was tidying up.'

Paula nods again, but then she says, 'I need that canvas. That's why I painted over it. I'm going to reuse it.'

'I'd like to keep it.' Jeanette stares at it while she speaks and after she looks away she can see its negative, a dark square, superimposed on the rest of the room.

'But it's blank!' Paula sounds exasperated.

'I know.' Words weigh heavy like stones in her mouth. Perhaps they will drown her.

'It was a trial run,' Paula says. She looks like she wants to say something else, perhaps elaborate on what she means by 'it'.

'I know.' Jeanette can't say out loud that right now the blank canvas seems more truthful than any other, more obvious, depiction. 'But I'd like to keep it, as a memento of — your work.'

'Oh...' There is a slight softness in the air now. She has appealed to Paula's vanity, her sense of importance. 'Perhaps I don't need it, for the time being. You might as well keep it.' She stands up. 'My show starts in two weeks. You can come to the opening, if you want to.'

Jeanette realises that she's not actually being invited to the opening, she's being given permission to come to it. She remembers the last show, the elegiac picture of Becca, and finally understands. 'Are you staying with Becca?'

Paula doesn't even look surprised. 'No.' She pauses as if trying to decide how much to tell Jeanette before continuing, 'No, I've met someone else.'

This, then, is the end. If she thought they'd got to the end before, she was wrong, because now they have reached the nub of it, and time stops here. She looks at Paula and sees something else in her face, a desire to tell her all about her new relationship mixed with her innate preference for keeping things secret.

'Will you be moving your stuff out?' It's an effort getting the words out, being practical.

Paula looks slightly taken aback. 'Well, I don't actually have anywhere to put them right now. Could I pick them up in a few days?'

'Of course.' They might be discussing a business arrangement, which could be all this ever was for Paula. A place to stay and regular sex. But she doesn't want to know. She could spend the rest of her life trying to guess what Paula's motivations and feelings were, and never know, because it's unknowable. There is no objective truth to this, there's just her feelings and Paula's feelings. And their feelings are different.

Paula stands up, 'I'll phone you. About the opening, and about picking up my stuff.'

She's almost out of the door when Jeanette allows herself to say, quietly, 'It was a good portrait. You shouldn't have painted over it.'

Paula pauses and speaks without facing her. 'It wasn't good enough.' And then she's gone.

When the door has slammed shut behind Paula, the balloon inside Jeanette bursts and she explodes into a million pieces. She flies up to the living room ceiling, crawls through the bedroom carpet, slip-slides down the kitchen tiles, comes to rest panting over the toilet bowl, where she is sick, before she takes flight again. She spends the rest of the night circling the bathroom, while her body slumps on the floor. She'd escape if she could, but she's not sure how. What would happen to her in the night air? Would she simply dissipate, her atoms floating away in the sky?

In the morning, she looks in the mirror and isn't surprised to see that she doesn't exist any more. The face looking back at her is Kate. This is what it means to have the past and present concertinaed together. Everything that has happened to her in the past is happening to her right now. Time has shut down. In a way, she's not surprised. As she stands there, brushing her teeth, she remembers what Einstein said; 'Time only exists to stop everything happening at once.'

She spits out her toothpaste and looks at Kate in the mirror again, seeing her freckled nose, her dark brown eyes. Kate looks back, impassive and still. When she was alive, she never stopped moving. She darted around their house, their school, the whole town. Jeanette was the quiet one, the steady one.

Jeanette sticks out her tongue but Kate doesn't react. She seems to be studying Jeanette, as if trying to decide something.

'Why?' Jeanette asks her. 'Why are you here, now? Why didn't you come back years ago?' When we needed you, she thinks.

Kate doesn't move, doesn't speak. Jeanette realises she can't stay in the flat with her dead sister so, even though it's Sunday, she goes to work.

Once she's there, she decides to go to the plate library. This is a little-used room where thousands of glass photographic plates are stored. Until the development of digital cameras, these plates were the only way of imaging large areas of the sky. Now they've been superseded by newer technology and the room has an abandoned, mournful feel to it.

Dust covers everything, blurring the edges of the shelves where the plates are stored. She's probably the only person in the department who comes in here anymore, and she wonders how long the plates can last before being thrown out.

She turns on the light table, but its yellow glow seems rather sickly, a poor copy of the daylight outside.

What she is doing here is archaic; she wants to look at photographic plates showing the portion of sky she plans to study. She could probably get better information from more recent electronic images, but she likes the way that the plates have captured light from these objects and preserved it like insects in the amber of the photographic emulsion. The tiny pieces of the objects right in front of her seem more substantial than images on a screen. Back in the days when all astronomy was carried out with glass plates, there must have been a weight, a heft, to people's studies of the sky.

She peers through the eyepiece at the plate, at the tiny images of stars and galaxies. Her fingers trace the unique patterns in the emulsion, as intently studied as the skin of any lover.

She used to find it odd looking at celestial objects no bigger than pin-heads. But now she's comfortable with her whole universe being inverted; unimaginably enormous and faraway galaxies have been shrunk to millimetre-sized dots on a glass plate in a lab. It's how she knows things. There are further inversions of reality in this material; the photograph is a negative; black sky is chalk white, and stars and galaxies are dark freckles. The plate is even back to front so that east is to the left and west to the right, a mirror image of real life.

Does time run backwards up there too? If something out there is observing her, would it see her leave this room, go to her flat, talk to her dead sister in the bathroom mirror?

She sits studying the plate through the eyeglass for some time, only pausing when the muscles in her shoulders seize from hunching over the table.

Then, as she straightens up, she sees someone else in the lab. Paula. Paula is sitting on the other side of the room, watching her. When Jeanette turns to look at her properly, she fades away, yet she can see her out of the corner of her eye. Paula is by the window, not speaking, just staring at her. Her outline is indistinct, as though the sunlight is wearing it away, but Jeanette can see that she's wearing the same paint-stained clothes as she wore the night before. Paula smiles at her.

She feels cold, angry. This is her space; Paula has no right to be there. 'What do you want?'

Paula remains silent. Jeanette realises she can see through her to the window, and the city beyond. She's more shadowy and less substantial than she was in the flat.

What will it take to get rid of her? She throws the eyeglass at her but Paula dodges it easily, and so she has to cross over to her side of the room to retrieve it.

'Happy now?' Jeanette asks her.

She doesn't look particularly happy. Her face is rather smudged, and her mouth seems almost wiped away. Her eyes are just dark hollows. As Jeanette looks at her, she seems to fade even more until parts of her are almost invisible.

Then Paula fractures into multiple images, and starts dancing around the room. Someone else appears, even darker and more vague, holding Paula's hands. It is herself. She watches the two of them silently dancing together, twisted like rope. The images are shadowy and monochrome as though caught on old photographs. Now, the dancing seems to be slowing down, and then Paula starts pulling at the other woman's hands. She seems to be resisting, she's trying to pull away but Paula's too strong, and the two of them recede to the far end of the lab, behind the tall shelves of books, out of sight.

What does Paula want with her? Why can't she leave her in peace? Jeanette approaches the back of the lab, creeping across the dusty linoleum so she can see what's going on. Her shoes squeak on the floor and so she gets down on her hands and knees and crawls through the dust. At the back of the room, behind the shelves, she can see the two figures huddled up against the wall. Still no sound from them. It's as if they are surrounded by a vacuum.

The figures are intertwined, their heads bent together, their hands stroking each other. She howls at them, and runs back to the light table, picks up the glass plate and hurls it at the shelves.

As it splinters, shards of the white sky shine in the air and tinkle onto the floor, disturbing the dust. When she dares to look again behind the shelves, Paula's gone. It seems that violence is the best way to deal with her.

She has to leave this place now, it's not safe anymore; but as she turns to go she realises that her hand has been cut by the broken glass. There's a scattering of blood on the floor, complementing the dark spots of stars. Blood is still dripping from the gash on her thumb, and there's a trail of drops leading from the shelves to where she's standing by the light table. The colour is beautiful, like the velvet dark roses her father used to grow for his lover.

Outside the sky is blue, the grass is green. She glances around her, at the east tower where Paula sketched her. As she looks at it, it bursts into flames. There is no noise, just a silent curtain of fire. She sees

Richard strolling along, hair caught in the wind. Jon is just behind him, deep in discussion with another lecturer. Other people amble through the blaze, and only she can see the shower of black smuts raining down on them.

Her father appears, holding a can of petrol. His arms are wrapped in bandages, but these are unfurling, trailing along the ground. Her mother walks out of the east tower and steps onto one of the bandages, preventing her father from moving. They stay still and silent, only connected by the pale bandage.

Above her the sky darkens to night. She can see the usual constellations for this time of year; Cassiopeia, Orion. And there is something else moving across the sky, rippling through it, making waves of particles shimmer in its wake. A girl swimming. Even as Jeanette watches, the girl fades away into dullness, the fire shrinks down, her parents dissolve. The unfurled bandage becomes a discarded hankie.

Her mother sits by the fire, knitting. The yarn is pink, always pink. Baby booties spill from the knitting needles into her lap, all connected to each other by a single thread of yarn. Her mother makes no attempt to cut this umbilical cord, she just carries on knitting. Outside the moon shines brightly, but her mother can only see by the electric blue of the television.

In a corner of the room, the Fates sit, waiting, watching the moon swing around the sky. They are waiting for it to get into the right position. Everything has to be just so, before they act. So they crouch, motionless, as the knitting needles clack.

When the moon is aligned with the window, and moonlight streaming through the room strikes her mother's lap, the Fates snip the yarn. The booties tumble to the floor. Kate's lips flutter as she lies on the side of the pool, one hand trailing into the water.

THEN

'Where is the Sun right now?'

It's a sunny day and the physics class is stuck inside, trying not to stare out of the lab's windows at the world beyond. There is silence. Jeanette is used to silence. The teacher talks, they write things down. When the teacher isn't talking, they're doing lab work and this too is done in silence. There are only five of them doing A-level physics, and she is the only girl. She didn't really notice at first, there are so many other ways to classify them. Such as willingness to answer the teacher's questions. She knows the answer to this question, but she also knows that always being able to answer the questions is enough to single her out, even more than being a girl. She isn't sure she wants to be so different from the others. So she sits on her hands and waits.

'Where is the Sun?' the teacher repeats. Someone points half-heartedly out of the window at the Sun, but doesn't speak.

'No!' The teacher sounds scornful.

They're doing the speed of light. They've worked their way up to it, from normal everyday speeds, people, bicycles, cars, to planes and rockets, to the speed of the Earth going round the Sun, and the Sun travelling around the Milky Way to the top speed. The biggest one of all.

Jeanette knows where the Sun is right now. At least, she knows where it isn't. It's never where it appears to be, because it has always moved on. You see the Sun as it was, eight minutes ago, because that is how long it takes for its light to get to the Earth. And eight minutes is enough for the Sun to travel about a hand span across the sky.

She puts up her hand. There is a pause while the teacher waits for someone else. She understands. It must be boring always to be faced with the same eagerness. But no one else moves and finally the teacher has to nod at her.

'It's not where we see it,' she says, and someone behind her snorts in disbelief.

'No? Why not?'

So she tells him, along with the rest of the class. As she talks, she realises for the first time that if the Sun is eight minutes away, and the next star, alpha Centauri, is four lightyears away, then beyond that are stars further back in time. The light she sees now from those stars has been emitted by them before Kate died. She has the power to see into the past, into a Universe which is innocent of Kate's death.

One evening she sees a comet. It has been predicted to appear but there's an uncertainty over how bright it will be. It's difficult to tell in advance, for various reasons. So Jeanette isn't very optimistic as she stands outside facing away from the house, from all the houses, to avoid as much artificial light as possible, training her binoculars into the night.

She finds the right part of the sky, and waits. The trick is to not look at it straight on. Faint objects are always best seen if you look to one side, to avoid the blind spot at the back of the eye. She doesn't find this so difficult, it's similar to the way she used to look at Alice.

At first it's a smudge on the sky, as if someone has left their fingerprint on a glass. Then, she notices the tail, a curling wisp. She stands and watches it for some time, able to see how it moves between the other objects in the sky, as if seeking out a place to rest, until it finally gets too close to the Moon and is drowned by light, like a moth plunging towards a lightbulb.

Comets are usually harbingers of disaster. But Jeanette can't imagine what could change in her life. Kate is dead and Alice has gone. All she does is plod through the days.

Sometimes when she walks home from school, she can convince

herself that by the time she arrives, something will have changed. But nothing changes. Their home is a desert devoid of time. Her mother occupies a space consisting of cigarettes and spoons of instant coffee and magazines and daytime TV. Her father does the same things every year to grow his vegetables and flowers. They're all trapped on a merry-go-round.

The only way to escape is to travel into atoms and stars. To learn that neutrons have a half-life of nine minutes once they've left the safety of the atom, and that their death is a spectacular karmic transformation into protons and electrons and anti-neutrinos. To uncover the ages of the Universe, like geological layers, and see how the constant expansion of the Universe makes time happen.

Perhaps that is the problem at home. Because nothing obvious ever changes, time itself can't intrude. But she herself is gradually, minutely, changing. She is now taller than Kate ever was. Her hair is lighter. But none of these changes triggers anything. They aren't enough to make her visible.

Only once does she emerge in front of her parents. She keeps a small photo of Alice in her purse. She's almost forgotten about it, until one day when her mother asks her for some change and it falls out.

'What's that?' Her mother sounds frightened. Perhaps for a moment she thought it was Kate. They both look at the scrap of paper and Alice looks back at them.

'It's only a photo.' She's stupidly relaxed; even the sight of Alice fills her with unexpected joy.

'But why...' her mother peers closer. 'Is that Alice? Why...'

'Why not?'

Her mother looks straight at her for the first time in years. 'Why have you got a photo of Alice in your purse?'

And she knows that her mother knows, that in spite of all the suffocating silences and fog of cigarette smoke, her mother can see perfectly well when she chooses to.

'It doesn't matter.' Her fingers scrabble to pick it up and tuck it back into the safety of her purse, where it belongs. 'It's nothing.'

Perhaps silence is better after all.

Orion is shining brightly. She's out in the garden, with her telescope. She doesn't really have anything in mind tonight, she's just aimlessly scanning the sky. The camera is bolted to the back of the telescope; in case anything interests her, it can be recorded. She locks the telescope onto Algol, the brightest star in Orion, almost absent-mindedly, and stands listening to the whirr of the motor as the telescope tracks the star across the sky, like a mechanical dog faithfully following its distant owner. Behind her squats the house and she knows that if she turns around, she'll be able to see through the glass into the living room where her parents sit, still and silent, soaked in the glare of the television. How long will it be before they absorb so much light from it that they start to glow blue themselves? She takes care to keep her back to them.

It's a clear night, one of the clearest for a long time. No moon either. Ideal for observing, for seeing the faintest objects that would otherwise be drowned out by cloud, or moonlight, or turbulence in the air. So she decides to have a go at Rigel, one of the many double stars in Orion. It's made up of a bright star and a fainter companion, which is usually too close to the bright one to be seen with her little telescope. She lines the brighter star up in the crosshairs of the telescope and sets the telescope off again, in search.

As she waits, the garden waits with her. She only ever comes out here at night. As its details merge into the dark, it loses a sense of its own history and is transformed into something more generic.

Later, she unloads the film, develops it and prints the contact strips. She watches the tank as the fainter star comes to life beneath the clear liquid. This is what she can do. Make the unseen, seen. Find things and know them. These things are real to her, even though she can't reach them.

She has to make a decision about her life, but for her it's no decision at all, because there's no choice. She is going to leave home and go to university. To study physics and astronomy. She's nervous about telling them, but she's not sure why. Will they be bothered, will they notice? And a quieter, sicker thought, will they be relieved if she goes? Perhaps they can pretend they don't have, have never had, any daughters.

Alice doesn't write. Jeanette has lost track of where she's supposed to be now, in her round-the-world gap year journey. She doesn't really want to think about the vast distances that separate her from Alice. She can't imagine Alice being capable of navigating herself home again. She prefers to conjure up that first memory of Alice, emerging from the darkroom, her small face lit by the deep glow of the safety light. As if they had met on another planet, orbiting around a red star.

'How did you and Dad first meet?' she asks her mother one weekend afternoon when her father is outside, out of view.

Her mother lays down her magazine and stares off into the middle distance as if looking back in time. 'It was at a train station. I got something in my eye and he offered me his hanky.' She smiles — a small, secret smile. Jeanette doesn't see her mother smile often. After a moment her mother picks up her magazine again. Jeanette can picture the two people standing on a platform, like mechanical dolls, one offering a hanky to the other, who takes it and dabs at her eye.

'He missed his train because of me.' Her mother looks like she's reading but Jeanette can still see the remains of the smile. She wishes she knew how to make it last. Perhaps it will work with her father too.

'How did you and Mum first meet?' They are outside and her father is digging in a vegetable patch. The windows to the house are opaque with reflected sunlight. No way of telling if her mother is looking out at them.

'It was at a station. I got something in my eye and she offered me her hanky. If I remember correctly, she missed her train and I sat with her until the next one arrived.' He grins, but Jeanette does not grin back. 'What's the matter?' he asks, but she just shakes her head.

Why is it so difficult, she thinks. Why is it impossible to ever really know anything about other people? Is it safer to stick to atoms and stars? It makes her sad that Kate never knew the beginning of her story. The true beginning, not the made-up one that her parents seem to have taken refuge in. So Jeanette will have to find out for her.

She discovers that Kate was born 13.7 billion years ago, in the Big Bang. The primordial explosion of space and time. At first it was too hot for anything to form, so there was just the promise of her, a whisper in the rapidly expanding vacuum, a quantum tremor in the plasma sea of quarks and gluons.

Then, a decision, a deliberation, a definite fluctuation. But still she could not be seen. Not until 300,000 years after the Big Bang, when protons and photons separated for the first time, and light was set free to travel.

Now she appears large on the sky. Hydrogen atoms form around her and gas flows towards her. Dark matter dances in attendance to her. She is written in the first stars. But these are too large and powerful for their own good, they grow quickly and die young. Their exploding ashes kick start the generation of the chemical elements, thrust out to fend for themselves.

She waits. She can wait.

More stars, smaller stars, are born. These last longer, long enough for the debris of their birth to settle into planets. Carbon and oxygen get swept up onto a planet where it's not too hot or too cold, and wait for life to form.

This must be the beginning of Kate. This version is knowable, understandable. One event leads to another and there is proper cause and effect. This is what she deserves. The other version is too uncertain, there are too many unknowns. One person could have missed the train, or got on a different carriage. The speck of dust would have taken a chaotic path through the atmosphere to hit that person's eye. It would have been bounced around by the wind, chased by raindrops, it could have hit another part of that person and lain on their skin or clothes, unnoticed.

Whose eye did it hit? Their mother's or father's? Who owned the handkerchief, conveniently washed and ready for its part in their conception? That story isn't even complete.

What about alternative theories? The Big Bang theory is not the only one they're taught. There is another one, the steady state theory, somewhat out of favour now and discarded. But Jeanette must consider it.

It's good enough, up to a point. It can create the elements in the stars, seed life on the planet. Galaxies come and go, stars are born and die, but overall everything stays exactly the same. There is no beginning to this story, just endless darkness. Kate deserves better. Kate deserves the beginning of the Universe.

NOW

At night the corridors go on forever. But it's just an illusion, caused by the darkness masking the end of the corridors. The lights turn on automatically above you, illuminating the piece of space that you happen to be occupying. Ahead of you as well as behind you, there is just darkness, and so you move on, in your small island of light towards an unseen dark end. Which may never arrive.

Jeanette works at night. It's better that way. Now it's dusk and she can hear her colleagues leaving the Observatory, going home. She is not going anywhere. She is going to work tonight, as she does most nights. She likes the Observatory in the dark and the silence. There's more room to breathe out, she feels an easing in her chest and she relaxes.

She's working on the map of her galaxies in her part of the universe. This map shows velocities as well as positions, so she can see not only where each galaxy is, but also where it's moving to. Each galaxy has a little arrow attached to its position, the length of the arrow shows how fast it is moving, and the direction shows where it is moving to. A map of the universe would show all galaxies moving away from all other galaxies. Each galaxy left behind in a perfect symmetry of isolated space.

At midnight she prints the map out and walks up the silent corridor to collect it from the server room where the printers are. She's done a large scale print, so she can pin it on the wall and take a step back to get an overall impression on what the galaxies are doing.

The corridor is silent and the light throbs above her. She stops moving, the light blinks off, and she's in the dark. The corridor expands, fills the universe. She is alone. She has to put a hand over her mouth to stop herself from crying out.

A dot of light appears wavering in the distance — the security guard. He flips the light switch at the end of the corridor and the whole space shrinks down, becomes ordinary again. She's able to go and collect her print and return to her office, even to reply to the guard when he speaks to her. She sees him every night, after all.

In her office, she shuts the door behind her. Looking out of the window at the smeared red sky, she feels like she's on a stalk high up over a dark field, and she imagines her office is the only one in the whole building, the light seen from miles away.

But as the light from here leaks out there, so does the dark from there leak into her room. She wonders where the boundary is, and how light and dark interchange there.

The map of her galaxies isn't what she expected. Until she looks at the map, she doesn't realise that she did actually expect anything, but now she knows that this was not it. She never does expect the reality of things. She should have learnt that by now.

What the map show her is the usual sprinkling of galaxies, represented by black dots, scattered across the white paper. This is normal, this is expected. But the arrows attached to the galaxies show them all moving in the same direction, away from the centre of this space. There should be enough of them to keep them together, but something is missing. At some point in the future, these galaxies will have left this space, will have forsaken it. There will be nothing there. She could weep for the future of this abandoned space. But she doesn't. She has work to do.

What defines this space is her interest in it. It has no other boundaries. But she has drawn an edge around it in order to learn about it. Does that make it real, she wonders? And taking her pencil, she traces a hole in the air in front of her.

Kate doesn't exist anymore, not even in Jeanette's head. The exploding rocket has killed her all over again. Jeanette can't even summon up her face. When she tries to, there's a blank, a vacuum. A white space hovering in mid-air, defying gravity.

And when she looks in the mirror at her own face, there's also a blankness. The individual features don't add up to anything anymore. She is not the sum of her parts.

Other people at work seem to avoid her. In the corridors, they walk past her quickly, calling out 'Hi!' behind them, without stopping to listen to her reply. Or they veer round her, as if getting too close to her is dangerous.

She's not surprised. She's realised from her latest project that voids exist in the universe. Nature abhors a vacuum, galaxies rush out of voids because there is not enough mass there to keep them in. She has her own void now. There is not enough of her to keep anyone else there.

She knows now that her work on the connected galaxies was all wrong. She and Maggie must have made a mistake because the universe is not about connections. It's about separation, vastness, coldness. One of the books that she's reading right now is called 'The Heat Death of the Universe'. It explains that due to the second law of thermodynamics, everything will run out of useable energy and wind down like broken clocks, reaching a sort of refrigerated equilibrium. She thinks she's reached this stage somewhat earlier than anyone else.

One day follows another. She makes her maps. She writes a paper about them and submits it to a scientific journal. It's accepted. She's not surprised, she's on the right track now. Not the short, sharp scramble, but the steady, slow plod. She even thinks more highly of Richard's everlasting data processing. Really, there's no point trying to form an opinion about the universe. It just is. The only thing to do is to observe it, and refrain from passing comment.

She goes back to Chile to work on the voids. She knows from her work with the glass plates that there are patches of sky that don't appear to have any galaxies, but the glass plates are not that sensitive and she wants better data to see whether there are faint galaxies that have been undetected so far, or alternatively if these apparent voids really are completely empty of any normal matter.

On the first night of her observing run she walks up the dusty path to the telescope, where the telescope operator is already waiting. He's not the same operator as the last time, and for that she's grateful. But this one seems to hardly speak any English either, and she starts to realise how much she normally relies on Maggie to act as interpreter. This is going to be difficult. She conveys in sign language and a few brief technical words how she wants the telescope to be set up.

Unlike all her previous observing runs, where each image taken by the telescope has contained galaxies or stars, now she is taking images where she hopes, if her initial work back home was correct, that there will be nothing to see. As predicted, the first image is dark and blank. The telescope operator turns to her questioningly but she nods, yes, this is right. We don't want to see anything. The second image is the same. She thinks she notices the telescope operator rolling his eyes as he lines up the telescope for the third blank image and picks up his newspaper.

As she can't remember his name, she has to cough to get his attention every time she wants him to move the telescope to the next patch of sky. But even though they manage to get into a routine, there's something not quite right. She can't figure it out at first. The room is quiet, all she can hear is the rustle of the newspaper and the distant hum of the telescope motor. Everything should be peaceful. Then she realises that each time they start a new observation, the telescope operator picks up his newspaper and she gets a glimpse of a large photo taking up nearly the whole of the front page. This photo shows some long bundles of cloth lying on the ground somewhere, with people standing around them, looking at the camera. It feels like they're looking directly at Jeanette. Their faces are serious, even accusing, although she doesn't understand what it is they're accusing her of. She can't make any sense of it, there's not enough information, so she looks away.

Then the telescope finishes its observation and the next image is displayed on the screen. From time to time she thinks how odd it is that she should be the first person to see these images; it feels like an unveiling. But there are no fanfares here. They both eat a lot of biscuits.

The next night is the same. The telescope operator is even reading the same newspaper, probably because nobody has come up the mountain since yesterday. She feels as if she's trapped in a bubble of time. If she can't move forward, how can she ever escape from Paula? From anything?

She realises with a sinking heart that all her images will look identical. She has never taken such dull images in her life. How will she be able to tell them apart when she gets home?

One of the images has a thin white line bisecting it. The operator points to it. 'Satellite track,' he says, looking faintly relieved that they have, at last, detected something. She tries to smile.

'We are being watched,' he continues.

'Sorry?'

But he just picks up his newspaper and falls silent again.

The next day another astronomer sits down next to her in the canteen. 'It will be cloudy tonight,' he announces. His accent is German.

'Really.' She says this louder than she means to, but the sky is spotless and there is no wind. She hates the way some astronomers, usually the older ones, act as if they know more than anyone else. She doesn't say anything more to him as they both watch the sky fade away over the empty landscape.

That night the operator's still reading the same newspaper and it's driving her nuts. Surely someone's been up the mountain from the nearest town with a more recent one?

Cloud appears at midnight so they have to stop the observations and wait. Without the hum of the telescope or the whir of the dome, it is silent in the control room. She stares at her hands, cursing the German astronomer. The operator reads on. He must have read the newspaper cover to cover by now.

She opens a few of the more recent images but when she looks at the screen all she can see is her own reflection. There is no point looking at these images. They are just images of herself. She will have to do it all by numbers.

And her own reflection looks back at her, pale and frightened. It's almost as bad as Paula's blanked out version of her. Perhaps this is what she really looks like.

'Biscuit?' The telescope operator is offering her a stale wafer. She shakes her head and starts to cry.

The next day she wants to avoid the German astronomer, so she goes out at lunchtime and wanders down the path. After a few hundred metres she finds a hollow in the ground, a convenient place to sit and watch the space around her. Peace. She feels the sun on her face, and leans back to rest against the earth. She shuts her eyes.

She doesn't know what has woken her up, only that she's been jolted back into the real world. The blue has faded from the sky; it's already sunset. She's been out here far too long, she should be at the telescope, preparing for the night. She tries to stand up but then she notices something standing nearby, watching her.

It's a wild dog. Small and yellow, with its snout pointed directly at her. She's too scared to shout. She tries moving her arm slowly but it snaps its teeth and so she has to lie still, just watching it. There's a thick layer of dust on its fur, the same colour as the sandy rocks. It could have crawled out of this landscape; it would be invisible from twenty metres away.

'Nice dog,' she mutters and it growls. She's close enough to note the utter blankness of its eyes, like a cloudy night sky. The sky is rapidly growing darker and she has to move; she can't be out here at night, she'd never find her way back to the observatory.

It starts slinking towards her, belly almost brushing against the ground. She fumbles around and finds a stone, hurls it at the dog. It misses but the dog springs away, kicking up a plume of dust before disappearing into the rocks.

Somehow she manages to stagger back up the path to the telescopes, her shadow creeping alongside her.

Tonight, there are too many layers of time in the control room. There is the distant past of the voids, brought to her in coded messages for her to unpick and explain. That is perhaps the easiest. Her own past has also taken up residence. It should have been left behind in Edinburgh, waiting for her when she gets home. Instead it's on her back, weighing her down. Insistent memories of Paula, of the connected galaxies, even of the ice woman, start surfacing and she knows that behind these memories are more distant and much worse ones. The present seems the least immediate of all these layers, even though she knows that the dog is outside.

'I saw a dog today,' she tells the operator.

'A dog?' He puts down his newspaper. 'Where?'

'Out there.' She waves her hand. How can anyone tell one part of this place from another? It all looks the same. Just one barren bit of sand after another.

'Yes. We have wild dogs here. They are fed by the cooks in the canteen.'

His English is much better than she thought. Perhaps he learns it from the astronomers. He folds his newspaper carefully into an old plastic bag, and she realises that this newspaper is important to him, for some reason. He looks expectantly at her, obviously waiting for her to say something.

'How often do you get a newspaper here?' It's all she can think of, but he doesn't seem surprised.

'Not often.' He pats the bag.

She has to go to the canteen the next day, and the German sits down next to her again. He has heard about the dog.

'Dangerous!' He shakes his head.

'I didn't think there was anything out there. Anything living.'

'The dogs have been here since the camp started.'

'Camp? What camp?' But she thinks of the photo on the front of the telescope operator's newspaper. The long bundles of cloth. Perhaps this is what bodies look like before they are buried.

'Chacabuco. It wasn't far from here.' He glares at her, but she's never heard this name before. She only knows the road between Santiago and the observatory. Then she remembers the first time she came here, years ago when she was a student, there was a roadblock manned by bored soldiers. They had inspected her passport, nothing more. But she remembers the excitement she had felt, coming from boring old democratic Britain. She had told people back home. Paula had been interested. Dear God, Paula. Had she used the tale of the roadblock to try and entice Paula, even at that stage in their friendship? How obscene.

She blushes now, and doesn't ask any more about the camp.

That night, she's staring at the latest image, and wondering if there are actually faint galaxies hidden in it, when the door to the control room bangs open and the German walks in. He doesn't say anything to her, just walks over to the telescope operator and holds out a hand.

'I am sorry,' he says.

The operator smiles and takes his outstretched hand. They stay like that for some time, their hands clasped together.

'What's going on?' Jeanette asks.

The German turns to her. 'The bodies at Chacabuco. One of them is his uncle.'

She stares at the operator. 'Your uncle?' She must sound stupid.

The German continues, 'People were sent to the concentration camp at Chacabuco when they challenged the regime, and they disappeared. Their relatives have been searching for them for years. The bodies have only just now been found.'

She walks over to the operator and looks down at his newspaper. But, as before, the photo offers little information. She imagines the relatives out in the desert, picking through the sand and rocks to try and find something like a photo or a scrap of cloth. A shoe. Or bones and ashes. It's too distressing to think of ashes.

She hopes whatever's wrapped up in the cloth is protected from the dogs.

Above the three of them the telescope continues to whirr, a steady comforting sound. She wonders if the people trapped in the concentration camp could see it. Did they hope that it would discover them? But you can't point a telescope at the ground; it would collapse under its own weight.

She wants to say something to the operator, but she can't think what. The telescope finishes its observation, and yet another blank image appears on the screen. They all stare at it in silence.

The next day she looks at the desert and realises it isn't empty anymore. The only emptiness is in her voids, her mind. Now that she knows what's going on out there, she thinks she can almost see the tiny people making their way back and forth across the surface like farmers sowing seeds, but in reverse. They are harvesting their own grief, but she has been careless with hers. It's lost, blown away, and she needs to find it again.

She has to prepare a talk for this conference she's been invited to, even though she's got nothing to say. Nothing about the link between the galaxies, anyway. Since the rocket explosion, neither she nor anyone else has worked out another way of testing the initial result. Maggie is too busy in California to spend time on it. Jeanette's colleagues seem happy not to mention it. She sometimes thinks she's almost the only person still bothered by it.

The conference is a small, prestigious affair, in an old house. It's by invitation only. She and about twenty other astronomers will tell each other about the latest developments in cosmology and the results will be published in a book called 'Frontiers of Modern Cosmology' which will be distributed to new PhD students. She knows it's an honour to be invited to contribute to this. It may even help her hang onto her lectureship. The Death Star pays attention to this sort of thing.

When she arrives at the house, she still doesn't know what she's going to say. She's got all the usual images of the linked galaxies, the ones that everyone's seen. She's got all the usual commentary down pat by now. She could just repeat herself. People repeat themselves all the time. They get one decent result, then they dine out on it for the rest of their careers. There's no harm in it. But she wants to break out of that little bubble.

She's also brought along the blank images of her voids from the last observing run, and after dinner on the first night, when she's left the rest of them downstairs in some old oak-panelled room self-consciously pouring each other glasses of port, she goes upstairs to her cold little bedroom and sits on the edge of the bed, looking at the voids. The absence of any galaxies in these little squares of darkness seems more real than her previous work on the linked galaxies. Nobody will question this absence. Although she's surprised at just how dark these images are. Her analysis shows that there is no hint of starlight, nor faint dust. Nothing at all, but emptiness.

The next morning she eats her breakfast by herself in the dining room. The others are complaining about their headaches. She slips away while they're still munching toast, and walks around outside for a bit. For some reason she's not bothered about having nothing to say. It seems more real than endlessly speaking, justifying, arguing.

They're due to give their lectures in the library so she goes there and waits.

She stares out of the window during the first lecture, on gamma ray bursters, and the second, which is on brown dwarfs. She doesn't get entangled in the inevitable argument on the possible contribution of brown dwarfs to dark matter. She bides her time.

After the coffee break she moves. She walks to the front of the room and, looking out of the window, she stands and waits. She's just not sure what she's waiting for. Then she realises that if the voids are as flawless as she thinks they are, they won't be able to transmit any sort of sound whatsoever. The void around her is perfect. It is cutting her off from the rest of the Universe. Even if she tries to speak to them, nobody will be able to hear her. She thinks about this for a bit, and then realises that she can still show her images. Sound can't be transmitted through a vacuum, but light can. So, in silence, she plugs her memory stick into the laptop and projects the images of the voids onto the screen.

It takes forty minutes to work her way through the entire set. During this time nobody else says anything either. They move around in their seats and look at each other, but they don't speak. She realises they are all lightyears away from her.

Although she can't speak, she can write. In her office, her hands wait above the keyboard as she tries to frame her thoughts and turn them into a logical narrative. That is how scientific papers are constructed. You present your initial idea, the hypothesis you want to test, and then you show the results of the data or the theory you've developed. On the page it is all supposed to come across as if the result is inevitable, as if nothing else could have happened. No satellites were harmed in the making of this experiment.

Reality is messier, of course. Reality intrudes with its unfocused images, equations that can't be solved, and diagrams that don't make sense. You don't know what's real and what isn't until you try to write it down and explain it all.

She knows that she has to start with a clear statement of her aims;

In this paper a set of images of voids has been analysed to give estimates of their diameters.

She pauses. There is something wrong with that sentence but she can't work out what it is. She carries on;

These diameters are used to calculate the volume of the voids, and hence upper limits to the star formation rates in these volumes.

It feels like she can see something out of the corner of her eye, but when she turns to look, there's nothing there.

In this paper the voids' size distribution has been used to put a constraint on the cosmological expansion history.

Now she realises what is wrong. Her paper is about her work but she's invisible in it. It's all written in the passive tense. Because, of course, that is the way that scientific papers are written. The use of the passive tense is deliberate to make the results appear objective and impartial. If you write out the woman with the messy hair and stained check shirt who actually did the work, other scientists may trust it more. That's the idea and she's usually happy to go along with it.

Her name is at the beginning of the paper, and she has to resist the urge to check if it's still there. She's written umpteen other papers, she should be used to the grammar of the universal scientist. But now, it feels as if she's disappeared into the white of the computer screen or the black of the voids. She twists in her chair to glance at the shelf of books behind her so she can see her thesis, with her name stamped in gold lettering down its black cloth spine. She takes a deep breath, lays her fingers gently on the keyboard and tries to think about the voids.

I stole the photo of Kate

She blinks at the screen. She didn't mean to write that, she wasn't even thinking it.

I stole the photo of Kate from their bedroom. The first time I've seen her for so many years. There's nothing left of her — nothing physical. Just memories and I don't even know if those are real or made up or dreamt or what.

She's not deliberately thinking any of this, it's just flowing out of her.

She appears in my head, in mirrors and then she disappears. How do I keep hold of her?

She doesn't know the answer to this.

No galaxies were detected in these voids, down to a central surface brightness of R=25. Nothing was detected at all.

And nothing will be detected in the future, no matter how hard you look.

Why did they keep the photo upstairs? Why wasn't it downstairs? Why did they keep it from me? Kate is invisible and now so am I.

She's crying now, tears dripping from her cheeks onto the keyboard, but she manages to carry on typing.

What I don't know about my sister's death:

She remembers the hospital. A room with peach coloured walls and her parents' faces wiped dumb and smooth. They don't see Kate.

They see her body, but it's not her. Kate's body is a bluish grey, the same colour as her finger nails. Her eyes are shut. There's no injury, no mark on her skin.

She's not there. This is the most certain thing that Jeanette has ever known or ever will know.

Their dad is still holding her swimming bag with her towel and her snack for later.

When someone's alive all you see of them is their body, until they die and you realise there is something else that was them and now it's gone. Then the body becomes a travesty, a mockery of the absent person. The body is still present, you can hold it (her father did), or kiss it (her mother did), or cry over it (both her parents did). But bodies are actually quite pointless substitutes for people.

After that, the day of the funeral. Maybe someone is in charge but she's not sure who; it isn't her parents. They still have those strange faces and shuffle around the house as if uncertain where they are, or who they are.

Someone has given her a flower to hold so she holds it. Someone else tells her to put the flower on the coffin, and as she approaches it she sees her face yellow and distorted in the shiny metal handles.

Lots of people are standing around in huddles, but they make way for her as if they don't want to touch her. As if something sets her apart. She is not attractive, she repels these people, she is anti-gravity. They look down at her and fall silent as she passes by them.

One of the cousins with sharp eyes comes up to her and says, 'Kate's in heaven now.'

'How did she get there?' she asks. She looks at the sky but all she can see up there are grey clouds and a tiny plane. Perhaps Kate's beyond that. She still doesn't know what heaven actually is and the cousin has moved off to talk to someone else.

Voids can expand faster than light. The universe itself expands faster than light. It just goes on and on, even after you get fed up with it and don't know how to explain it any more.

Now all I can remember is the photo and not the actual face. The photo is a substitute for the real thing. The images are not the universe.

The day is bright, almond-scented by the gorse bushes on the hill. The Observatory rises up from the steep bank of grass. All this is just like a normal day. She can hear the birds above her. She can see her colleagues and students in the distance, but she doesn't approach them. Since the conference last week, people have been problematic. Silence lays thick on her tongue. She can't remember the last time she spoke. Today might be difficult; she is supposed to give a lecture to the third year students on the birth and death of galaxies. Not for the first time, she wonders why astronomy has to use metaphors relating to life. Aren't there other ways of describing the beginnings and endings of inanimate objects?

She goes to her office and stares at a picture taken by the Hubble telescope of a supernova, the remains of a once-bright star shrouded in filaments of multi-coloured gas. The dead star itself is anonymous, you wouldn't know it had caused a massive explosion unless you imaged the velocity field of the gas and saw the shock waves all emanating from the pale dot off to one side of the picture.

It is unusually silent in her office; even her computer's hum seems dulled. All she can hear are footsteps in the distance getting louder, clumping up the spiral staircase of the tower. Then the door opens and the Death Star appears. He's wearing one of his more flamboyant tweed jackets, with a tie that doesn't match.

'Aren't you due to lecture the third years today?' he asks.

She nods.

'How are you going to do that if you can't talk?'

How does he know this? Did someone tell him about the silent seminar on voids?

They look at each other. She quite likes this absence of words. It makes people look at her more carefully, as if they really have to think about what they're seeing. They can't just rely on the same old noise coming out of their mouths. She knows he is thinking about her, he's puzzled, trying to put it all together so it adds up.

'Are you alright?' he asks finally.

She looks at the supernova again. It's amazing how far gas can escape from the surface of a dying star. When a heavy star explodes it can be one of the brightest things in the Universe.

'You've been working hard lately. Perhaps you need a break.'

A break?

'I think you've been overdoing it. All these invited seminars, on top of your new lecturing duties.'

She wishes he'd stop being nice to her. If he carries on, she'll get upset.

'Perhaps you need a change of scenery. To recharge your batteries. You could go away somewhere?'

At least he still looks stern, he hasn't smiled at her yet. That's a relief. She's not sure she could cope with anyone smiling at her.

'Why don't you go home? To your parents?'

'Home?' The word surprises them both, and she falls silent again. Her parents. Yes, perhaps. Perhaps it's time. She's studying voids, after all. She can go home and study them.

Back at the flat, she takes a bag and packs some things in it. A toothbrush, enough underwear for a few days, and then she unhooks the white canvas from the wall and puts that in the bag as well. It seems the right thing to do.

Outside on the street again, she pauses for a moment, before setting off. This will be an adventure. The bag's bulky because of the canvas, so she has to clutch it to her chest. She doesn't know what the canvas actually is, any more. It's not a picture, not a normal one anyway. But it's not blank because there is information on it, if you look hard enough. It's a thing that doesn't seem to have a name. It has a place, though. Its place is with her.

In the station, she's doubtful for a moment or two, until she buys her ticket. She doesn't usually like stations. People rushing around at random, as if they don't know where they're going. Today isn't so bad, because of the vacuum tucked around her that makes everyone else look very far away, as if she's looking at them through the wrong end of the telescope.

She feels better when she's actually sitting on the train, watching the land outside slide away from her, but she should have brought her maps of voids. She takes the canvas out of the bag and looks at it for a bit. It's smooth under her fingertips, and slightly warm. Not so different from skin. She can feel the woman next to her shift slightly in her seat, trying to create more space between them. It doesn't matter. She lifts the canvas to her face and breathes in deeply. The woman gets up and walks down the aisle, even though the train isn't due to stop anywhere for some time.

The thing's a palimpsest now. It has its own history; Paula's first portrait of her, just showing the superficial aspects, then the second portrait in pure white, a truer account of her. And now this, a cosmic void. There is nothing more she can say about herself. It's complete.

Some hours later, the train arrives. When she gets off, she feels confused for a moment, unsure about her route. It's been a long day, so much has happened already. She climbs the long, shallow hill that meanders away from the station and up to the house where her parents live.

She doesn't know why she's come here but she does know that this is the only route she could have taken, like a curving ball or a beam of light following its path through space.

Her mother opens the front door, looking puzzled.

Jeanette rests the bag against her feet. 'Can I stay a few days?'

During dinner, she watches them as they talk in soft voices about ·nothing much. She doesn't say much but they don't seem to notice. As she sits at the old kitchen table, listening to them tell her about the neighbours and the weather and problems with the local post office, she feels drowsy in this blanket of warm sound.

After dinner they all watch television. She doesn't remember doing this before, when she was a child she spent her evenings upstairs in her bedroom, away from them. Even now she feels an itching to go to the window, to turn her back on the room and gaze into the night.

They have a new television, an enormous screen on which the newsreaders' faces appear larger than life and their voices boom out, deep and powerful. It's almost too much to take in. She's not used to so much information, she's used to scrabbling around in the noise, trying to find out facts, trying to infer what she can about the world.

At some uncertain point in the night she wakes up. She gets out of bed, walks down the corridor and stands outside the locked door. When she finally turns the handle the door opens, as she knew it would.

She's entered the void, the underworld. Inside Kate's room, she sits on the edge of the bed and waits. It's cold in here, so she gets under the covers. At first her mind is blank, and then it becomes crowded with images, photographs, snippets of film. Some of these are memories, others are things she's never seen before. Everything's all jumbled. Sometimes the images are speeded up, other times they slow down. To start with, she's watching other people, and then something flexes in her and she becomes these people. She becomes:

Her mother knitting booties, the wool trailing through her hands.

Her father trimming roses, pricking his finger on a thorn.

Alice in the darkroom, her face flushed red.

Paula painting a picture of a naked man.

Kate in the pool, swimming up and down, navigating the boundary between air and water. Blue above her, she can see the sky through the glass ceiling. Blue beneath her, she's suspended above the tiled floor. Back and forth. Touch the end of the pool with her fingertips, and flip and twist, and start again. Her movement creates waves eddying around her.

This is the shortest distance between the ends of the pool but it doesn't seem that short. And as she swims, she has time to notice the small intrusions into this world from outside. Near one corner of the pool a pink plaster lurks and bobs, like some mutant sea life. Pain inside her, ringing like a distant bell. There has never been pain before.

She swims for ages. At one point the other kids come and join her, then they leave her again. The bell dies down, starts up again. Her coach is always there, walking up and down on the tiles, keeping pace with her like a metronome. He's shouting at her, he's always shouting at her, but it's silent apart from the bell inside her.

Above her, the sky dims to grey before turning black. It's night-time. The lights in the pool are turned off. There is no light in here, she can't see her coach any more. Even though she couldn't hear him, she misses him. She shouldn't be able to see where she is going, but she can. It takes some time, a few laps, to realise that she is emitting light herself. She is the only source of light in here. The water glows around her, as if she is radioactive.

She can't stop swimming. Swimming is what she does, she's the swimming girl. Sleek and armoured in her swimming suit, she knows what she's doing, as long as she keeps going.

She swims in time with the bell, feeling it knock against her ribs, toll in her head. It counts out laps, rings each time she starts a new one.

Her light fades, dies away. Now she is swimming in utter, blank darkness. The bell gets louder. The noise beats in her head, in her stomach, in her chest. She puts her hands over her ears to try and block it out.

Silence.

When Jeanette wakes up in her own bed the next morning, she feels confused. The room is the same as the one where she grew up, and also not the same. Time and entropy have done their work here. The curtains are faded from the sun, cracks run along the length of the ceiling, the wallpaper is frayed around the door.

As she struggles from the sheets, she automatically glances at the chair, half expecting to see her school uniform draped on it.

Downstairs, both her parents are waiting for her at the kitchen table, a rerun of dinner last night. There's something in the way they're sitting, their heads slightly inclined to each other, that makes her think of binary systems, two stars locked into a single stable orbit.

Her mother smiles at her. 'Since you're here, I should give you this.' She picks up the photo of Kate and offers it to her.

'Thank you.' She doesn't really want it, not now she's realised that images don't matter. There's no point pinning Kate down on paper. Kate's everywhere and nowhere. But she does have something she can offer in response to the photo. She fishes the white canvas out of the bag and hands it to her parents. 'Here.'

The white paint almost glows, a vacuum humming with particles and unsaid words, unvoiced thoughts.

'What's this?'

'It's a portrait of me.'

'But...' They look at it, puzzled.

'You never put up any pictures of me, when I lived here. When I was a kid. So I thought you might like one, now. It matches the rest of the house, doesn't it? All the nothingness, the blanks.'

She's crying now, so she stops to wipe her cheeks. Then she realises her parents are crying too. Tears are running down her father's face, her mother is rummaging around for a hankie.

'Why didn't you talk to me? We didn't both die. I don't even know how she died. You never told me anything!' She rips the photo of Kate into two pieces. Then she remembers doing this to the star certificate that her mother gave her, all those years ago. She stands there, clutching half of Kate in each hand, her anger subsiding. Perhaps, then and now, her mother was trying to reach out, to make a connection.

'Jeanette,' her father sighs, 'you are the only thing that kept us going. Without you we really would be nothing.'

'I'm sorry,' she says.

'Don't be,' her mother grabs hold of her hand, 'The truth is we don't know how she died. We don't really know anything about it at all.' She squeezes her hand before continuing, 'How could we talk about it when we didn't know what to say? You were so young, even younger than Kate.' Her mother nudges her father, 'You should tell her what you do know. About the death. What happened that morning.'

Her father sighs, and passes a hand over his face. 'All of it?'

'All of it.' Her mother sounds definite. They glance at each other before her father starts to talk.

'I haven't ever talked about this since the inquest. Never.' And now his voice does sound a bit creaky, as though it hasn't been used very often. He sits up a bit straighter.

'When Kate first started training in the mornings, before school, and I'd take her to the pool, I'd stay and watch. I liked to watch her swim; it was so exact. She turned it into a science. And she was so unselfconscious about it. She never cared if anyone watched her or not. She just got on with it.

'But it was always the same routine, every morning. Or at least if it was different, I couldn't spot the differences; they were too subtle for me. So, quite often I'd go out to get a coffee. That morning, I went outside into the carpark. It was a clear bright day, pale morning sky. It was always quieter out there. The swimming pool was incredibly noisy, it all just bounced around between the walls and ceiling. I liked going outside where sounds could fly away and leave me in silence.

'The carpark faced the pool, and one side of the pool was glass so you could see in. But it was sunny that morning and the glass just reflected back the sky. I couldn't see what was going on inside. Usually I drank my coffee quickly and went back inside. But that morning there was a woman in the carpark. She asked me to help. She'd lost something, I can't remember what.'

He pauses and wipes his eyes, 'She wore dark glasses and she wanted to borrow some money to make a phone call, so I rummaged through my pockets looking for change. I couldn't see her eyes because of the glasses.

'And then someone came running outside. One of the other girls. She was barefoot and still in her swimsuit. She could hardly speak, she was huddled, dripping wet, cold and goosepimpled. But she managed to say that something had gone wrong with Kate. Those were the words she used. Gone wrong. As if the machinery of Kate's perfect swimming had broken down.

'She and I ran back inside. The woman didn't move, she just stayed there, immobile. I have always tried to remember what I was thinking at that point, but I don't remember anything. 'After the event I can reconstruct the fear, that I must have felt somewhere in my body, that my daughter was injured. That something had happened to her.

But I think my mind was blank. Perhaps I was still thinking about the woman, or even just the coffee which I'd hardly begun to drink. Perhaps I was just intent on not spilling my coffee.

'Kate was...' he wipes his eyes again, 'lying on the side of the pool. One arm was trailing in the pool and it was still moving. When I saw this, I thought she was ok. But she wasn't. She'd already gone by this point but we didn't know that then. Her arm was moving because the water was pushing it around.

'The coach was doing CPR. Blowing into her mouth and pressing down on her chest. I asked the girl what had happened but she didn't know. She didn't see anything until the coach jumped into the water because Kate was on the bottom of the pool. Sunk. We found out afterwards that there was water in her lungs so she'd already drowned before the coach could get to her.

'Nobody saw anything. That's the point. It was all invisible. If I'd been there I might have seen her get into trouble. Or I might not. I don't know.

'I wonder what the woman did after I left her in the carpark. I can't remember what the problem was. I felt I should go back and ask, or tell her why I'd run away. But of course I never did, I never did.

'It makes no sense, no matter how many times I tell it. One minute she's alive, the next she isn't. The post-mortem couldn't answer any questions. And at the inquest nobody could work out what had happened. Why she slipped under the surface of the water, into darkness. There weren't any marks on her body. No bruises. She didn't die because she hit her head on the edge of the pool. She just died and nobody saw her do it. They say nothing happens unless you observe it, don't they?' He looks at Jeanette, who nods slowly, doubtfully.

'But nobody saw her. So how can she have died?'

Her mother says, 'You should have stayed, you shouldn't have gone out for the coffee,' and he says, 'What difference would it have made.'

'At least you would have been there.'

'Yes, I would have been there,' and he cries some more.

Like looking down a microscope into the past, Jeanette remembers the coach standing in their hallway, saying to her mother, 'You weren't there.'

'That's what the coach meant, that day,' she says.

'He made a point of it during the inquest, but the coroner slapped him down. He was there and he didn't see anything. He was just trying to divert attention from himself,' her mother says.

'Well, we don't know that. Clearly, he felt awful, but it made us feel awful too. I couldn't have done anything. I wouldn't even have seen her slip under the water from where I was sitting.'

The woman. 'Did you ever see the woman again?' she asks.

'He found another one,' her mother says, sharp. 'It makes no difference, one woman or another.'

Her father says nothing.

What difference would it have made if her father had been there? Even if he couldn't do anything about it? She has spent so long assuming that they knew what happened but didn't tell her, that she feels almost giddy with the realisation that they know as little as her. It makes her feel as grown up as them. There is no difference between them any more and perhaps there never has been, not since that day.

Perhaps it is right that this death was unseen. Death is never understandable, it is the only thing we cannot know. She's always hoped for some explanation, but Kate's death is still too large to encompass in her model of the universe.

And perhaps that's why her father has another woman, to take him back to that last moment before he knew about Kate. The gap between his words and what has happened is infinite because the facts are unknowable, so all they have are his words. The realisation shocks her, there is no external reality. No balance, even, between objective and subjective.

Kate's death, that hard crystalline ever-present feature of her life, is dissolving into red sunset, a smear of colour washed across the sky. She still doesn't know anything about it, it is a meaningless event. But if this means nothing, then what about all the other information she has fought and struggled so hard to find? What meaning does any of that have? And for a moment her mind tips beyond the see-saw balance down into the vacuum.

But even in nothing there is always something. Nothingness never actually exists. Nothing plus the uncertainty principle will always make something, particles of energy that pop into being and out again. The higher their energies, the shorter their lives. That'll do for her. She can play with that.

'That's it,' her mother says. 'I know you think we never thought about you, but we used to lie awake at night worrying about what to tell you, how to talk to you about it. It was just too difficult. But we should have. Anyway, now you know it all.'

Now she knows what they know, but there is still one secret left. Hers. She hugs herself, wondering if she should let it go.

The rest of the day is peaceful. They go for a walk to a nearby park, where the path is just wide enough for the three of them to walk side by side.

As they walk quietly through the almost deserted park, she thinks about the future, her life beyond the voids. She can finish the void project soon, and then what? If her lectureship gets renewed, she'll have to start thinking about next year's courses. If it doesn't get renewed, there will be nothing for her in Edinburgh and she'll have to look for jobs elsewhere. Instead of panicking, this feels like an opportunity. Perhaps she's been there long enough. Perhaps she should go to new places, get away from what she knows. Leave Paula behind.

She may be able to predict the future of galaxies or even stars but there's something exhilarating in not being able to know her own future. To be the ghost in the machine.

Later that afternoon in her parent's house, they're all drinking tea when the phone rings.

'Jeanette,' her mother says, 'There's a woman on the phone for you.'

It is Becca. Jeanette has forgotten that Becca would have had this number, from years ago.

'Jeanette, are you alright? I phoned your flat but there's no reply. Paula doesn't know where you are...'

'Paula...'

'Do you want me to tell Paula where you are? When you're coming home?'

'No. Don't tell her anything. Please.' She's aware of her parents standing nearby, listening.

'Ok.' Becca doesn't sound surprised.

'I'm fine.'

'Good.' Becca pauses. 'Will you be back by the weekend? I could come round for a cup of tea, if you like. I haven't seen you for ages.'

'That would be great. Thanks.'

After she's hung up, she remembers her father making his secret phone calls from this same spot.

'Who was that?' her mother asks.

'She's a friend.' And this seems as good a way of telling them as any other so she carries on, 'she's not my girlfriend.' As she says it, she's not sure why she ever hid it from them in the first place.

'I know,' says her mother. 'You're living with your girlfriend, aren't you? You tried to convince me she was your flatmate but I could tell.' She turns to Jeanette's dad. 'She looked just like she did when Alice Airy was around. She looked happy.'

'Paula's not my girlfriend either. Not any more,' and she bursts into tears.

'It's ok.' Her mother strokes her hair. 'It'll be ok. You're going to be fine. You'll be happy again. I promise.'

When she arrives home, Paula's sitting on the sofa, painting her fingernails. She's got black hair and red lipstick, with traces of blue paint worked into the creases of her white fingers. She looks at Jeanette standing in the doorway of the living room and says, 'I won't be long, I just stopped by,' before returning her attention to her nails.

'I don't mind,' Jeanette replies. 'Do what you like.'

Paula takes off her shoes and socks, and starts painting her toenails. Jeanette watches her, admiring the precision with which she covers up the pale extremities of her feet, and the way she gently strokes the brush three times; centre, left, right, down the tip of each toe.

'Where have you been?' asks Paula.

The nail polish is dark red, a fashionable shade of blood. Paula's fingernails glitter wetly, as though she has been working in a butcher's shop. Perhaps she has.

'Where have you been?' she asks again, and this time she pauses, her brush held in the air like a tiny wand, as though what Jeanette is about to say matters to her.

'My sister died twenty years ago,' says Jeanette. 'I missed the beginning of her death.'

A bead of nail polish drips off the brush onto the sofa, but Paula stays motionless. Her mouth is slightly open, so that Jeanette can see into the soft, damp cavern.

'Do you know why the Ancient Greeks thought that dead people lost their memories in the underworld? Why they drank from the waters of forgetfulness when they died?'

Paula slowly shakes her head.

'Because death is outside time and you need time to construct your memories. You need past, present, future. A beginning, a middle, and an end. But death is too constant for that. Too unchanging.'

Paula shakes her head again but it's not clear whether she's disagreeing with Jeanette.

'But the Universe isn't that unchanging. So you see — death is outside everything. It can't be explained by anything.'

'Did you go to visit your parents?' asks Paula. Jeanette nods. 'You always go a bit doo-lally after you've seen your parents,' and she returns to her nails.

Jeanette flops down suddenly, without her body warning her, on the floor. Paula looks up again, 'Are you ok?' and she screws the lid onto the bottle of nail polish. 'Shall I make us some tea?' She pads off into the kitchen, her feet slightly splayed to avoid disturbing the wet nails.

Jeanette listens to her bustle and clatter. An old tune begins to play in her head. Something forgotten that's now being remembered.

When Paula returns with two steaming mugs she doesn't go back to the sofa, but sits down on the floor next to Jeanette. Her eyes are as blue as the daytime sky. Jeanette has gazed at this colour countless times, waiting for the night.

'I've stopped doing portraits,' says Paula. 'I'm onto less representational stuff now. More abstract.' She sips her tea. But it's still too hot for Jeanette. 'What do you want for supper?' She holds her fingers out in front of her, admiring them.

'Supper?'

'I could make us something comforting, like kedgeree.' The fingernails are only inches from Jeanette's face, they hang between her and everything else in the room. She looks away and sees a suitcase next to the sofa.

'Have you come to pick up your stuff?' she asks.

The fingernails falter in the air, 'I don't actually have a new place sorted out yet. I thought I would by now, but it — didn't work out.'

'You can't stay here.' Jeanette starts drinking her tea which has finally cooled to the right temperature. The fingernails flutter down onto Jeanette's knees. She regards them, a set of blood-filled leeches.

'No?' There is a slight pressure from the fingertips now, she can sense the leeches are waiting for orders to inch their way up her legs, try and get inside her.

Her body shudders against the hand and bucks it off her knee.

She stands up. 'No. It's over. It belongs to the past.' After she's spoken, a pure, deep, rich silence spreads inside her, expanding out through the pores of her skin. She knows she doesn't need to say anything more.

Paula doesn't seem hear the silence. She waits for a few more moments, for something else to be said, before finally giving up. 'Guess I'd better get a move on, then.'

At work she checks her emails. There is one from a journalist at New Scientist who is working on a story about unusual results in science, and who wants to talk to Jeanette about the connected galaxies and the difficulties of interpreting data. She replies, agreeing to be interviewed by him as long as he talks to Maggie as well.

There's another paper by the consortium published today and, as with the last paper, Richard's name is submerged in the lengthy list of authors. She thinks it might be a bit higher up than the last time, maybe he is rising to the surface. Perhaps she should go and ask him.

She finds him in his office, unpacking a new computer. White polystyrene shapes have settled on every surface, like fake snow.

'New toy?'

'Yup.' He's grinning. Not quite at her.

'What are you going to use it for?' She's almost jealous of it. She's not really that interested in computers, but this one looks so obviously newer and faster than hers.

'Running simulations. It's the next step of the project. We'll be doing more detailed simulations of the Universe to compare with our data.' He positions the computer just so on his desk and stands back to admire it.

'And what if they don't agree with each other? Which would be wrong? Your simulations or your data?' She shouldn't wind him up, she is genuinely impressed. Simulations are fun, building your own toy universe in the privacy of your computer. Actually doing what scientists are always accused of doing — playing God.

He glares at her. 'The simulations of course. The data are always right.'

'Of course.' She tries not to think about her own data. 'And you're writing the code for the simulation?'

'Some of it.'

'Are you going to put in humans? Little tiny people running around your artificial stars and galaxies?'

Now he grins at her properly. 'That would be fun. You could model yourself. And predict your own future.'

'And at what point do you model yourself running a model of the Universe and the whole thing disappears up its own arse?'

'Ha! I don't care, as long as they give me the money. I've just been awarded three more years of dosh to do this.'

'That's fantastic.' She means it, too. 'And well done on the latest paper.'

'Oh, that.' He waves his hand dismissively. 'There'll be another five papers published by Christmas. They're coming thick and fast out of the sausage machine now.'

'And all with you as a co-author?'

'Yup. Buried in the *et al.*' He quotes her easily, almost jokingly, but it's clear from the fact that he's remembered it that he's been thinking about it. 'Surrounded by all the other drones.'

'No, you're each doing your own thing and it all fits together. That's what we all work on, isn't it? Little pieces of the puzzle.' She's almost uneasy at his demonstration of humility. Does it make up for him and Paula? Nothing cancels that out, but for the first time she can see that perhaps it doesn't matter. And not just because of the usual cosmic reasons, that they are all just dead stardust floating around one of billions of stars in one of billions of galaxies. There's a better reason; she doesn't care anymore. Paula hurt her and that's the end of it. It's in the past. Lots of stuff has happened in the past and she is where she is.

He interrupts her thoughts. 'I saw your paper on the void

distribution has been published too. Nice job.'

'Thanks. It may help save my bacon here. With the Death Star.'

'And you were the sole author. So you can take all the glory for yourself.' Just a hint of sarcasm there, but then he continues, 'It's funny how we concentrate on the things we can see, the galaxies and stars, and we forget about the absences. All the spaces in between. But they're just as important. Trying to work out why things *aren't* there is just as important as why they are.'

That afternoon she's in the seminar room with everyone else, perched on one of the uncomfortable little fold-down seats. This week's seminar is about the recent discovery that the expansion of the Universe appears to be accelerating, not slowing down as used to be thought. This acceleration can be explained by invoking a substance called dark energy.

The seminar speaker reminds the audience that only four percent of the Universe is ordinary visible matter and everything else is dark. Jeanette thinks about all of this dark stuff; the stars too dim to be seen, the black holes, the elementary particles that don't interact with light, and the gaps between things are all dark. The ordinary stuff makes a sort of surface crust of light which is scarcely consequential anymore, like dead autumn leaves on a swimming pool. Dark is where it's at.

And all these unseen things have so much effect. They can slow things down, speed things up. Push people apart, pull families together. She may never be able to see Kate, but the effect is always there. It lives on.

She watches the Death Star snoring in the front row, his bow tie quivering with each exhalation. One of the students asks the speaker, if dark energy is so important then why has nobody found it before now? How can there suddenly be a new substance that accounts for most of the Universe? The speaker just shrugs; that's the way it works. The student writes something in her notebook.

It is night. Becca has just gone home after sharing a pizza with her, and she's sitting outside in her garden with a pair of binoculars, waiting. She's not sure the binoculars will help that much. Sometimes they don't when you're trying to see really faint things.

She's expecting the comet at half past eight. It should appear in the south-east, above the roof of the old hospital. The comet's officially named after the Japanese astronomer who first discovered it twenty years ago, but she prefers to think of it as nameless.

Comets used to be harbingers of doom. She has no answer to that, she knows what happened the last time the comet was in this part of the solar system. But still, she feels hopeful. It cannot be any worse than last time. It is not likely to be the same. The comet will perturb the orbits of other objects around it. It's difficult to say how far away the influence of the comet will be felt, given the complex movements of everything else in its neighbourhood.

A smudge appears in the sky. Even as she sees it, it gradually gets brighter until finally she can look at it face on. It looks painted onto the rest of the sky, you can tell it doesn't really belong here. It's as if a glamorous neighbour has just popped in.

She continues to watch it as it sweeps across to the west of the city and sinks beneath the rooftops.

As she goes inside, she wonders what she'll be doing with her life the next time she sees it.

Acknowledgements

I wrote this book partly because I wanted to bring to life the process of doing astronomy and show both the beauty and the uncertainty of that process. So, I would like to thank my fellow astronomers; in particular Alan Heavens, Marek Kukula, Bob Mann, Lance Miller, Seb Oliver, Michael Rowan-Robinson and Suzie Ramsay, from whom I have learnt much over the years.

This book would not have happened without the terrific guidance and hard work of Adrian Searle and Helen Sedgwick at Freight Books.

I'm very grateful for the various types of help that I've received from fellow writers during the journey of writing this book. Mary Paulson-Ellis has offered detailed advice on several drafts. At the University of Glasgow Michael Schmidt, Alan Bissett, Colette Paul, as well as Kate Tough and the other student members of Group D, saw and commented on parts of an early draft. All the members of the editorial group Ink Inc; George Anderson, Jenni Brooks, Sophie Cooke, Roy Gill, Theresa Muñoz and Allan Radcliffe have provided much needed feedback, wine and laughter. Ken MacLeod, John Ward and Zoë Beck have been endlessly kind and supportive.

Since 2010 the ESRC Genomics Policy and Research Forum has generously provided a haven in which I could write. I'm very grateful to their support which continued long after it was officially supposed to end. I also acknowledge a Scottish Books Trust New Writers Award for 2011/2012.

Lastly and most importantly I'm grateful for the love and guidance from my family and other animals; Graeme Busfield, Herb Goldschmidt, Belle Brett and all the cats.